THE EZEKIEL PROJECT

A NOVEL

ISBN: 1493575473
ISBN-13: 978-1493575473

Jillian,
Thank you so
much for your

THE EZEKIEL PROJECT

A NOVEL

encouragement and
friendship!
Christina Knowles

Christina Knowles

PROLOGUE

Minnesota 1967

REID woke in a cold sweat, the gun blast ringing in his ears. A dream, it was only a dream. In it his older brother, Hayden, had been shot in a hunting accident. The one Reid had been begging to go on. Hayden still hadn't told him if he would be invited or not. Now, he wasn't sure he wanted to be. In two days, Hayden and two of his friends were going deer hunting, and Hayden told Reid that maybe he could tag along and even bring his .22. He could shoot some rabbits or something, as long they had already gotten their licenses filled. Until then, he would have to be very quiet and just watch.

In his dream, Reid had gone with them, and so had Hayden's friend, Billy Johnson. They had been walking up a steep hill, and at the top they reached a barbed-wire fence. Hayden pulled down on the wire while each boy stepped carefully over. When it was Billy's turn, he stumbled, and his rifle slipped and leveled on Hayden. Billy grabbed at the rifle instinctively to keep it from falling to the ground and inadvertently squeezed the trigger; the bullet of the .243 Winchester rifle tore through Hayden at close range. The bullet ripped open his gut, spraying flesh and flannel all over Joey Bradford, who was standing right behind him, mixing large intestine with small intestine. Lucky for Joey, the bullet went through at an angle and missed him coming out the other side. The scene in Reid's dream played out in slow motion for him, and he saw every gory detail as if it were one of the old monster movies he loved to watch at the local cinema on Saturdays, although this horror movie was in color, unlike the ones on the big screen.

Afterward, over breakfast, Reid told his parents about the dream in the presence of Hayden and his two younger sisters, Peggy and Susan. His father laughed heartily and his mother frowned.

"I told you he was too young to see those movies, Howard," Carol Tessier told her husband. "Now he's having nightmares."

"He's okay. The boy has a vivid imagination, that's all."

"What are you trying to do, Squirt?" his brother asked. "I've been looking forward to this hunt all summer. And I was going to tell you that you could come. Are you chickening out?"

Reid had the same dream the next night and was convinced that he was seeing a warning about the future. Reid stayed home while Hayden and his friends went hunting. He was grounded for not dropping the subject of his brother's impending death; his entire family had grown weary of it. Even Hayden, whom Reid admired and loved, laughed and told his friends about Reid's belief that he could see the future in a dream. They all laughed and teased him — even Billy Johnson. They'd left without him that morning, and Billy and Joey had come back early from the hunt, licenses unfilled and without Hayden.

CHAPTER 1

*C*LOUDS *of dust and gases fill the hot desert air as the soldiers of B Company, 151st battalion, United States Army, desperately try to attach their gas masks to their grimy, sweat-stained faces. The confused soldiers fumble blindly through the fog of chemicals, searching for their masks or struggling with the straps while attaching them to their faces. Some dazed and unsure of what exactly is happening, fall chokingly to the ground, fighting uselessly for air. Sergeant Joel Carpenter, holding a dirty white cloth tightly around his face to block the poisonous gas from his lungs, scans the area, taking in the sight of his fellow soldiers strewn about the desert sands, watching others stumble incoherently in circles around the many already dead bodies. As if in a dream, the sounds all around Joel are muffled, and everything is hazy; no doubt a result of the gas-filled air. Joel's gaze falls on a dead soldier lying on his back, his eyes staring blindly into the night sky, his gas mask still attached to the back of his pack which he holds tightly in his arms.*

Marty. Why didn't you put on the damn mask? Joel kneels down beside Marty and gently closes the eyes of his friend. He unfastens the buckle attaching the mask to Marty's pack, unwraps the makeshift turban from his face, and shutting his eyes tightly, he dons the mask himself, tightening the straps around the back of his head. He takes in a deep breath, filling his tight burning lungs with long-awaited air.

* * *

Ft. Clairemont Research Facility
Spring Forest, Colorado
13 December 2002

Joel sat straight up in his bed, gasping for air, sweat beading on his forehead. He looked around the dim, near empty room in confusion. Recognition slowly came over him as he realized that he had been dreaming again. If that's what you could call it. Dreaming of Iraq was always a nightmare. But then again, so was waking up in the Department of Scientific Research Medical Facility. Joel threw back the covers from the small cot and stood up weakly and headed for the john. He wore what appeared to be a uniform that looked like army-green surgical scrubs, except that the letters USDSR were printed boldly across both the front and the back of his shirt. USDSR stood for United States Department of Scientific Research.

Gazing into the mirror, he barely recognized his haggard and pale reflection, his haunted eyes that looked about a hundred years old, at least in their experiences. These eyes had seen too much for a man of thirty-one. He rubbed the week-old stubble on his chin, and then ran his fingers through his long, matted, and sweaty hair.

Women had once loved running their fingers through his thick, black wavy hair. He doubted they would love it right now. He needed a shower and some coffee—strong coffee and a fix.

Joel was a junky. Not heroin, cocaine, or crack, but Anasymine. Anasymine was a drug developed by the Department of Scientific Research, specifically by Colonel Reid Tessier, to enhance the psychic abilities of vets with Gulf War Syndrome. Joel began to shake, and he gripped the sink in front of him. It had been about six hours since his last injection, and he was beginning to feel the absence of the drug his body craved.

"It's time for your tests, Sergeant." The voice came from behind him in the doorway of his small bathroom. Joel didn't turn around, but his gaze rose back to the mirror. He stared steadily at Adam Blancett in the reflection.

Blancett was an army nurse at the research facility, which seemed sometimes more like a mental ward than a research hospital. Blancett took his job way too seriously. Of course, working in a place that held the country's finest captive for the purpose of conducting secret experiments on them was hardly a place that allowed too jovial an attitude. Joel stared back at Blancett with disgust, not so much because of Blancett himself, but of what he represented. The blind obedience of the army soldier. Once Joel had been like that. Once, long ago when he'd been an integral part of the infantry's well-oiled machine.

"I need my medication," Joel said solemnly, still regarding Blancett in the mirror without turning around, more out of fear of letting go of the sink and falling to the floor than out of any defiance.

"Hang on, hang on. You know the drill. We gotta get your vitals first." Blancett put two strong arms under Joel's elbows and led him back to the bed to sit down. Blancett was a large, hulking man who worked out religiously, and it showed in his bulging biceps. He even had muscles on his neck. Maybe this was a reaction to the teasing he regularly endured about being a "nurse." A nurse in the research facility, however, was more akin to a bouncer than to the noble profession; he was ready to subdue any unruly subject in an instant.

Joel was no small man himself. At 6'2", he was once a healthy one hundred and ninety pounds, but had dwindled to one hundred and seventy-five and falling since his return from the Persian Gulf. He still had fairly good muscle tone and with training in several martial arts, he could handle himself even with his illness.

Blancett fastened the blood pressure cuff to Joel's arm and began pumping.

"Good. You're doing better. Dr. Andrzejczak will be relieved."

"I'm lucky to have such a caring doctor," Joel said sarcastically as he turned so that the inside of his arm was up and resting on the table in front of him, anxious for the injection.

"Dr. Andrzejczak cares about all of his little experiments. You're very valuable to him." Blancett inserted a needle into a small bottle, and the light green liquid slowly rose to the top of the hypo. Blancett flicked the end of the needle with his finger and a small amount of the drug squirted out the top, releasing the deadly air pockets. Blancett leaned over Joel and swabbed his inner arm with an alcohol pad with one hand, and then inserted the needle with the other. As the Anasymine flooded his veins, Joel breathed a sigh of relief and relaxed back into the pillow, eyes closed.

"Wake up, Sleeping Beauty. You've got work to do."

Blancett helped Joel to his feet. "Dr. Andrzejczak is conducting the tests, today."

Joel opened his eyes and gazed up at Blancett, wondering if the nurse was trying to make a sick joke.

"He doesn't like to be kept waiting. Let's go," Blancett said, losing his minute amount of patience.

Dr. Andrzejczak? That meant telekinetic testing. Dr. Andrzejczak was fond of telekinetics. More likely, he was fond of putting people in pain. The more pain, the better. Telekinesis, moving objects from one place to another with his mind, weakened Joel more than anything else, except maybe mind manipulation. But so far, he thought they were unaware of his ability to influence others psychically. He'd hidden it from them well, not only because whenever he tried it, he was bed-ridden for the rest of the day and once he'd nearly gone into a coma, but because he knew it was what they wanted from him most of all. And he only cooperated when absolutely necessary. If they knew he had the ability to control the minds of others, they would use any sort of coercion to force his compliance. Andrzejczak used this type of intimidation regularly to secure Joel's cooperation, even when it wasn't necessary. This intimidation always involved other subjects, usually the weakest and most helpless.

"I said let's get a move on," Blancett said angrily, jerking Joel up by the arm. Joel acquiesced and followed Blancett down the hall.

CHAPTER 2

Spring Forest, Colorado

DROPPING a few of her carefully chosen Christmas packages, Elaina Valdez-Tessier was stunned by the strong, dirty stranger gripping her arm. Staring intently into her startled eyes, the hobo-ish looking man seemed to be in pain as he issued his warning, unmindful of the crowds of December mall shoppers.

"He knows what yer up to. Don't try it," the stranger slurred out of his painfully twisted face. "Don't do it." He shook his head. "Don't do it." He swayed back and forth as the words came out in a singsong manner. "He knows, he knows. You can't get away with it," he sang. Then he pressed his lips to her ear, and the cold wetness of his lips sent shivers down her spine. "He'll find you," he whispered. "He finds us all."

Elaina stood frozen, too shocked to move and not comprehending what the strange man was talking about, or why he was holding her by the arm so tightly. Her son, Luke, standing next to her, moved forward.

"Mom, who is this guy?"

Luke's voice brought her out of her paralysis, but his presence added to her fear. The implications of being accosted by a lunatic in the mall with her eight year old son was even worse than being alone. Elaina tried to pull her arm free, but his grip was too strong.

"Let go of me before I scream for security." A few people had already begun to notice the filthy man holding on to the beautiful dark haired woman with the small boy.

The man's eyes seemed to focus, and he reluctantly released her and smiled, revealing yellow teeth. When he smiled, Elaina realized that the man must only be in his early thirties, but his unshaven and haggard appearance made him seem much older.

"You've been warned, E-lai-na," he pronounced her name very slowly and carefully. "Just do as you're told, and you'll be okay. You've got the boy to think of. Keep your thoughts pure and be a good little wifey. And remember—we can see," he said mysteriously as he tapped the side of her head with one gloved finger. Laughing, he turned and fled as quickly as he had appeared. Shaking, Elaina bent down and embraced Luke. He pulled away.

"Luke, have you ever seen that man before?" Elaina asked him, staring directly into his eyes. "At Daddy's work, on post, or around the neighborhood?"

"No." Luke shook his head. "You think he knows Dad?"

"No. I just thought maybe—never mind. Just some crazy. Let's go." Elaina bent down and picked up the packages she had dropped and hurried Luke through the mall.

Elaina pulled into the snow-covered drive of a small

Victorian house on a tree-lined street and turned off the engine of her black Jeep. Elaina slammed the door to the Jeep, juggling her Christmas packages and two bags of groceries.

"Luke, can you get the rest, please?" she asked, her bags threatening to spill onto the pavement as she rushed up the icy driveway, snow beginning to fall lightly.

"Hurry, Luke! It's almost five! He'll be home any minute." There was real fear in her voice, not just impatience.

Luke slowly alighted from the Jeep and sullenly made his way to the front of the house with two packages. Elaina shuffled the bags into one arm and fumbled with the keys.

"You know, you could give me a little help here," she called to Luke, who was still walking stubbornly slow up the front walk behind her.

"Why don't we just order a pizza?"

Elaina didn't know why Luke refused to grasp the gravity of the situation. Colonel Reid Tessier, commanding officer in charge of the Department of Scientific Research in Forest Springs, Colorado for the United States Army, would not want pizza for dinner. Not so much because he preferred more elegant, gourmet-type meals, but because he would assume that Elaina was slacking off in some way. Not living up to her responsibilities as wife and mother to a very important man. He took his role as her husband as seriously as he took his commission at the army post, and he would never allow her to throw aside her duty to prepare a fitting feast for the family anymore than he would allow his subordinates to disobey a direct order.

Dropping the bags of celery, lettuce, manicotti, and wine on the counter breathlessly, she flipped on the water tap in the sink and simultaneously turned on the oven.

"Luke, go turn on the Christmas lights. Make it look like we've been home for awhile."

Luke went grudgingly out over to the large artificial tree in the living room and plugged in the lights.

"Don't forget the outside lights," Elaina called from the kitchen as she beat the ricotta and Parmesan cheese with raw egg. Luke walked through the kitchen on his way to the garage to turn on the lights and stopped, peeking around Elaina at the stove to see what was being made for dinner.

"Dad likes you to make the homemade kind." Luke observed his mother stuffing the hard manicotti with the egg and cheese mixture.

"The instant kind is faster. He'll never know the difference," she paused and looked meaningfully into Luke's eyes, "unless you tell him."

"I won't," Luke gave in, "but don't forget to throw away the box."

"Thanks, Luke. I knew I could count on you, Buddy." Elaina gave his hair a tousle and grabbed the empty manicotti box and threw it into the trash, covering it with paper towels to hide it.

It was a relief to have Luke on her side for a change. Sometimes Luke could be so difficult, almost as if he was trying to make trouble between her and Reid. When she tried to hide things from Reid, just to keep the peace, Luke occasionally found some kind of pleasure in telling Reid all about them. But when she least expected it, he came through. Not that she wanted him to take sides; she just didn't want him to always be on Reid's instead of her own.

She had married Reid young. Only twenty years old, and she had been very naïve. Reid was seventeen years older than her and had never been married before, even though he was incredibly handsome and charming. And still was, at least handsome. He could still be charming, though only on rare occasion.

She supposed she had been trying to escape her parents at the time, strict Catholic parents. Mexican immigrants, who believed in a tight-knit family and the practicality of hard work. Reid had seemed like a dream come true. Someone who loved her just the way she was—impractical and creative, a dancer. That hadn't lasted long. As soon as they were married, Reid had started criticizing her for an assortment of things. She soon became pregnant and thought that Reid would appreciate her as a mother to his son. Although Reid adored his son, he blamed Elaina for getting pregnant too soon. It didn't match his idea of how the perfect marriage should go. He had timelines and rules for everything. Everything had to happen on his timetable and according to his ideal, or he lost control. And he liked to be in control.

She attributed this to his work. He was a very important person with a very important position that caused him great anxiety. Elaina tried to do everything she could to please him and make the home more peaceful, mainly for Luke's sake, but no matter how hard she tried, she couldn't be perfect. It was worse than living with her parents. Far worse.

"Elaina!" She heard the shout from the living room and almost dropped the pan of manicotti as she was putting it into the oven. Reid strolled into the kitchen with a briefcase in his hands. "Is dinner ready? I've got a lot of work to do tonight, and I'm starved."

"It'll be just a while longer. I-we-there was a huge line at the market and the roads were bad, so I got a little bit of a late start, but it won't be much longer." Turning to face him, she smiled up at him. "I made manicotti."

"Shit. I don't know if my stomach can handle all that tomato sauce and cheese. I feel like I'm going to get an ulcer, all this shit I've got to deal with at work. Everything's coming down around my ears," he said pulling off his uniform coat, revealing his still perfect physique. "If I don't come up with something tangible they can use, they're going to shitcan the whole project. But no, go ahead and kill me with that Italian shit! What's the difference to you? The army's got great life insurance." With that he stomped out of the room and headed for his home office.

Luke came in from the garage wearing his Discman turned up loud enough for anyone near him to hear the faint sounds of the music he was listening to. Removing the headphones momentarily, he asked, "Is Dad home?"

"In the office," Elaina replied and turned to wash the vegetables for the salad.

Luke went into the office and found his father sitting behind the computer, rubbing his head slowly. Looking up and seeing Luke, his face softened.

"Hey, Squirt. How're you doing?"

"Good." Luke climbed into his lap behind the desk. Although eight years old, Luke still loved to sit in his father's lap. He idolized Reid. His father was a scientist—a microbiologist and a chemist. Luke was impressed by his father's degrees and his position of authority, and the fact that he was in the army was pretty cool, too.

In Spring Forest, a lot of people were in the army because there was a post nearby on the outskirts of town, but most of his friends' fathers were not colonels, nor did they work in the Department of Scientific Research. Luke wanted to be like his father when he grew up, only not so serious. His dad did get a little too uptight about everything. But he couldn't help it. He had a lot on his mind.

His mother should understand that and try harder. Still, Luke wished his mother didn't cry so easily about his dad's angry outbursts. He always forgot he was mad a few hours later. Only sometimes he did hear yelling after he went to bed, and occasionally even some loud noises like something being thrown or broken, and then his mom crying. He heard a lot of noise that night after he went to bed.

The next morning, everyone was sitting around the kitchen table, Reid reading the newspaper and drinking coffee, his plate empty, his breakfast already eaten. A bruise was forming on the left side of Elaina's jaw from the encounter with Reid the night before. Elaina was staring at Luke, who had his Discman on, turned up loud enough for everyone to hear again and only picking at his full plate of pancakes and eggs. Elaina got up from the table, frustrated, and began clearing away the plates from the table.

"Luke! Turn that down! And eat your breakfast; we're going to be late again if you don't hurry up." Elaina leaned over the table and turned the volume down on his Discman.

"I don't eat breakfast," Luke replied.

"Yes, you do." Elaina glared at him.

"Why don't you give the poor kid a break? If he's not hungry, he's not hungry." Reid looked up from his newspaper momentarily before once again ignoring them.

Elaina reached over and snatched the untouched plate of food from in front of Luke and tossed it into the sink. "Go get dressed," she told Luke without turning around. Turning on the faucet and scraping the food down the disposal, Elaina was startled and repulsed to feel Reid's arms encircle her waist and his head on her shoulder as he whispered into her ear.

"I'm sorry about last night, Baby. I was just really stressed out about things at work. I didn't mean to take it out on you," he said as he turned her around to face him and nuzzled up closer to her body.

"It's okay," she could barely bring herself to look him in the eyes as she told the lie.

"It won't happen again." He bent his head and tried to kiss her, but she turned her head away. This infuriated Reid. *Bitch*, he thought, *after everything I've done for her, this family, and she acts like she's too good to be touched*. Letting go of her, he turned to the stairs and started up them. "I'd better get ready for work."

Elaina relaxed back against the sink, and tears began to roll down her face as she watched Reid run up the stairs. She wasn't crying because he was angry again. She was crying because she didn't care anymore. She hadn't wanted to work things out for a long time now. She would have left him a long time ago, but she was afraid. Afraid of being on her own, afraid of raising a son by herself, and most of all afraid of what Reid would do. Wiping away her tears on the dishtowel, Elaina followed him up the stairs to get dressed. Life goes on and this was hers. She had to be strong for Luke. She went upstairs to get dressed for her day at the dance studio and to take Luke to school.

Elaina owned a small dance studio where she was the only teacher a few blocks away in the small and quaint downtown area of Spring Forest. She had always dreamed of being a dancer. A real dancer, on stage performing before a crowd of appreciative onlookers, but Reid had never encouraged her to perform. In fact, he forbade her to, except in small local shows that she and her students put on for their families. That had been one of the reasons she had left home. Her parents hadn't liked the idea of her being a dancer. Her father had thought it immoral, and her mother thought it impractical. Elaina knew her father was bitterly disappointed in her for running a dance studio, but at least she had married well and had a son. Her mother liked Reid, and she believed in the marriage vow. She would never encourage Elaina to leave her husband, even if she knew how cruel he could be.

She had tried to get Reid to go to counseling, but of course, he had refused. There was nothing wrong with him. His behavior was always perfectly understandable under the circumstances. Regrettable, but understandable, and if she tried harder not to upset him, then he would have an easier time not losing his temper.

When Elaina reached the top of the stairs, Reid was already showering in the adjoining master bath. She could see the steam drifting through the open door, and the mirror was completely fogged over. Reid loved his showers hot. From the corner of her eye, Elaina noticed Reid's black leather briefcase sitting on the bed. It wasn't like Reid to bring his briefcase upstairs. He almost always left it down in his office, which he kept locked when he wasn't using it. His briefcase was top-secret. Everything was always top-secret. His work was so important, thought Elaina resentfully. She blamed many of their marital problems on his work. And why not? Reid always blamed everything he did on work — the horrible and unrelenting stress of work — as if no one else in the world had a difficult job. At least that was when he wasn't blaming Elaina for his problems. Most of the time Elaina felt guilty because she believed she wasn't a very good wife. Especially because she knew she didn't love Reid anymore. She supposed she never really did, seeing as she'd never really known the real Reid until after they married.

But right now she felt like maybe their problems weren't really about her. Maybe no matter how great she was, it wouldn't matter. It was Reid, and he would be like this no matter whom he was with. A moment of clarity like this didn't come very often, and Elaina grabbed onto it. She should leave. But where would she go? If she stayed in town, she could probably live off her dance studio. Not well, but she could survive. But what about Luke? He preferred his father to her most of the time, and he wouldn't want to leave. And she knew it was only a matter of time before Luke would get in his way and cause some violent outburst from Reid. She couldn't allow that to happen. Besides she could never be without Luke. He was her only happiness in life. But Reid would never let her live in the same town as him. He would be humiliated and afraid of what his colleagues would think. He would bring her back, and there would be hell to pay. And Luke. He would never let Luke go. According to Reid, Luke was the only thing she ever did right. Of all his many faults, the man did love his son.

The briefcase caught her eye again. Curiosity overwhelmed her, and she walked over to it, glancing at the bathroom where Reid showered. The water was still running. Fog still rolled from the doorway. Reid was even humming in there. He must have gotten over his anger already. Unable to resist, she unlatched the buckle fastening the flap and opened the case quietly, nervously. Reid would be furious if he caught her going through his things. Especially, his top-secret government business. She slowly inched out the folder inside and glanced again at the door to the bathroom. Still showering. Her heart began to hammer as she pulled out the folder and opened it.

On the first page in bold letters was typewritten, THE EZEKIEL PROJECT, SERGEANT JOEL CARPENTER, SUBJECT #33. Underneath, there was a photograph of a soldier, late twenties, clean-shaven, military haircut, in uniform, a slightly closed-mouth smile on his lips, dark, closely cropped hair, and strikingly bright blue eyes. Penetrating eyes that seemed to lock on to her own and hold them. There was something about the picture of this man that mesmerized Elaina. Elaina thought he was very good looking, but it was more than that. She finally forced herself to flip to the next page and read on.

The document was a combination of typewritten and handwritten reports about Sgt. Joel Carpenter and his experiences as a test subject for The Ezekiel Project, some medical records, and statistics about something. One page caught Elaina's attention, a summary of Joel Carpenter's condition. It read: JOEL CARPENTER, PERSIAN GULF WAR VETERAN, DISPLAYS SYMPTOMS OF GULF WAR SYNDROME. PYRIDOSTIGMENE WAS ADMINISTERED AS A PREVENTATIVE MEASURE AGAINST POSSIBLE EXPOSURE TO CHEMICAL WEAPONS, SPECIFICALLY, THE NERVE GAS, SARIN. Elaina read on. The report stated that Joel Carpenter was exposed to significant amounts of Sarin gas when stationed in Iraq and a weapons site was bombed by an American air strike. The document reported that Joel Carpenter was diagnosed with Gulf War Syndrome in 1992, significantly earlier than many other veterans. His symptoms were listed as being mostly neurological in nature. The report also detailed Joel Carpenter's sleep pattern disruptions, numbness in limbs, headaches, and memory problems. The summary ended by reporting that he was being treated with something called Anasymine to enhance his "viability for use by the government," whatever that meant.

As Elaina flipped to the last page, she began reading the results of the tests that Joel Carpenter underwent as a subject in the project. The tests indicated a high tolerance for pain, a high I.Q., and a strong propensity for Extra Sensory Perception, including, but not limited to, precognition and telekinetics. EEG results showed significantly altered brain activity, especially sleep patterns. *Precogni-*

tion? So Reid had finally discovered something after all these years of trying to convince his peers of the possibility of psychic abilities in humans. No wonder he had been so fanatical about his work here. As Elaina studied the file intently, she noticed that the shower had stopped running. She stiffened, and the hairs on the back of her neck prickled.

"What the hell do you think you're doing with that?" he shouted. "That's top-secret government information!"

Elaina whirled around, dropping the file to the floor where it scattered in all directions and faced Reid glaring at her, wrapped in a towel. Reid's face was red with anger and his jaw clenched and twitched, as it always did before he lost control.

CHAPTER 3

Ft. Clairemont Medical Research Facility
13 December 2002

BLANCETT led Joel down the sterile, white halls of the hospital, through the day lounge where many other test subjects watched television with unresponsive faces as if under some hypnotic suggestion emitted from "Jeopardy." Entering a different wing of the hospital, Joel continued to follow Blancett through the corridor until they reached the lab. The lab was a large room surrounded by one-way reflective windows, so that doctors and scientists were able to see in, but research subjects were not able to see out. Inside, the room was filled with computers, electronic monitoring devices, something that looked like a polygraph, an EEG machine, an EKG machine, and what looked like electric shock equipment. One man with USDSR printed on his shirt stretched out on a table with electrodes connected to his temples while being shown images on a screen. Another sat in a chair across from a technician with picture cards, only the backs of the cards visible to the subject. The technician asked the man to identify which card was the elephant. As Joel entered the room, Dr. Andrzejczak approached him. Andrzejczak, a balding man of about forty-five years old with small wire-rimmed glasses, was deceivingly harmless looking.

"Okay, Sergeant. Sit down." Andrzejczak motioned to a chair in front of a long table with electric shock equipment on it. "This should be easy."

Joel sat down in the chair uneasily, glancing toward the shock equipment while Andrzejczak placed a keyboard in front of him. Surprised, Joel looked up at Andrzejczak warily.

"Just a few precog questions to warm up, okay?" But Andrzejczak's tone wasn't questioning. He stared at Joel with a smirk barely playing across his mouth. "What will be the outcome of the Moran trial in Philadelphia, guilty or not?" The precognition tests often included easily veri-fiable information that could be confirmed within a day or two, like the results of a trial or a political vote. Even the horse races, which was a popular one for some of the techs.

"I don't know," Joel responded thoughtfully as if thinking very hard. "But your wife, Anne — isn't it? She's thinking about sleeping with your brother, Jim."

Dr. Andrzejczak's face turned beet red, and he clenched his fists, glaring at Joel. Joel couldn't hide his smile of amusement.

"Let's go on to the telekinetic portion of the testing, shall we?" Andrzejczak controlled his anger and spoke through his tight jaw. He would soon make up for Joel's humor. "Let's see if you find this as amusing, Sergeant."

Andrzejczak motioned to one of the technicians, and the man left the room briefly and returned with another subject, a frightened and gaunt man with a beard and wildly unkempt hair.

"Please, Man, no. I don't wanna do this. Come on, give me a break!"

"Hello, Joel," Dr. Rivers greeted him as he walked through the door, ignoring the other screaming subject. Joel stared up at Rivers trying to hide his revulsion.

"Don't do this. You don't need him." Joel struggled to keep his voice calm.

The man screamed as if in agony as Dr. Rivers and Dr. Andrzejczak strapped him into a chair.

"No, Man! Please!" the man pleaded as Andrzejczak began hooking up electrodes to the subject's temples, and Rivers attached a monitor to Joel's head. Joel struggled against the doctor, and two technicians rushed over to help hold Joel in the chair.

"Calm down, Sergeant. This will be over before you know it," Rivers told Joel.

"Charlie, it's okay, Man. Don't worry," Joel said to the screaming man as Andrzejczak finished securing him to the chair, and the electrodes were in place.

"Of course, Charlie will be fine. That's all up to you, isn't it, Joel?" Andrzejczak warned him.

"This isn't necessary. You know I can do this—you've seen me." Joel looked pleadingly at Andrzejczak, but he didn't acknowledge him.

"We need to record your brain patterns during the process." Rivers took it upon himself to explain what should have been obvious to the sergeant. "Telekinesis involves a lot more of the brain, and we need to know exactly why it seems to drain you like it does."

"You don't need him. I'll do whatever you want. I can move anything you want. It doesn't need to be like this," Joel begged Rivers, who always seemed to have more compassion than Andrzejczak.

"Joel, you seem to forget that without motivation, you've been very uncooperative in the past," Rivers answered.

Seeing this was getting him nowhere, Joel turned abruptly away from Rivers and focused on Andrzejczak with a fierce concentration. Joel shook violently, but he held on, and the intensity with which he stared at Andrzejczak increased. The veins stood out along Joel's neck, and sweat began to form on his brow. The room began to fade, and everything seemed to slow down and expand for Joel. It seemed to him that he could see the particles, even the atoms making up the electrodes on Charlie's temples.

Suddenly, the electrodes snapped off of Charlie and swung over to Andrzejczak, attaching to his head. Andrzejczak, shocked, slapped and pulled at the wires, but could not free himself of them. Joel fixed his gaze on the control panel of the box on the table. Suddenly, the knob for the intensity level spontaneously turned to full, and the power switch flipped on. Andrzejczak frantically pulled at the wires to no avail. He shook tremendously as the surge of electricity ran through him. His mouth opened to scream, but no sound came out. He fell to his knees, writhing in pain, spittle forming on his lips. Everyone else in the room, including Rivers, stood frozen with fear and stared in shock. Finally, Rivers rushed over to the wall to unplug the machine, but Joel seeing him, stretched out his hand toward him, and he fell to the floor as if he had hit a force field of some kind. Joel, exhausted, slumped over in his chair and lost consciousness. Two psych techs and Blancett burst in the door to help Andrzejczak. The techs freed Andrzejczak from the electrodes while Blancett helped Rivers to his feet.

"Help him." Rivers pointed to Joel. "Make sure he's okay."

Blancett went to Joel's side and checked his pulse, and then holding one lid open, shined a light into his eye.

"His pulse is racing, and his pupils are unresponsive," Blancett informed Rivers.

The two technicians helped Andrzejczak to his feet, but he could barely stand, and not at all on his own. Still he tried to speak, pointing at Joel.

"I want him tied down — isolaaation," Andrzejczak slurred his words together, barely coherent. "Give him — Thorazine — unconscious. I wan — him unconscious."

"Take Dr. Andrzejczak into my office. Have him lie down in there. Check his vitals," Rivers told Blancett. "I'll take over here."

Dr. Rivers bent down to check Joel over himself. Joel seemed to be conscious, but not coherent. Rivers pulled Joel to his feet, and with the help of another nurse, took him to a viewing room next to the lab. Joel looked around and tried to make sense of what he was seeing. Rows of white-sheeted beds, medical equipment, cameras. He looked up and saw a dark haired nurse with a moustache, and he felt the prick of a needle as the nurse injected him with a sedative. Joel relaxed back against the bed where they laid him. Rivers turned to two scientists in charge of the viewing room.

"Call me if anything significant happens." Rivers left Joel sedated in the viewing room.

The room was long with a few patients lying unconscious on the beds and wires and monitors attached to their heads, chests, and arms. Most of the beds were empty. On the outside of the rooms, TV monitors recorded and charted the results of the monitoring devices. Below these screens sat computer keyboards recessed into the wall. The two army scientists typed on the keyboards. Joel slept on one of the beds, already wired to the monitors, his eyes closed and his face relaxed. His eyes began to move rapidly beneath his lids, appearing to dream.

"His blood pressure is way up. That's weird," said one scientist, a short man with blond hair who couldn't have been more than twenty-five. The name on his badge read Clark. "His pulse is racing. Come here, Carlson."

The other scientist, Carlson, came over to look at Joel through the viewing window. He was much taller, with brown hair and much older, probably about forty.

"They sedated him, didn't they?" Carlson asked.

"Yeah. Enough to put a horse out for the night," Clark replied. "Hey, take a look at this." Clark pointed to the monitor. "Sergeant Carpenter." Clark typed something furiously on the keyboard. "Brain activity's extremely unusual. It's like he's conscious and in REM sleep at the same time. Breathing, heart rate, brain activity—all suggest he's fully conscious, but he's completely sedated, and he's showing dream cycles."

Carlson began typing on the keyboard next to Clark, and a different screen appeared on a second monitor. Clark moved over to Carlson to take a closer look.

"It doesn't make any sense. His REM patterns are off the chart, and one of the side effects of the sedative is an absence of REM sleep." As Clark said this, he and Carlson stared curiously at Joel in the television monitor. Suddenly, as if he knew they were watching, Joel's eyes popped open, and he stared directly into the closed circuit television camera. Joel seemed to be fully conscious and alert, not dazed as if he had just awoke.

"What the—?" Carlson took over the keyboard, checking the information for himself. "His readings haven't changed at all. The REM patterns are the same." Carlson shook his head as if this would clear everything up. "Unbelievable. Fucking impossible. Is he asleep or not?"

"He never was asleep. That's the point! He's operating in the conscious and the unconscious at the same time!" Clark seemed to think he had everything figured out. Carlson wished someone would explain it to him.

As they stared at the monitor, Joel Carpenter stared back, and suddenly, as he closed his eyes, the television monitor went to nothing but static, as if it had lost its signal.

"We'd better call Rivers." Clark stared at the screen of static.

CHAPTER 4

Morning
14 December 2002

YOU stupid bitch! How many times do I have to tell you to mind your own damn business?" Elaina fell backwards on the bed as Reid's fist caught the side of her head. The room was blurry and going dark as Elaina groped for something to hang on to. She slid off the bed and landed at Reid's feet. Reaching down, he picked her up by the back of her hair and the belt of her robe and slung her out of his way, so he could pick up the scattered pages of his precious file. When Reid had finished gathering up the pages of the file on The Ezekiel Project, Elaina got to her feet. She was still dazed, but her vision was clearer now. She felt a small amount of blood trickling down the side of her face. Reid went to her side. Frightened, she tried to block another blow, but Reid had calmed down.

"I-I'm sorry," she tried to explain before he could hit

her again. "I was just curious—it was lying open on the bed; I just glanced through it. I didn't see anything." Reid let go of her, and she managed to stand on her own. He put the papers back into his briefcase. Moving towards her again, he reached out and held her by the arms.

"I'm so sorry, Baby. I didn't mean to lose my temper like that," he said piteously.

"I didn't—I couldn't see—tell anything. I just started looking at it when you came in," she lied. "I was just curious. I'm really sorry."

"It's just that this work is classified, and I could get in a lot of trouble if someone found out I let you see it," Reid explained, smoothing her hair back from her face. He grabbed a tissue from the dresser and began dabbing the blood from the small mark his ring made on the side of her face. He pulled her into his arms and rubbed her back, holding her closely. She stiffened involuntarily at his touch. Reid let her go abruptly and a flash of anger crossed his face again. He turned away and began dressing for work.

As Elaina sat on the edge of the bed trying to regain control of her body, something caught her eye under the chair next to the bed. It was a few pages of the file that had drifted under the chair. Somehow Reid had missed them when he picked up the rest of the file. Elaina glanced over at Reid. He was pulling on his pants, then tucking in his shirt before zipping them up. She looked back down at the papers under the chair. Silently, she stood and walked closer to the chair. Without looking down, she stretched out her foot and kicked the papers under the bed, hiding them under the dust skirt. Reid glanced over at her.

"I'd better get Luke to school," she said running her fingers nervously through her hair. She headed for the master bath and shut herself inside. She cleaned her face and brushed her teeth, and when she thought he might be gone, she opened the door and found the bedroom empty. She dressed quickly and raced down the stairs to get Luke.

When she entered the kitchen, Luke was packing his lunch, and Reid was still there, pouring some coffee into a travel mug. Luke was very self sufficient for a third grader. He was used to packing his own lunch and even making his lunch on weekends. His mother and father were often preoccupied with arguing and fighting, so he stayed out of their way until they were done.

"Ready, Luke?" Elaina tried to sound cheerful, although her swollen and red face gave her away. The bruise from yesterday's blow was clearly visible on the left side of her cheek, and now the right side of her forehead was turning from red to purple. A small bandage covered the cut Reid's ring had made on her temple. Luke looked at his mother and then to his father, concerned.

"You'd better get going, Squirt," Reid answered Luke's gaze with a forced smile. Then he turned to Elaina, "Are you going to be at the studio, today?"

Of course, she went there every day. Her small dance studio downtown in the old but stylish part of Spring Forest, where she taught both children and adults jazz and ballet, was her only escape from the reality of her life. It wasn't the same as performing, but at least she could dance. Dancing took her away from all her troubles and made her feel free.

At first Reid had wanted her to stay home, but eventually he had bought her the dance studio out of guilt. Luke had just started school at the time. She had become pregnant again and was suffering from severe morning sickness. She hadn't done the laundry, and the house was a mess when Reid came home from work one day. He lost his temper and threw her down the stairs where the laundry room was located, suggesting she finish ironing his shirts. The fall caused her to lose the baby. She decided she wouldn't try to have any more children for awhile. Without another little one to take up her time at home, Reid gave in and let her open the studio to keep her busy. It was his way of apologizing for having lost his temper.

"Yeah. I have one ballet this morning, one at noon, and a jazz at one. I'll call you when I get a break," she replied without looking up. She just wanted to leave without any more conflict. She was already beginning to plot her escape. Not permanently, of course, but she had to get away for awhile.

She could go visit her mother and father in Arizona. Reid wouldn't get too upset over that. In fact, he approved of her occasional visits to see her parents. She would have to call him later and make it sound as if it had been her parents' idea to come. The only problem would be convincing him to let Luke miss a few days of school in the middle of the year. He wouldn't want Luke to miss school, and he might be suspicious if she pressed him. She had to try. She had to get away for a few days and clear her head, decide what to do. Maybe even get up the courage to leave Reid for good.

Suddenly, the memory of the man in the mall came to her, and she heard his voice in her head, *Don't do it. He knows, he knows.* Of course, he couldn't know. It was just her paranoia talking, and that guy was just a crazy person. Reid couldn't possibly know. She looked up at Reid and thought she saw suspicion on his face.

"Okay. I just want to make sure you're going to be there in case I need to call you or something. I wouldn't want to get your machine. You know how I hate talking to answering machines." He stared at her.

A lump rose in her throat. *There is no way he knows*

what I'm thinking. Oh God, I am getting paranoid. He's not God. She managed to smile.

"I know," she breathed, and her voice cracked. "Let's go, Honey." She reached for Luke and put her hand on his shoulder. Reid stepped over to her and put his arms around her and squeezed.

"It's going to be okay, Baby. I promise. As soon as the problems in this project get ironed out, everything will be back to normal," he attempted to reassure her. The only problem was that this was how normal was at their house. Reid bent down and high-fived Luke and smiled at him. Luke smiled back, all problems and concerns about what had happened between his mother and father seemingly forgotten.

"See ya, Squirt. Do good in school. Maybe you'll grow up to be just like your old man."

"Okay, Dad." Luke wanted to be smart and powerful and have an important job in the army just like his dad someday.

Elaina fought back tears as she drove Luke to school. Luke stared silently out the window. Lately they hadn't talked and joked around like they used to. Luke was becoming quiet and sullen. Elaina worried about his emotional stability, growing up in a house full of anger, violence, and fear. She just thanked God, if he was out there somewhere, that so far Luke hadn't been the target of Reid's anger. Still, she knew that it affected him. It had to.

"Luke, what do you think about going down to Arizona to see Papa and Nana for awhile?" Elaina looked over at Luke tentatively. Luke finally turned his eyes away from the window long enough to give Elaina a defiant expression.

"Why ask me? You don't care what I think."

"Yes, I do." Elaina's heart broke that he thought that.

"Okay, I don't want to go," Luke called her bluff.

Elaina took a deep breath and tried to think how she could turn it around so that it at least seemed like she was being fair, but she couldn't think of anything, and the fact that her eight year old son could outwit her, frustrated her deeply.

"Why do you have to be like that?" Elaina asked him. "I just want us to get away for awhile. It'll be fun."

"You mean get away from Dad, right?" Luke looked at her as if she was Judas Iscariot and Reid was Jesus Christ.

"Look, you know your dad and I haven't been getting along lately," Elaina tried the honest approach. There was no use lying to him; he seemed to be on top of things. "And I thought a little time away from each other might help."

"Why do I have to go just because you can't get along with him? You go. I want to stay here with him." Luke turned angrily towards the window again.

There was no way in hell that Elaina was leaving Luke here alone with Reid. Without her to be his punching bag, how long would it take Reid to start using Luke to relieve his stress just because he was convenient?

"I want you with me," Elaina replied sincerely.

"Maybe Dad does, too," Luke came back with his own logic.

"I'm sure he does," Elaina answered carefully, "but he works late, and who'll pick you up from school?" Elaina thought she had beaten his logic now.

"Maybe Nathan's mom could give me a ride." It didn't even take him a second to counter her arguments. What would she do when he was teenager? She shuddered to think.

"No, we're going together. It'll be fun," Elaina said cheerfully, trying to lighten the mood that hung like fog over the Jeep. "You'll get to miss school." She thought that would surely get him to change his mind, but he just shook his head, leaned over, and began playing with the radio, flipping from station to station. He stopped on one and turned it up. Elaina leaned over and turned it back down, desperate to feel like she still had some control as his mother. He glared at her with his amazing green eyes, and she had trouble staying angry with him. They were Reid's eyes, the shade of grass in springtime, and he had Elaina's dark skin to set them off perfectly. *He's going to be something with the ladies when he grows up,* she thought. She just hoped it wouldn't be something like Reid.

She pulled into the school parking lot of Washington Carver Elementary School and stopped in front of the large red doors. Luke reached down and grabbed his backpack from the floor and jumped out, slamming the door shut without so much as a goodbye. Elaina rolled the window down and stuck her head out the window to shout to him.

"I'll pack some things and get you right after school!" she yelled but Luke never turned around. She was sure he had heard her but was just being stubborn. She thought of the man in the mall again, and as an eerie feeling of dread came over her, she began to think that it might have been better to have gone right then. Just kept going right past the school without looking back. It would give them more time to get out of Colorado before Reid noticed they were gone, if he didn't already know what she was planning.

This was crazy. He didn't know. Besides she needed to get some things together and let her students know she was going to be gone for a little while, or she might not have any students left when she got back. *If I ever come back.* Of course, she was coming back. She couldn't stay at her mother's forever. Even if she could stand it, which she didn't think she could, Reid would know exactly where to find her, and he would bring her back. Or Luke back. Elaina wasn't so sure that Reid wouldn't be glad to get rid of her, but she knew he would want Luke. She was thinking things out too much again. *I might as well call Mama*, she thought. She dug in her purse for her cell phone at the first stop light, found it, and dialed before the light changed.

"Mama, how are you?" Elaina forced herself to sound excited to hear her mother's voice and not to cry. The urge to spill out all her marital troubles to her mother was overwhelming, but Teresa would never understand. She had stayed with Francisco no matter what and dealt with her marital problems in silence, except for the occasional weeping Elaina heard at night when her father was not at home. Although, Elaina's father had not been physically abusive, he had been overbearing and emotionally cruel at times. Teresa would never approve of her daughter running from a problem. Besides, she thought that somehow she was responsible for bringing out the worst in Reid and was too ashamed to tell her mother that her marriage had sunk to the point that it had.

"I'm all right, now that your papa has sold the extra cattle he was so worried about. You know how he gets this time of year, and how are you getting along, Honey?" Teresa asked, sounding tired.

"Good, really good," Elaina lied, unable to just let the truth out. "Hey, uh, I thought maybe, um, Luke and I would take a ride down there to see you and Papa. Wouldn't that be—"

"Well, what about Reid, Dear? Doesn't he want to come? I'm sure he won't want you driving all that way by yourselves."

"No, Reid has to work. He's been working really hard on this project, and he can't get away," Elaina replied.

"I don't think it's a good idea to leave your husband all alone when he has so much on his mind with work and everything. Hadn't you better stay and make sure he has everything he needs? You can come when things calm down at his army pole." Although Teresa spoke excellent English, she hadn't quite mastered the military terms.

"Post, Mama," she said, rolling her eyes as she listened to her mother go on about poor helpless Reid. If only she could tell her mother what she really thought about Reid. But her mother would be shocked and might even be angry and, no doubt, disapproving. Elaina didn't think she could handle that right now on top of everything else.

"We just thought it would be nice to come now. It's nice in Tucson in the winter, and it's been so cold here. Besides, we haven't spent a Christmas together in so long. Luke would really love to spend an old fashioned Christmas on the ranch," Elaina reasoned, suddenly deciding that Christmas would be a good excuse to stay away longer.

"You mean you want to stay until Christmas? You can't leave Reid alone at Christmas."

"He might join us by then, if he's through with what he's doing. Until then, he won't have time to notice we've gone anyway, Mama." Elaina wished that were true. "Mama, Reid will be fine by himself. He's really too busy this year to care about Christmas, okay?" There was no answer on the other end.

"Look, we just want to come, all right? Is it okay?" Elaina tried one last time and put a note of desperation into her voice that her mother didn't quite understand, but felt she couldn't ignore.

"Of course, Elaina. It's always fine for you to come. We'll see you in a couple of days. Drive carefully."

"I always drive carefully, Mama, and thank you. Bye,

Mama." Elaina sighed with relief. If it was always fine, then why did she have to go through so much pleading and explaining to get her to agree to one little visit?

Elaina pressed "End" on the phone and tossed it onto the seat beside her. She ran her fingers through her long dark hair, a nervous habit she'd never outgrown, and let out a deep sigh.

Arriving at the studio, she parked the Jeep in her usual spot, a few rows from the front of the building to leave the closer parking for her students, not that she had that many. Although business was good, she had a small clientele that consisted mostly of adults. Working only during school hours, limited her business potential dramatically. She only had one preschool class of ballet, then two adult ballet classes, one with only four students and the other with eight, and finally an adult jazz class with five students. Because Reid was an old fashioned husband and wanted Elaina home when he was home and didn't want Luke to be hanging out in a dance studio, either, she couldn't take the school age children that brought in the most business. She had tried to convince him to let her teach on Saturday; however, Reid had insisted that she needed to be available for weekend trips, which they never took, but just in case, she needed to be available. She didn't have any students coming for a couple of hours, but she liked to get there early to do paper work, straighten up, and to dance. In fact, mostly to dance.

Juggling two bags of supplies, her purse, and a gym bag, Elaina stepped out of her Jeep and shut the door with her hip. The studio was located in a small strip mall next to an interior design studio and a chiropractor. Walking carefully up the icy steps to her dance studio, she reached the door with no hands available to open it. The name on the door read: SPRING FOREST SCHOOL OF DANCE, Proprietor: Elaina Tessier.

She liked to go by Elaina Valdez-Tessier, proud of her Mexican heritage, but Reid was against the hyphenated maiden name. He thought when a woman married, she should leave all traces of her former identity behind and gladly be branded his property. There was a large wreath on the door and Merry Christmas was written on the window in Santa Snow. Elaina loved to decorate for Christmas. Christmas had always been her favorite holiday home on the cattle ranch in Arizona. She and her mother had gone all out decorating the large ranch style home from one end to the other, and it had been a good time, a warm and happy time. Now, just surrounding herself with Christmas décor brought back feelings that soothed her trampled soul slightly.

As Elaina struggled to turn the key in the lock, the phone inside began ringing. Shifting everything to one arm, she managed to get the door open and the key out of the lock. Entering the building, she punched in the code to disarm the alarm quickly, dropped the bags on the reception counter, and grabbed the telephone from the wall where it hung.

"Spring Forest School of Dance, may I help you?" Elaina answered the phone breathlessly.

There was a pause on the other end of the phone, and Elaina could hear muffled noises in the background. Then a man's deep voice spoke tentatively.

"Elaina Tessier?"

"Yes."

"Are you married to Colonel Reid Tessier?" the man asked, and Elaina swore it sounded like he was trying to disguise his voice somehow. A shiver went down her spine, and she was intuitively frightened. She gripped the phone tighter.

"Who is this?" she asked slowly.

"Do you know him?" the voice on the phone asked, and Elaina thought this must be some kind of prank or trick question. Did she know him? If she was married to him, she must know him.

"What?" Elaina asked, mildly perturbed now.

"Do you *really* know him? Because I don't think you do. I don't think you could be with him if you really knew him."

"What the hell do you want?" Now she was getting angry. First the guy in the mall and now this? Someone was trying to mess with her, and she had a feeling Reid was behind it. Trying to scare her, most likely. Maybe he did know she was planning to leave. Of course, it wouldn't take a genius to figure out that she might think about leaving after he bruised her face twice in a twenty-four hour period. "Tell me who this is?" she shouted into the phone.

"I can't." The voice seemed genuinely sorry, then became matter-of-fact sounding. "Just listen to me. You're in danger. I can't explain how I know this, and you probably won't believe me anyway, but I'm telling you the truth. He's going to try to kill you. You have to be careful. There could be someone following you right now."

Elaina turned toward the window and pulled the blinds apart to peer through them. A cold feeling of dread passed over her as she glanced up and down the street in front of the strip mall. It was pretty quiet this time of day, but there were a few cars parked along the edge of the street and in the parking lot. She could make out figures in some of them, but couldn't see well enough to know if they were looking at her or not. She felt like she was being watched, though. *Calm down*, she told herself. *It's just this guy on the phone making you feel that way.*

"Look," she said angrily into the phone, "I don't know

why you're doing this, but if you call here again, I'm calling the police." Elaina slammed the phone down on the hook and tried to get a grip on herself. She pulled up the blinds slightly again and peeked out. A man was standing right in front of the window smoking a cigarette. She almost screamed, and then he crushed it out and walked a few doors down and unlocked the nearby dry cleaning store. It was Mr. Chen, her neighbor. *I've really got to get a grip*, she thought.

CHAPTER 5

Ft. Clairemont Medical Research Facility
14 December 2002

COLONEL Reid Tessier sat in his office looking through his papers on his desk when Colonel Thomas Pierce thumped heavily on the glass pane of the door's window. He couldn't quite see through the glass. It was a milky beveled glass that allowed shapes and some colors through, but no details. Reid called out for whoever it was to enter. He regretted the decision to allow the unknown person to enter without identifying himself when he realized that it was Tom Pierce. Reid thought Pierce was a self-righteous pompous ass, and now he stood in front of him, angry and hurling accusations.

Pierce had been an old friend and colleague of Reid's going back to Ft. Huachuca, Arizona, seventy miles southeast of Tucson, where he was stationed when he met Elaina. Reid had been stationed there with Pierce, working on counteracting biological and chemical toxins and developing antitoxins when the United States government decided that this threat was an actual possibility in the very near future. Pierce was an idealist, believing that their work only involved the counter agents to these diseases, not the development of our own biological and chemical weapons arsenal. Reid, however, always knew that staying ahead of the arms race included having these types of neurological based weapons. It was the future, after all, and they were interested in the long term. It would save millions of dollars to fight an entire war without destroying a building, shooting down planes, sinking ships, not to mention all the priceless art and architecture that would be preserved in this more civilized type of war. Although anyone having seen the effects of chemical and biological agents would hardly consider them civilized. Yes, Reid was a realist. He had gladly worked on developing neurotoxins, similar to those used in the Middle East, and then went to work dutifully on their antitoxins. It wouldn't be prudent to have a weapon without also having the protection from that weapon, of course.

It was because of his excellent work in Arizona that he was transferred to Colorado and given a chance to work on his own project. To develop something of his own. Something that had been important to him all his life: The Ezekiel Project, or more specifically, the psychic abilities of human beings. The belief that the human brain had such untapped potential had never been a difficult concept for Reid to accept. The disbelief and ridicule he endured from his colleagues, however, caused him to become obsessed with proving the reality of this phenomenon professionally. He had the good fortune of meeting a like-minded person in the field with enough authority to begin the project.

Pierce had come along for the ride. Having worked

with Reid in the past, he was an obvious choice to partner with on the project. Pierce was never completely in the loop on things, though, because he was too squeamish about doing what needed to be done. He was, nevertheless, a brilliant scientist and a specialist in his area of brain chemistry, so Reid had accepted him into his group of scientists. Now it appeared, he would regret that decision.

Pierce thrust his hand down hard on Reid's desk, shaking the coffee and causing little droplets to spurt out and stain the papers underneath them. Reid looked at Pierce, annoyed, and mopped up the drops with a tissue.

"You did this! I can't believe this project is that important to you! These are our own men you—"

"Don't lecture me about my men!" Reid interrupted. "Everything I've ever done has been about duty—they understand that—why can't you?"

"They don't know that you're responsible, and I don't think anyone will be understanding when they find out you engineered this." Pierce looked at Reid incredulously.

Furious, Reid stood up, knocking his chair over behind him and grabbed Pierce by the shirt collar, pushing him back. They stood facing each other.

"Lower your voice, Pierce. This is a Level Five security project, and if you so much as let out one word of any of the details of this project to anyone without the proper clearance, I'll make sure you go down for treason!" Reid threatened.

"That's bullshit! You expect me to believe that Speare sanctioned this? And that he's agreed to use untested drugs in experiments on his own men? He'd never back you on this." Pierce shook his head confidently.

Before Reid could answer, Dr. Simms stuck his head in the open door.

"Sir, excuse me. I need to talk to you real quick," said Simms, looking from one man to the other.

Reid glanced at Pierce.

"Excuse us, please. I think we're through here, Colonel." Reid looked meaningfully at Pierce. "Come on in, Doctor."

Pierce reluctantly left and closed the door behind him as Simms entered and sat across from Reid's desk.

"It's Montoya and Thompson. They've both died," Simms said quietly, looking at the top of Reid's desk, avoiding his gaze. "Thompson, late last night, and Montoya, early this morning. As you know, they've been declining for some time now."

"What caused it?" Reid controlled his anger.

"We're not sure."

"What the hell is going on here?" Reid bellowed, finally losing some of his carefully constructed control.

"What I mean to say is that we're not exactly sure. We have some ideas, but we're still trying to determine if it was a result of the drug, or the altered brain patterns shorting out the normal functions of the brain, or just the disease itself, or—" Simms paused.

"Or what?" Reid asked impatiently.

"Or a combination of all three," Simms finished.

"Well, I'm glad you have it narrowed down," Reid said sarcastically.

"Colonel, this drug hasn't been tested. Very little is known about Gulf War Syndrome. There have been some documented deaths."

"We're testing the drug now. That's why we call them

test subjects." Again Reid could not keep the sarcasm from his voice.

"We're not testing the drug for safety in a controlled test group. We're testing it for its ability to enhance psychic abilities. It is definitely doing all that we had hoped in that regard, but we don't know what its long-term effects are. We're just now sure that it's highly addictive, similar to narcotics, causing severe withdrawals and even death when it's removed," Simms said gravely.

"How does this relate to Montoya and Thompson?" Reid seemed totally unconcerned with the long-term effects of the drug. "They weren't taken off the drug."

"No, but they were on it the longest. No one else has been on the medication for so many years," Simms explained.

"The 151st has been on it almost as long. They were the second group. Most of them seem fine," Reid countered. "Look, Simms, I need to know exactly what is causing my men to die. I need to know now. Sort it out. I don't care what it takes. Do your controlled test groups. I don't care. Just don't change anything with my best group. I need them right now. Carpenter, Marks, Garcia, Donner, and Blaine are needed for an assignment."

"Carpenter's not doing so well, Colonel. He just got out of the infirmary. I don't know if he'll be ready."

"He's just screwing off. He's getting stronger, but when he uses it all at once, this happens." Reid looked seriously at Simms. "Carpenter is the best I've got. I need him on his game, quickly."

"Sir, Carpenter has his own agenda, sometimes. He's not the most cooperative," Simms said carefully.

"That's okay. The best are always hard to control," Reid said proudly. "Now if you'll excuse me, I seem to have misplaced something very important."

Simms left the office, shutting the door behind him. Reid shuffled through his papers on his desk as he had been doing when Pierce first arrived, followed by Simms. It was amazing that he could accomplish anything with everyone poking their heads into his office every five minutes. And where was the rest of the file?

Reid suddenly lifted his head and stared blankly at the wall, remembering Elaina dropping all the papers, scattering them across the floor. But he had picked them all up, he thought. Stupid bitch, always giving him more work. He scooped all his papers into his briefcase and left the office.

* * *

Joel Carpenter sat in the corner of the day lounge watching the show, amused. The activities of the research hospital were not always so amusing, but today everything couldn't have gone better if he planned it. He didn't plan it. He knew he would take the opportunity whenever it presented itself, and he did.

Several nurses and psychiatric technicians were checking blood pressure, administering medication, and subduing angry and confused patients. Joel usually thought of the subjects in the Department of Scientific Research as patients in a mental ward more than as test subjects. He couldn't help it. Most of the subjects suffered from one kind of delusion or another. Many were psychotic at times. All of them were afflicted with terrifying images running through their minds at any given time, some without provocation. Some could control their precognitive abilities better than others, like himself. But even he suffered from an occasional uninvited image taking over his reality—seeing the deaths, murders, crimes, and even accidents of others involuntarily. His visions were mostly like this. He couldn't consciously distinguish between the types of visions he saw, so there must be something in his own mind that focused in on that type of precognition. Controlled, perhaps, in the same way other dreams came. A result of individual personalities and preconceived ideas, as well as the events in one's life at the time. Perhaps, there was a raison d'être within him that necessitated this type of revelation. Maybe a divine destiny, conferring upon him these warnings, forcing him to intervene or be found unworthy by some holy being. The only thing was he knew where his visions came from, and they weren't from God. Oh, they liked to think of themselves as gods, but they weren't quite there, yet. Joel wasn't ready to see the government or the military as hallowed after what they had put him through for the past ten years or so. Had it been that long? He couldn't keep track anymore. He had always accepted his responsibilities as a soldier, just like he had done during the war. But what had that got him? In here.

"Get 'em outta my head!" Charlie shouted. Charlie Marks was going off again. Charlie, whom he had saved from electrocution in the lab. Was it this morning, yesterday morning? Yes. He was sure it had been yesterday. Joel had left the infirmary this morning. The sedative had worn off sufficiently enough for him to be conscious of the chaos around him, and his vitals had gone back to normal after peaking during his telekinetic performance for the doctors. Rivers had been impressed; he could tell. But Andrzejczak had gone home, probably for the rest of the week after being in the infirmary for a couple of hours himself. Andrzejczak would be hell to deal with when he got back.

"I want 'em out, out!" Charlie shouted. Joel knew what it was like to hear the voices in his head. Sometimes he wanted them out, too. Especially, Elaina's. He thought she was very beautiful. A dark haired intelligent looking beauty in her twenties. Judging by the age of the boy in the photograph, she was probably closer to her late twenties. He assumed she was his mother. He had seen her photograph on Colonel Tessier's desk. He had asked about her, but Colonel Tessier hadn't appreciated his interest. He looked up Colonel Tessier's family information in the laboratory computer when Dr. Rivers hadn't been watching him very closely a couple of weeks ago. He found out that her name was Elaina, and their son's name was Luke. Knowing this didn't make seeing her in his premonitions any easier.

He tried to put her out of his mind, but she continued to visit him regularly in his dreams and while awake in his visions. Her dark eyes pleaded with him, and she seemed so alone. She was reaching for her son but couldn't find him. He was taken from her, he felt. Not yet, maybe, but soon. She often interrupted him when he was on assignment, making him unable to predict anything about what he was asked, only seeing her desperate face.

Still, when she disappeared for a few days, he missed her and would try to see her. That's when he'd taken the photo from Tessier's office. He had it hidden in his room, and he would take it out and look at her. Then he started getting the feeling that she was in danger, not just her son. In fact, he sensed she was in far more danger than the boy.

"I need my medication!" shouted Charlie.

Nurse Blancett and a young psychiatric technician tried to calm Charlie. As the psych tech held Charlie's arm, and Blancett prepared an injection of Thorazine, Joel saw his opportunity.

CHAPTER 6

14 DECEMBER 2002

A S Elaina hung up the phone, she ran her fingers nervously through her hair. The phone rang again almost immediately. Practically jumping out of her chair, she took a deep breath and stared at it while it rang a few more times. Finally, getting up her nerve, she answered it.

"Hello," she said cautiously, skipping the memorized greeting she always used, assuming that it was the anonymous caller once again. It was not.

"Elaina." It was Reid.

"Reid," she said, relaxing back against the chair. She couldn't remember the last time she was relieved to get a call from him. "What is it?"

"I just wanted to tell you again, how sorry I am about this morning. I want to make it up to you tonight. Let's go out to dinner and forget about work for awhile."

"Uh—I was going to call you. I talked to Mama this morning, and she wants me to bring Luke for a visit. I told her we'd leave this evening. I think it would be good for Luke to get away for a while and have some fun." Elaina held her breath, waiting for a negative reply.

"Okay. I'll miss you though," he said suspiciously. "We'll have that dinner when you get back then."

"Sure," she said, breathing again, but still feeling out of breath. She was a terrible liar.

"Elaina," he began, "about that file—I only got so mad because I could get in a lot of trouble if anything happened to it or anybody saw it; do you understand?"

"Of course, I understand. It won't happen again; I promise. We're leaving after school, so I'll see you when I get back," she replied carefully, hardly believing she was going to get off this easily. Sometimes when Reid was feeling guilty for losing his temper, he would be extremely understanding for a couple of days, and although she was glad about that, she couldn't know how long it would last.

"Drive safe." His warning sounding a little more threatening than the typical admonition. "Love you, Baby. Kiss Luke for me."

"You, too, and I will." She hung up the phone and automatically peeked through the blind again. She couldn't get the caller or the man in the mall out of her head. The crazy mall guy seemed to be sent by Reid. But if Reid had known she was planning to leave and thought she wasn't coming back, then why didn't he say anything on the phone just now? And the other man, the caller—he seemed to be trying to warn her against Reid. Either way she just wanted to get out of here for a while and get some perspective.

As Reid hung up the phone in the bedroom of their

small Victorian house, he looked around the disheveled room. After being unable to locate the missing papers in the file, he had gone back home to have a look. The bedroom looked like a tornado had torn through it. Drawers were open and clothes were strewn from one end of the room to the other. Chairs had been overturned and the coverlet had been thrown off the bed.

"They've got to be here somewhere," he muttered to himself. He couldn't believe that Elaina would take the papers, but he made it a habit not to trust anyone; after all, she was reading the file this morning.

The phone began to ring, and he abandoned his search to answer it.

"Excuse me, Sir," apologized Captain Patrick Carlson, "Lieutenant Sheldon is missing."

"Missing?" Reid asked.

"He never showed up for the meeting today, and no one has seen him at all. He's not picking up on his mobile or at home," the captain informed him.

"It's not like Sheldon to miss the meeting," mused Reid. Sheldon was in charge of the security in the research facility, and every Monday they had a staff meeting. "Is everything else okay?" Reid asked.

"Seems so, Sir," replied Carlson.

"All right. Let me know if he comes in. It's probably nothing," Reid informed him, but he was concerned, not for the lieutenant, of course, but for the security of the facility. Reid hung up the phone, opened the closet, and began opening shoeboxes and dumping their contents to the floor.

At the dance studio, Elaina applied some more makeup to her bruises and changed into a leotard and dance sweats to get ready for her first class. She couldn't have the preschoolers asking how she got her face all bruised up. The "I walked into the door; aren't I clumsy?" line was getting old. Who really believed that anyway? Even if it were true, people would think you were lying.

Elaina passed out stickers to her morning preschoolers as they filed out of the studio with their mothers and a couple of fathers. She waved good-bye to the last of them and sat down to do some paperwork. She probably ought to have canceled her adult classes for the rest of the day and gone home to pack. Something was telling her she needed to alter her plans a little. She went to the window and pulled the blinds apart and peered out, remembering the man on the phone earlier. He didn't sound like the same person who had accosted her in the mall the day before. She didn't see anyone out there, except a dawdling child from her class and her impatient mother trying to shoo her into the car.

It was beginning to snow again. Thick, heavy, wet snowflakes fell slowly from the white sky. Elaina loved when the sky was like that, totally and mysteriously white without a trace of blue. Even the clouds were not recognizable, as if the whole sky was one enormous snow cloud, so full and overflowing that it wasn't dark like most storm clouds. It was glowing white because it was so overfull of fat, white flakes ready to dump on the unsuspecting people below. It was the kind of snow that stuck together perfectly for snowballs and snowmen. The kind that built up and deepened to three or four feet. Enough to tromp playfully through and unfortunately ended up muddy and sloppy on the sides of the road after people drove on it all day. Why did all of her nice thoughts have to turn dark and depressing all the time?

She shut the blinds and picked up the phone and

stared at it. Maybe she should call Reid and tell him she was not going to her mother's after all. Then she wouldn't have to be so afraid he was going to find out what she was planning. It would be less suspicious. She pulled out the scrunchy holding up her hair and let it fall in a cascade around her bare shoulders. She ran her fingers nervously through it, thoughtfully. Shivering suddenly, she pulled a University of Arizona sweatshirt over her skimpy dance leotard.

She had attended the University of Arizona when she met and fell in love with Reid, who was stationed at the nearby Ft. Huachuca army installation. During summers off from school, she worked part-time as a receptionist in the research building there, Civil Service. Her father thought that Civil Service was the best thing she could do with her life and had insisted that Elaina get some good, practical work experience as long as he was going to foot the bill for her "artsy" education. She dropped out in her second year and went with Reid to Colorado to start a new life together as Mrs. Reid Tessier. She always planned on transferring to a Colorado university, but Reid always said that it wasn't a good time. Maybe next year, he'd say, but next year wasn't ever any better. She wanted to take Fine Arts, maybe get her license to teach since she couldn't perform. Reid had said she didn't need college to teach dance if she had her own studio. She wanted to take some business classes, but he didn't think that was necessary either. She'd done okay without finishing college, though. She had a very good mind for business and didn't even hire someone to do her taxes. She was very proud of that.

Maybe someday she would get the nerve to leave Reid for good and start her own dance studio somewhere else. And she could have a couple of night and weekend classes, too, to make more money to support herself and Luke. *If only Reid would get hit by a truck or something,* she thought. That thought that had probably entered her mind a hundred or more times through the years, made her feel dark and sinister, and though, with this thought came a wonderful feeling of freedom, there also came a heavy and overwhelming feeling of guilt. What kind of person was she that she could entertain such morbid thoughts about the person with whom she had at one time fallen in love? Even if he wasn't that person anymore. Maybe he never was.

She was not a very good person, nor was she a very good mother. She knew it. If she were able to keep Reid happy, then he wouldn't let the stress of things at work get to him so much. And she wasn't a very good mother because sometimes, when she was so concerned about Reid, she neglected Luke. Instead of caring how Luke was handling something, she was only concerned about how Reid would react in any given situation.

Shrugging off her thoughts, Elaina noticed that her next class was about to start.

CHAPTER 7

Ft. Clairemont Research Facility
14 December 2002

JOEL Carpenter wasted no time once he saw his opening. While Blancett and the private were calming Charlie, Joel got up from his chair and covertly slipped behind the empty nurses' station. He rummaged through the cabinets Blancett had left open when Charlie began his desperate tirade.

"Hey, that's Thorazine, Man. I need Anas—" Charlie railed.

"It's okay, Charlie. I'm gonna get you your medication right now," Blancett informed the now crying Charlie. Blancett headed toward the nurses' station, and Joel ducked down just in time to avoid being seen. He edged his way around the counter to hide as Blancett unlocked a cabinet to the right of him and removed a small bottle labeled, Anasymine, and a hypodermic needle. Blancett left the cabinet open once again and hurried over to Charlie.

Joel crawled back over to the open cabinet and sorted through the bottles, checking their labels until he found several filled with the curiously green liquid marked, Anasymine. Charlie began to scream again, and Blancett struggled to inject the wailing man with the medication.

"Hurry up, Man!" Charlie shouted at Blancett. The soldier held his arm still so that Blancett could find the vein. Charlie sank to the floor as the medication took effect.

Joel boosted five bottles of the Anasymine and a handful of syringes and shoved them inside his pants pockets. He heard Blancett groan as he and the psych tech picked up Charlie, one under his arms and the other under his feet. Joel got to his feet and slowly walked towards the sleep hall, where the subjects' rooms were located. Blancett and the psych tech were too busy carrying Charlie through the day lounge to notice the bulging pockets of Joel's pants.

In his room, Joel opened his footlocker and removed a small Ziploc bag from the bottom. After placing the bottles of medication and syringes into the bag, Joel wedged the bag in the bottom of the footlocker underneath a few pairs of boxers and some books. Joel noticed a couple of photographs hanging out of one of the books. One was of his mother, who died shortly after he was born, with his father, who had raised him in the logging country of Washington, right outside the small town of Olalla. His father was dead now, too. He had died when Joel had just gotten back stateside after the war. Joel hadn't been able to attend the funeral. He was drafted into The Ezekiel Project by then. And Colonel Tessier wasn't big on letting his soldiers out on leave.

The other photograph was of Elaina and a much younger Luke, the one he'd taken from Tessier's office. Sometimes he wondered what had made him take the photograph when she was constantly invading his dreams anyway. But he did like to look at her picture. He took the photo of Elaina and Luke and sat down on the bed to look at it for awhile when he began convulsing uncontrollably. Joel fell backwards in pain, seized by a precognitive vision.

He is in the dark warehouse, the only light coming from a small, swinging lamp overhead, casting strange shadows all around. He thinks of Plato's "Allegory of the Cave" and imagines figures dancing in the corners. He turns his head and scans the warehouse. In the shadows, Joel makes out army Jeeps and trucks that are parked in rows on one side, one with the engine pulled out and the hood open. On the other side of the warehouse is a desk and next to it boxes of files and a couple of dust-covered filing cabinets and Reid Tessier pointing a gun at — he struggles to see in the dark. It looks like Elaina, yes, and Luke, standing behind Tessier. Elaina is upset, crying, he thinks, and she is pleading with Tessier. She begs him to let their son go.

Joel doubled over in pain as the vision intensified.

"Reid, please — just let him go. It's not too late," Elaina cried. "You can let us go and run. Get away before they come for you."

Tessier, still looking at Elaina and pointing the gun at her, speaks to Luke, still standing behind him, "Luke, I want you to close your eyes, son, and turn around and face the other way."

"No!" Elaina screams. "Run, Luke, run!"

Joel came out of his vision drained, sweating, and in terrible pain. His head felt as if it had been caught in an invisible vise. His breath was shallow, and he strained to get more oxygen. Regaining his bearings, looking around the room, he saw Blancett and Simms staring down at him closely. Looking up at them, he discreetly shoved the photo of Luke and Elaina underneath the edge of the blanket. Simms stepped forward and shone a bright light in first one eye, and then the other. Simms turned to Blancett.

"Get a blood pressure reading," Simms told Blancett. Blancett complied, and Joel concentrated on slowing his breathing, calming his pulse. He began to feel normal once again and sat up, glaring at the two men.

"Were you having a psychic episode, Sergeant?" Simms asked, continuing to examine his eyes.

"A psychic episode?" Joel asked in a mocking tone.

"A vision—a premonition of the future, or of the past, or a telepathic vision from one of our minds here in the present?" Simms leaned backward and turned off the light.

Annoyed, Joel scratched his sweat-drenched head and tried to appear nonchalant.

"No. I just zoned out for a minute. I need some sleep—I haven't slept in four days. It makes you kinda spacey, you know? That's all." Joel didn't want to be hooked up to a bunch of monitors in the viewing room again. Twice in one twenty-four hour period would be too much. Besides, he had plans. Joel hoped he looked convincing. He had no idea how long they had been watching him, but it was likely they had seen him writhing in pain. "I've had this stomach problem. I think it was the chili they served last night. You're lucky you don't have to eat here."

"According to your chart, you were heavily sedated last night. And we have an EEG of your REM patterns from early this morning," Simms told him with a troubled expression.

Irritated, Joel lost his patience. "Look, I told you I haven't slept. I don't care what your chart says. That sedative doesn't work. It just makes me groggy." That was the truth, and Joel hoped they would leave him alone thinking he needed the rest. It had been a long time since he'd slept well. Since before the war, in fact.

"Sergeant Carpenter, we're going to increase your medication a small amount. It'll help make your thoughts clearer," Simms told him in a condescendingly calm voice.

Joel didn't know if Simms thought he was losing it, or if he just wanted to enhance the visions, now that he knew Joel was having some heavy duty ones.

"My thoughts clearer? Don't you mean my 'psychic episodes'?" Joel asked sarcastically. Joel pushed Blancett's hand away from his arm and tried to get to his feet, but he began convulsing again.

"He needs his shot," Blancett told Simms as he reached in his pocket and began to prepare the injection.

"Go ahead. Increase by three cc's."

"Hurry up." Joel shook violently.

As Blancett injected him with Anasymine, Joel relaxed back onto the bed, feeling better immediately.

"Very well. We have you scheduled for some more tests tomorrow. Get some rest today. And Sergeant Carpenter, let's try to be a little more cooperative, tomorrow. Goodbye." Simms was obviously referring to the incident yesterday morning. What was their problem? They wanted him to use his telekinetic abilities, and he did.

"Dr. Rivers had to go home and will probably not return this entire week because of your little stunt." Joel suppressed a smile.

As soon as they were gone, Joel rose from the bed and knelt by his footlocker. Opening it, he shoved two pieces of gum in his mouth to kill the bitter taste, one of the many side effects of the Anasymine. Joel rummaged through the locker until he found a large brown paper bag hidden in the bottom under his clothes and books. Opening the bag, he pulled out an army uniform. He gathered up the Anasymine and syringes he had placed in the locker earlier and placed them in the bag, along with three packages of gum.

Stripping off his clothes, Joel peeked out the door and checked to make sure no one was coming before changing into the uniform. Buttoning the uniform, Joel stared at himself in the mirror. The uniform he was wearing said SHELDON across the left front pocket. Joel wondered if they would be missing him, Sheldon, soon. He would need to be out of the facility before anyone became aware that Sheldon was missing.

Joel hadn't wanted to resort to violence, but knocking out Sheldon and taking his uniform had been an unfortunate necessity. Tying him up and dragging him into the janitor's closet had been risky, but not nearly as risky as hanging around in the lounge waiting for a chance to get into the medication cabinet had been. Sheldon would be okay, and they were bound to find him before the end of the day. At least by the time Morris, the janitor, arrived. Sheldon would have a major headache, but his pulse had been strong when Joel left him, and with any luck, Joel would be long gone by the time they found him. Joel rubbed his whiskers. Three or four days worth of stubble wouldn't help him appear to be an active duty soldier, but because of the potential threat the telekinetics posed, they were only given the opportunity to shave once or twice a week under the scrutiny of an armed guard.

Joel piled some clothes and his pillow under the blankets of his cot and tried to form the shape of a sleeping man, hoping that would buy him a little more time before they noticed his escape. He gathered the bag under his arm, then remembering the photograph of Elaina, he returned to the bed and retrieved it from under the blankets. He looked at it briefly and tucked it into the bag, returned to the footlocker, and took the photo of his mother and father and tucked it down next to Elaina's. Joel cautiously opened the door to his room and stuck his head out. He looked up and down the hall. Seeing no one, he sneaked down the hall toward the kitchen entrance, past the hospital rooms where patients slept. This was the best exit because he didn't have to pass the day lounge or the nurses' station.

Reaching the kitchen, he found it empty. It was past lunchtime and the kitchen appeared quietly deserted; the pots and pans shone in the light that streamed in through the window above the large stainless steel sink. Everything had been cleaned and neatly put away. The kitchen crew was gone, just as Joel had hoped. *Maybe things are going to work out for a change,* Joel thought cheerfully, as he opened the back door and stepped out without setting off any alarms. This door was generally left unlocked during meal times, so the crew could take their cigarette breaks, and he had hoped that the last person coming through the door had forgotten to lock it. So far, so good.

Stepping off the cement steps and around the can that served as an ashtray for the kitchen personnel, he turned the corner and ran smack into Stevens, the cook, smoking a cigarette. Joel's breath caught in his throat, and thinking quickly, he saluted the man and continued walking. Stevens quickly changed hands holding the cigarette and straightened up, standing at attention, saluting Joel in return before recognition came suddenly over his face. His troubled gaze followed Joel as he walked past. Dropping his cigarette and grinding it under his boot, Stevens stepped forward and called to him.

"Hey! Whatta you doing out here—in that uniform?"

Joel stopped and turned around striding back towards Stevens, smiling as if he had a perfectly reasonable explanation.

"Well, see —," Joel began and interrupted himself by throwing a hard right punch to Stevens' jaw, knocking him sideways on top of some trash barrels. Making far more noise than Joel would have liked, Stevens landed unconscious, sprawled across a spilled trashcan. Joel looked hesitantly around, wondering if anyone had heard the loud crash. He bent down next to Stevens and lifted his wrist, checking his pulse before running away through the lot behind the building and into the thick cover of trees surrounding the facility.

Miraculously, Joel didn't see anybody following him through the thick underbrush of the forest right outside the research facility's main building. He ran fast through the pinions and lodge poles, ducking low, his clothes catching on low branches and snapping some dry twigs not yet covered in snow. Barely keeping his balance as the hill sloped downward and picking up speed, he ran forward. His knees weak from his disease, his lack of sleep, and the leftover heaviness of the recent sedatives, he hardly kept himself from falling and tumbling headlong down the hill. If he fell, he would surely sustain injury, at the very least being cut by the low, sharp branches of the dense trees. Reaching the bottom of the hill where the pines thinned, he found himself in an aspen grove where the sun shone through much brighter. Still, he heard no unwanted footsteps over his own ragged breathing. He was ashamed at his current physical condition. Once a strong and formidable soldier, he shuddered at what he'd become.

Past the trees, Joel reached the outer perimeter of the post marked by a twelve-foot electrified fence. Joel stopped in front of it, reading the high-voltage warning signs posted on the fence. His eyes located the transformer box on the far edge, next to the fence, standing on a pole. Joel focused his breathing and concentrated intently, using his telekinetic power to explode the box in a dazzling display of sparks before it caught into flames. A loud buzzing sound emanated from the fence itself until there was a loud pop as the fence was neutralized. Releasing his control over the transformer box, Joel dropped to his knees, severely weakened from the effort. But hearing distant voices shouting from the other side of the hill, Joel staggered to his feet and climbed the now impotent fence.

CHAPTER 8

14 December 2002
1400 Hours

IN the research facility, everyone was in an uproar over Joel's escape. Stevens hadn't been out long, and as soon as he'd come to, he had reported Joel's actions. Stevens had also mentioned that Joel wore Sheldon's uniform, which prompted a thorough search of the building and grounds for not only Joel, but for Sheldon as well. Sheldon was found in a utility closet, bound and gagged, but not in bad condition. Joel had hit him on the back of the head, earlier that morning and removed his uniform, leaving Sheldon in his undershirt and boxers. After tying him up and covering his mouth with duct tape, Joel had gone to the day lounge and sat, waiting for his opportunity to get at the medication in the cabinet. He wouldn't last long on the outside without it. One of the soldiers on guard duty, a corporal named Bill Fishe, explained what he had learned from Sheldon to Dr. Simms. Dr. Simms was surprised to find that Joel had been in any condition to escape, especially if it required the knocking out of military personnel, particularly after his experiences the day before.

"Find him, now. I don't want to have to explain this to the colonel," Simms said grimly.

"Sir," interrupted another guard named Conway, entering the room breathlessly, "it looks like the subject made it over the electric fence. It's been shorted out somehow."

"Get out there and find him!" shouted Simms. Now he would have to report it. He dreaded calling the colonel. Simms picked up the phone on his desk reluctantly and dialed Colonel Tessier's cell number.

Reid was still going through Elaina's things when his cell phone rang.

"Yeah?"

"Colonel, it's Simms. Carpenter is gone, escaped. About two hours ago, near as we can figure."

"Carpenter?" Reid was now very irritated. First his file, now Carpenter. "Joel Carpenter?"

"He's obviously been planning this. He attacked Lt. Sheldon sometime this morning. Tied him up in a closet, took his uniform. After lunch he attacked the cook and went out the back. Took out an electric fence. His powers are getting stronger."

"I want him back before anyone gets wind of this. Find him and make sure he doesn't get hurt. Use the tracking system. Activate the chip. He's the key to this whole project. Make sure you debrief anyone who knows about this. I want them to understand that no one mentions this to anyone, especially not Speare."

"Yes, Colonel. I've already got a team on it," Simms assured him.

Reid hung up the phone and tossed it into his briefcase. What else could go wrong today? The missing pages from the file obviously weren't here. Elaina probably took them with her. But what could she possibly want with them? And now Carpenter had escaped.

Reid grabbed his briefcase and headed downstairs. He heard the sound of a car pulling into the driveway, then a door slamming shut. Putting down his briefcase, Reid went to the window and parted the curtains for a look. Colonel Pierce was walking up the front steps. Reid stepped back and smiled. At least one thing was working out better than he had planned. He had thought he would have to go after Tom, but here Tom was making it easy by coming to him.

The doorbell rang and Reid immediately opened the door, motioning for him to come in. As Tom entered, Reid glanced quickly up and down the street to see if anyone had witnessed his entrance to the house. No one was usually home this time of day on his street, and he saw that today was no exception. He smiled and shut the door.

CHAPTER 9

Spring Forest, Colorado
14 December 2002
1400 Hours

ELAINA walked out with Valerie, a student from her modern jazz class, the last class of the day. Valerie Fielding was a friend of Elaina's and often stayed after the other students left, but today Elaina hurried her out. Hanging out a "Closed" sign on the door and setting the alarm, Elaina grabbed her purse, gym bag, and Valerie by the arm and left the studio.

"You sure are in a hurry to go on that trip. You haven't even changed. That's not like you. Is everything okay?" Valerie looked at Elaina with a curious expression.

"Yeah. It's just that it's a long drive, and I have to go home and pack if I want to leave straight from the school after I pick up Luke."

"Are you leaving him?" Valerie asked softly. "The makeup doesn't quite cover those bruises."

"I fell in the shower this morning; I told you," Elaina tried to look irritated by the question, but she was touched by the concern and embarrassed at the same time. She felt her face flush and feared that the sweat on her face would wear off the makeup even more. "Reid and I just need a break."

"So how long are you going to be gone?"

"Just a week or two." Elaina resumed walking to the car, not wanting to waste more time.

"Do you really think that's going to change anything?"

Elaina stopped and looked angrily at Valerie. She knew Val was trying to help, but interference, well intentioned or not, always made Elaina angry. She supposed the thing that annoyed her the most was that Valerie could see through her lies and knew the truth she was trying to hide. Ashamed, she wondered how many others knew the truth as well.

Elaina didn't answer. Reaching her Jeep, she opened the door and threw in her gym bag and purse.

"Okay, okay. I'll mind my own business, for now. Have a good time." Valerie leaned forward and gave Elaina a friendly hug.

"Thanks," Elaina said, more grateful for Valerie dropping the subject than for the wish for a good time. "See you when I get back."

Elaina glanced at the dashboard clock. 2:00 PM. She had an hour and a half before Luke got out of school. She headed home.

Arriving home, she noticed a strange car in the driveway. She parked behind it, wondering who would be at her house this time of day. There was no other car around, only the blue Honda that she didn't recognize. It could be someone to see Reid, but he was never home at this time of day, and his car wasn't out front, but of course, it could be parked in the garage. If Reid were home, she wouldn't be able to pack freely without risking another confrontation as she'd hoped. She didn't have time to waste, however, so she decided to go in. Anyway, Reid would be busy with the person visiting and wouldn't bother her.

As she opened the front door, she heard loud and angry voices coming from inside. Entering the house cautiously, she stopped and listened, trying to figure out who the other person was. One of the voices was obviously Reid, but the other, although she recognized it, couldn't be placed right away. By the sound of it, they were arguing over something related to work. Elaina crept quietly across the foyer, thinking she could sneak upstairs and leave them to their argument. Apparently they had not heard her Jeep pull up, and Elaina was glad. She could still avoid an uncomfortable confrontation. She stopped when, from the corner of her eye, she glimpsed them in the kitchen.

Her view into the kitchen was mostly obstructed by the hallway wall, but she could see the far left side of the kitchen. Occasionally, the man arguing with Reid would back up far enough for her to see him. She recognized him as a colleague of Reid's, Tom Pierce, someone that they'd known from Arizona. She remembered Reid mentioning that Tom was transferring to Colorado from Ft. Huachuca to work in the research facility with Reid. He'd been glad about it at the time.

Elaina made her way silently to the edge of the foyer and pressed herself up against the wall, trying to remain unseen. She heard Reid trying to reason, albeit loudly, with Tom.

"We had to try the drug now. By the time they approved it, the research would have leaked out, and China and every other country with their noses up our ass would know what we're doing!" Reid paused. "It's working, Tom. I know it."

She saw Tom clearly now as he leaned back against the countertop and looked at Reid with disgust.

"What have you done? You're a colonel in the United States Army, and a respected expert in the field of chemistry and biology—a scientist, and you've turned your back on every ethical practice—"

Reid moved closer to him, and Elaina could see a little of his face as he glared at Tom.

"You don't know what I've done! What I've sacrificed for this project," Reid interrupted passionately, as if he were a politician playing the indignant to an audience.

"It's true, isn't it? You did this to them. You gave them the disease, so you could study them." Tom let go of the countertop and stood up straight, meeting Reid's gaze with his own defiant one. "Blancett asked me if it was true, but I couldn't believe—"

"Blancett overhears too much," Reid lowered his voice slightly and took a step back out of Elaina's view. "The first soldiers that were exposed to Sarin—that wasn't our fault. But when we treated them, we found out what they were capable of—only the ones that were immunized first—the Sarin—it changed them," Reid reflected thoughtfully as if he had gone back in time and couldn't understand how anyone could question what he'd done under the circumstances.

"You quit treating them and started experimenting on them." Tom didn't try to hide the disdain in his voice.

Elaina couldn't believe what she was hearing. Did this have anything to do with the Ezekiel Project? No wonder he didn't want anyone reading about it. She crept forward, risking being seen to get a better view of the kitchen.

"The Myotrophin used for treating their symptoms retarded the paranormal abilities, permanently," Reid justified. He wondered if Tom could understand if he knew the whole story. Maybe he wouldn't have to eliminate him. After all Tom had been a close friend, one of the only ones Reid had ever had. But he didn't trust him now, not after threatening to expose the project. Reid didn't think he could ever trust Tom again.

"So you needed a new group of test subjects," Tom finished for him.

Reid nodded, "A group of hand-selected soldiers, all tested for a higher than normal sensory ability, all immunized against Sarin—we knew they would live," he suggested as if this justified the whole thing. "It was just a matter of changing the coordinates of the bombing a few degrees and making sure the men would be there at the right time." Reid began to get excited, thinking of the brilliance of his plan. "Don't you see, we weren't trying to kill them—we were just making a better soldier. And the drug I developed—we developed, it was better than we'd hoped. The Anasymine—it's growing new pathways in their brains to handle their new abilities."

"It's killing them," Tom responded.

"We don't know what's killing them." Reid's enthusiasm was dampened by Tom's remark.

"Who else is involved? You couldn't have engineered all of this alone."

"The pilots didn't know what they were shooting at— they were just following orders. But it was worth it, Tom. Look what we've done."

"Yeah, look what we've done. They're dying, Reid.

They can't sleep, they're all addicted to Anasymine, and they're becoming psychotic! All because we want a new weapon." Tom's voice began to get louder, and he stepped toward Reid, full of righteous indignation. "And all you care about is getting the credit—everyone knowing how you were right all along—but do you really believe that Speare will agree with what you've done? I know he'd never go along with this. He'll can this whole project when he gets back and finds out two men have died and how this whole project came to be."

"He isn't going to find out." Reid stepped forward, forcing Tom to back up.

"Have you lost it? You can't keep something this big a secret. Two subjects are dead! One is missing, and the rest are fucking lunatic junkies! And I've heard you've got some of them walking the streets doing errands for you, following your wife; God knows why. What happens when one of them goes off in public?" Tom ran his fingers through his sweaty hair and shook his head before going on. "I'm not going along with this anymore. I don't know what's happened to you, Reid, but I don't want any part of this."

Furious, Reid grabbed Tom by the throat and threw him up against the wall. Now Elaina could see both of them clearly. She couldn't believe what she'd heard or what she was seeing. She held her breath as Reid continued to choke him. It was clear that Tom could not breathe, and Reid had no intention of letting him go. Horrified, Elaina was unable to move, frozen with fear. As the life passed out of Tom, he slid slowly to the floor.

Elaina gasped, and Reid turned abruptly toward the foyer. Their eyes met, hers wide with fear and disbelief, and his narrowed with the realization that she had heard everything that they had said. And she had seen everything. He wondered exactly how long she'd been standing there. It made little difference. She had certainly seen enough to guarantee him life in a military prison.

Finally able to respond, Elaina spun and ran towards the front door. It was only a few steps away, but her legs felt like lead, and she seemed to be moving in slow motion, as if in a dream. The doorknob seemed a complicated thing as she struggled to open it, hearing Reid's footsteps on the foyer tile behind her. Flinging the door open, she didn't bother to close it as she raced down the steps to her Jeep. Thank God, she had put her keys in her coat pocket rather than in her purse. She found them easily as she reached the Jeep, but her fingers did not cooperate as she fumbled for the correct key. The Jeep was unlocked, but she wanted the key ready as soon as she got in. *Never mind*, she thought, *when I get in, I can lock the door and then find it*, but just as she made this decision, her nervous fingers dropped the keys, and she saw them slide under the Jeep, aided by the slippery ice.

Reid was sliding on the ice next to the blue Honda, struggling to keep his balance. Elaina fell to her knees and slapped her hands around blindly under the Jeep, staring uselessly at Reid coming toward her. Her fingers struck the keys and slid them farther under. Tearing her eyes from Reid, her heart, a ball-peen hammer striking her ribs in an arrhythmic beat, she dropped her head to the ground and saw the keys inches out of reach. She lowered her stomach to the ground and stretched her arm farther under the vehicle. Her fingers fought frantically for the keys, and she hooked the ring on one finger and pulled them forward, clutching them tightly in her hand. She knocked her head on the bottom of the Jeep as she pulled up from her position. Scrambling to her feet, she couldn't help but turn to see why Reid had not yet reached her. He was also scrambling to his feet, having fallen on the ice just past the Honda. Only seconds had passed, but it seemed an eternity since she'd fled the house.

Getting to her feet, she felt as if she were moving under water, struggling against the current. She pulled the door to the Jeep open and hurled herself inside, slamming it shut and trying desperately to locate the lock button without taking her eyes off Reid who was now next to her, reaching for the door handle. Her fingers found the lock button, and she began to cry as she heard the beautiful click of the door locking. She managed to start the engine and put it in reverse. She hit the gas, looking behind her through the rearview mirror. When she turned forward to see what Reid was doing, he was staring after her, punching numbers into his cell phone. Finally, hitting dry pavement, she squealed out of the driveway and headed away from the house.

CHAPTER 10

Spring Forest, Colorado
14 December 2002
1430 Hours

SERGEANT Joel Carpenter walked down the streets of Spring Forest, Colorado, free for the first time in over ten years. He scarcely had time to enjoy the crisp mountain air, the mysteriously white sky, or gaze at the snowcapped mountains surrounding the small town. He wanted to run but avoided drawing attention to himself and restrained his gait to a brisk walk. The people of Spring Forest were, of course, used to seeing military personnel walking around town in uniform with an army installation so nearby, but Sheldon's uniform was ill fitting, showing his socks underneath his pants. Besides, he expected the USDSR staff to be covering the entire area very soon. He needed a change of clothing and a car. The car would be easy enough to get. He knew how to hotwire most types of vehicles, and most people in Spring Forest didn't lock their cars. But getting a change of clothes with no money would be a more difficult matter. He had just about decided that he should get the car first and worry about the clothing in the next town when he spotted a laundromat across the street. Joel entered the brightly lit, but run down establishment and tried to look natural, which was difficult without any laundry. He avoided looking directly at any of the few patrons inside. Just inside the door and staring suspiciously at him was an old woman who looked like a bag lady with frizzy, white, unkempt hair and a dirty house dress, covered with two mismatched sweaters and a puffy vest, the down feathers creeping out of the several holes in the material. On her feet, were very worn combat boots. Across the room was a couple, a boy and a girl of possibly eighteen, making out in the corner, not even aware of his existence. He sat down in one of the elementary school-style chairs lining the edge of the windowed wall. The bag lady began checking the payphones in the corner for change that might have been unwittingly left by those more fortunate than herself. After thumbing through a magazine for a few minutes, he heard the buzzer sound in one of the dryers. He watched for a moment to see if anyone of those in attendance would go over and empty the machine. When after a moment none of them did, he nonchalantly acquired one of the provided rolling baskets, wheeled it over to the dryer, and began unloading it. He had hoped that some of the machines were being used by people who had chosen not to stay and wait for their clothes, but those who would return after completing some errand.

The bag lady watched him skeptically, but she made no attempt to claim the clothing. In fact she probably was not there to do laundry at all, but to get in from out of the cold. It had been snowing on and off all day, and the ground was still covered in yesterday's snow. The snow that had begun melting the day before was now slick ice. Joel rummaged through the clothes until he found a flannel shirt and a pair of jeans that seemed to be his size. Turning his back to the bag lady, he tucked the clothes under his arm and covered them with the paper bag he was carrying. If he tried to stuff the clothing into the bag, she would surely notice and think it odd. Thinking the clothing hidden, he pushed the basket past the dryers and over to a table by the door when the old lady shouted at him.

"Hey!" she bellowed as if she were the personal security guard policing the laundromat.

Startled, Joel abandoned being sneaky and fled through the door into the cold air. She followed him outside, shouting after him.

"Hey, them ain't yer clothes, Boy! You bring 'em back here 'fore I call the police!"

Joel ran to the edge of the building and decided to go around behind it to check for an unlocked car. The bag lady was drawing looks from passersby.

"You some kinda pervert?" he heard her yell as he rounded the building. To his dismay, there were no cars parked in the alley at all. He cut through a couple of empty parking lots and noticed that this area of town had a lot of closed businesses that had gone under and were vacant. Turning right on Dale Street, he walked about two blocks and came to a more populated area. The temperature seemed to be dropping, and Joel stuffed his hands in his pockets, the clothes and bag stuffed into the crook of his elbow. He felt some coins in one of his pockets.

He was passing a small diner festively decorated for Christmas with the smell of strong coffee wafting out every time a person pushed open the front door to leave or enter. The front window was edged with Santa Snow, and twinkle lights blinked around the inside border. Unable to resist, he went into the coffee shop and sat on a stool at the front counter. Besides, he would need to change his clothes somewhere and the sooner the better.

Garlands hung from the ceiling of the diner, and there were more Christmas lights inside. Joel remembered that it was December 14th, but at the facility they hadn't even put up the three-foot fake tree, yet. Every year the staff would try to make a big deal out of getting the subjects to help decorate it, but it was a joke. A poor attempt at normalcy considering everything that had been done to them. It would have been better not do anything in observance of the holiday. Instead, it served to remind them of all they'd lost.

The waitress behind the counter was cute with short, wavy auburn hair and a friendly smile. The tag pinned to the front of her uniform said that her name was Angie. Her smile widened when she saw Joel, and she immediately leaned over the counter provocatively and held a pen to her pad of paper.

"What can I get you, Sweetie?" she asked flirtatiously, looking him up and down.

"Just coffee. Please." Joel lowered his gaze, her stare unnerving him.

Angie picked up the coffee pot off of the hot plate and began pouring.

"Ain't you got some pretty blue eyes?" she said bending her head to get a better look. "Want some sugar, Sugar?"

Joel shook his head and stared at his steaming coffee. Angie looked at him curiously.

"No need to be shy, Honey." She laughed, assuming her overpowering sensuality had embarrassed him. He was embarrassed; after all he hadn't been around women in a very long time. Every once in a while a female soldier worked in the facility, but by and large, men were the majority because all the subjects were men and it was a live-in facility, and the army frowned upon such fraternization. But Joel was too concerned with anyone getting a good look at him to be flattered. It was good that she thought him shy instead of suspicious. He sipped at his coffee quietly.

"That'll be ninety-five cents, Hon," she said with a wink, not giving up.

Joel reached into his pockets and brought the coins out and laid them on the counter. He fingered through them, counting. Three quarters, two dimes, and three pennies. He was relieved that he had enough to pay. He had no idea how much anything cost anymore, but he realized three cents was not an adequate tip.

"I'm sorry—it's not much of a tip. It's all I have at the moment." He looked at her apologetically. Angie smiled seductively and covered his hand with her own.

"Don't you worry about it, Sweetie."

Joel never heard what she said. Her touched electrified him, and he grasped her hand on top of his and clung to it. The room went dark and he began to shake. *He sees Angie standing before him, but not here, in a small bedroom with a burgundy satin comforter on the bed and a candle burning on the bedside table. She is wearing a red silk teddy, and she is unbuttoning his uniform shirt. She caresses his bare chest, and then her hands rise to his shoulders and pull the shirt down over his arms. She leans forward and whispers in his ear.*

"I'll take my tip now, Soldier," she breathes in his ear.

Joel jerked his hand away from hers suddenly and stood up shakily. He grasped the edge of the counter for support. Angie was surprised, but she looked at him with concern.

"Are you all right, Sugar?" she asked.

Joel regained his composure and tried to smile.

"I'm not feeling so good. Have you got a restroom I could use?"

"Sure," she said a little disappointed. "On the left." She pointed down a hallway to the left of the entrance.

"Thanks," he said. Picking up his coffee and his belongings, he headed for the restroom to change.

"You take care of yourself, Hon," she called after him, checking out his butt as he walked away.

Joel found the tiny, dirty restroom and locked the door behind him. He set his coffee on the sink and quickly changed out of his army pants and into the jeans. They fit well, even the length, which was surprising because he was so tall. Joel took off his uniform shirt and dropped it to the floor. His hands were shaking as he tried to take a drink of his coffee, and it spilled over the edges. He looked up at himself in the mirror with disgust. His body was still in good condition, at least it seemed so to the eye. His chest was well-muscled, and he still had a six-pack across his stomach, a result of numerous push ups, pull ups, and sit ups done in the sleepless hours spent alone in his room.

He dumped the Anasymine, syringes, and three packages of gum out of the paper bag and tore the plastic wrapper from one of the needles. He opened the bottle of Anasymine and poked the needle through the small opening and pulled back on the hypo, filling the syringe. Lifting it up in front of him, he flicked it lightly with his finger and squirted a small amount out into the air to prevent deadly air bubbles from entering his blood stream. He flexed the fist of his left hand open and shut until he could locate the vein in his arm. His inner arm was filled with needle tracks just like a heroin junky. Again, an overwhelming sense of disgust washed over him. He injected the Anasymine and relief flooded through him as the drug made its way through his veins. He stopped shaking immediately and leaned back against the wall for a moment. His breathing returned to normal. Turning on the cold water, he splashed his face several times, then dried it on paper towels.

Joel reached down and picked up the blue flannel shirt and put it on. It, too, fit well. He put Sheldon's army boots back on and thought that they would be good in the cold weather. He didn't have any others anyway, and no one would think black boots odd this time of year, especially in Colorado. Joel picked up Sheldon's uniform shirt and began to roll it into a ball, but he felt something inside. He reached into the inside pocket of the uniform shirt and found a wallet. Going through the contents of the wallet, Joel found a Visa card and Sheldon's military ID as well as his driver's license inside. No cash. He pocketed the wallet and stuffed the uniform into the paper bag along with all of the medication and syringes. Bending over, he picked up the photos of his father and of Elaina and Luke and put them into the bag as well. He stuffed two pieces of gum in his mouth and put the rest of it in his pants pocket. He lifted his coffee from the edge of the sink and sipped it. It was already getting cold. He left it on the edge of the sink, picked up his paper bag, and left the restroom.

He looked towards the counter to see if Angie was looking. She might think it was strange that he'd changed, or she might just want to talk to him again. Either way, he couldn't afford the time or the attention. He sneaked past her and out the front door when she had her back turned, talking to the cook. He wandered through the parking lot, checking doors of vehicles until he came to an open white truck. It was kind of old, but there wasn't much of a selection, at least unlocked. *Times must be getting worse if everyone locked their doors in a place like Spring Forest,* he thought. He took a quick look around to make sure he was unnoticed and didn't see anyone. He jumped in and pulled the wires out from under the steering column.

CHAPTER 11

Spring Forest
14 December 2002
1430 Hours

ELAINA swung the Jeep recklessly into the parking lot of Washington Carver Elementary School and pulled into a space so quickly that she hit the curb before she stopped and threw it into park. Breathing hard and her heart still racing, Elaina sprang from the vehicle and raced into the building. She passed the office and headed straight for Luke's classroom. She didn't have time to go through the procedures of signing him out, having his room called, and then waiting while he slowly packed up his things and met her in the office. After all, those procedures were for his safety, but in this case his safety depended on her getting him out of town and away from his father as soon as humanly possible. After narrowly escaping from her own home, she wasn't about to wait for school to get out or for the office to follow their procedures.

She wondered what Reid would have actually done if he had caught her. She hadn't waited to find out, yet she had a hard time believing that he would be capable of killing her, even after what she'd seen. She supposed that she was being naïve. After all, hadn't he struck her that very morning, as well as the night before? All of a sudden, she remembered the anonymous phone call asking if she really knew her husband. She supposed she didn't, but had no idea who might be calling, and if they were trying to warn or threaten her. Seen in conjunction with the strange man at the mall, it seemed it was more likely a threat, something aimed at scaring her. It had worked, but that was a moot point now. Nothing could have scared her more than what she'd just witnessed—and heard. Her mind started going through Reid and Tom's conversation and attempted to make sense of it, and then she forcefully put it out of her mind. She didn't have time for that right now, or the concentration. She just needed to get Luke and get as far away from here as she could, as quickly as she could.

Lost in thought, Elaina burst into Luke's classroom, throwing open the door to the quietly reading class with a loud clang. Mrs. Cox and the entire class turned and stared at Elaina in surprise. Luke flushed a deep red and glared at his mother, deeply embarrassed by the appearance of his mother in class. One little girl with red braids announced that the visitor was Mrs. Tessier, Luke's mother. She recognized her from a field trip for which Elaina had volunteered to drive. Luke lowered his gaze to his desk in complete humiliation.

"May I help you?" Mrs. Cox inquired, coldly polite.

"I need to pick up Luke, now. We're on our way out of town," Elaina stammered, waiting for the inevitable information about procedures.

"You'll have to sign him out," Mrs. Cox informed her

patiently. Elaina did not respond, but instead walked over to the coat hooks and took Luke's coat from the brass hook protruding from the wall and scanned the cubbyholes for his black and green backpack.

"At the office," Mrs. Cox continued. "First door on the left as you enter the building."

"Sure. I'll do that on the way out." Elaina found his backpack, snatched it up, and motioned for Luke to follow her. "Come on, Luke. We're in a hurry."

When Luke didn't immediately get up, Elaina went to his desk and began placing his books in the backpack. Luke got out of his seat, now looking more confused than embarrassed or angry, even concerned.

"What's wrong, Mom? Why are you here so early?" Luke asked.

"I'm sorry, Mrs. Tessier—" Mrs. Cox began.

"Okay, we'll be sure and check with the office on our way out." Elaina turned to Luke and helped him on with his coat. "Let's go," she told Luke, ignoring the protests from his teacher. She pulled Luke by the arm, out the door, and straight past the office without stopping. Luke stared at his mom in confusion, running to keep from being dragged out of the building. Once outside, Elaina ran for the Jeep, still pulling Luke by the arm.

"Get in!" Elaina yelled to him when they reached the Jeep, and she jumped in the driver's side while Luke got in the passenger side. Elaina tore out of the parking lot, burning rubber once again. She bounced down the curb and started out into the street without seeing a car headed her way. Slamming on the brakes, she barely missed hitting the car passing in front of her.

"Coño, shit!" Elaina slumped forward on the steering wheel as the driver beeped his horn at her and drove

<figure>- 91 -</figure>

on. She ran her fingers through her hair and took a deep breath, trying to regain control.

"Mom, what's going on?"

Elaina pulled herself together and pulled back out on the road, this time checking the intersection carefully, both directions. *That's right, get us killed in a car accident while trying to escape getting killed*, she thought, disgusted with herself. Still driving too fast, she sped down the road with a white-knuckle grip on the wheel, staring straight ahead.

"Mom," he began again.

"I want to get to Nana's," Elaina explained lamely.

"Mom, would you slow down? What's wrong with you?

"Luke, something has happened, and we need to leave in a hurry. Everything's going to be okay. Just relax."

"You relax! You're the one racing down the street." Luke turned around looking for his things in the backseat. "Where's my stuff?"

"I didn't have time to pack anything."

"We're leaving for Nana's without anything? Why?"

"I told you I didn't have time! Don't ask me any more questions, okay?" She looked over at Luke for the first time, taking her eyes from the road. She thought he looked terrified. "Look, we'll just buy new stuff when we get there."

"Coooool." Luke smiled, temporarily placated. Elaina slowed down slightly when she entered SR-9, the highway toward Breckenridge, and Luke relaxed. He bent down and rifled through his school backpack and pulled out a Gameboy and headphones. "At least I've got this with me," he said. He put on his headphones and began playing.

"Luke, I'm sorry I didn't pack your stuff," Elaina apologized.

Luke pulled off the headphones and looked angrily at his mother.

"You don't care about my stuff," he said, his anger and hurt coming out in the tone of his voice. "You don't care that I don't want to go on this stupid trip." Luke put his headphones back on before Elaina could reply and went back to his game, remaining silent for several miles. His angry remarks stabbed Elaina in the chest, and she took a deep breath, letting it out in a ragged sigh, stifling any useless response. She couldn't ever seem to think of the right thing to say to him anymore. More and more it seemed like all they ever did was fight. She stared at the road and concentrated on her driving, periodically checking her rearview mirror for Reid.

Reid Tessier spoke on the phone hanging from the kitchen wall. Already, there was no sign of a body, no sign of a struggle. Of course, strangulation did not leave much mess.

"Let me take care of her. Please—my son is with her. Let me handle this my own way," Reid pleaded into the phone. He listened for a moment and then replied, "I promise I won't let you down. I have as much at stake here as you do." He listened again. "Yes, Sir. I'll be in touch." Reid hung up the phone and ran upstairs to pack a bag.

The man on the other end of the line hung up the phone and nodded to the large man in front of him.

"Go ahead—you're on this," he said gravely. "You can't expect a man to deal with his own family. Let's track her cell phone and credit card activity. If that doesn't work, we'll put out a warrant on her, but I prefer to avoid that."

"What about the kid?" Harris asked.

"You can't let him live."

Nodding, Harris picked up his cell phone and made the call to start tracking Elaina and Luke.

CHAPTER 12

On The Road
14 December 2002

ELAINA drove east to Denver on autopilot, and Luke stretched restlessly in the seat next to her. It was the route she normally took to her parents' place. Although out of the way, she liked to go through Denver, stopping at her favorite restaurant for an Italian meal, and then heading south on I-25 all the way to Sante Fe to spend the night in the enchanted southwestern city. She usually went this way when she was alone, preferring the shorter route when traveling with her restless son.

Castle Rock, a small town just south of Denver, came into view, and Luke sat up hopefully.

"Can we stop here and eat?" he asked when the town came into view.

"Let's wait till Colorado Springs," she said wanting to get more distance between them and home.

"I'm tired. Where are we going to sleep?" he asked.

"In Colorado Springs, I guess," she said, checking the dashboard clock. It was nearly seven o'clock. She hadn't realized it was that late. No wonder he was hungry.

Reaching Colorado Springs at just after eight, they checked wearily into a hotel, looking forward to having something hot to eat and a warm bed for the night. Elaina had to give the clerk her credit card number as security for the room, but she didn't like it.

Up in their room, Elaina looked through her purse and counted her money. Sixty-seven dollars and forty-two cents. That wouldn't get them very far. Her cell phone suddenly began ringing and almost made her drop her purse. She sat staring at the ringing phone, and for an instant she considered answering it. Then she remembered how people could be traced even more easily through a cell phone than a landline.

"Aren't you going to answer it?" Luke asked.

"No," Elaina said punching the power button on the phone. "We'd better leave this thing off." She considered throwing it away for a moment, and then decided to keep it and just leave it turned off. She might need it in case of an emergency. She threw it in her gym bag, stretched out on the bed, and ordered room service. Luke tried to talk her into going down to the pool, but she told him no, and now he sulked on the bed in front of the television set.

She needed to start getting smart. She couldn't go around charging hotel rooms on her credit card and using her cell phone when Reid was surely looking for her. He had no choice but to find her, she thought, after what she'd witnessed. The thought made her shiver, and she kicked off her shoes and got under the covers, waiting for dinner to arrive.

"What if Nana tries to call?" asked Luke out of the blue.

Suddenly, Elaina realized that there was no way they could go to her parents' house. What had she been thinking? She had told Reid she was going to her parents. And even if she hadn't, that would be the first place he would look. She had been too preoccupied with getting out of town and too blown away by what she'd seen to stop and think about where they should go.

"Mom, did you hear me?" he asked.

"Yeah. We'll call her. We have to tell her that we're not coming after all."

"What?" He looked at her, shocked. "Where are we going?"

"I don't know, yet. I think we'll still head south for awhile, then maybe east," she said thinking she would rather stay in as familiar territory as she could.

"Do we still get to buy new stuff?" he asked.

"Yeah," she said, smiling at him.

Elaina had dozed off from sheer exhaustion built up from the day's events when a knock at the door startled her awake. She sat up in bed with a start before she remembered that she had ordered a pizza and some soda from the kitchen. She threw the covers back and heaved her feet off the edge of the bed, still groggy from her nap cut short when Luke scurried to his feet and for the door with the intention of paying for the food. He snatched up the twenty-dollar bill she'd left on the table.

"The food's here, Mom," he said as he ran for the door.

Her stomach dropped as she saw him unlatching the dead bolt on the door before she could stop him.

"Luke, no!" she yelled sharply. "Don't you open that door!"

But he had already turned the handle and the door swung open a few inches as Luke turned to see why his mother was so upset. The man in the hall wearing a hotel uniform looked in curiously, wondering why his arrival with the pizza had caused such a stir.

Elaina was up on her feet and to the door in an instant. She smiled at the man and took the pizza and drinks from him.

"Go ahead and pay him," she said to Luke, and he did.

When the man had gone Elaina turned to Luke angrily.

"I am the only one who answers doors or phones on this trip. Understand?"

Luke nodded silently, withholding any smart remarks for the moment. He had never seen her like this. She wasn't usually this bossy.

They ate the pizza and watched an old movie on the television, *Scavenger Hunt*. It had Cloris Leachman among a group of family members required to complete a bizarre scavenger hunt in order to win the inheritance of their deceased relative. Luke loved it, and Elaina had to admit that it was pretty funny, too. It grabbed her attention for long enough intervals to allow her to laugh and loosen up a little, releasing some tension.

At ten-thirty, Elaina checked the dead bolt and shut off the light before slipping into the bed next to Luke. A loud clanging ring jarred her from her restless sleep where she dreamed of Reid strangling her in her own kitchen while Luke watched. She sat up and struggled to make sense of the absurdly loud jangling, and she saw the telephone sitting on the nightstand with its red light blinking and realized that it was the source of the racket. Her stomach knotted up as she looked at the bedside clock and noticed that it was two-thirty in the morning. She could think of no one who would have a reason to call her from the hotel at this time of night. Luke mumbled something next to her that sounded like "answer the phone."

She leaned over the nightstand and lifted the receiver from its cradle and merely listened without saying anything. She wasn't going to purposefully give herself away, even if whoever it was surely knew it was she on the answering end of the call.

"Get out, now! Get out of the hotel, right now," the deep male voice on the other end of the line enunciated the last two words carefully, putting special emphasis on the urgency of his advice.

Fear shot through her, and her chest constricted as she listened to the exigency of his command. Familiarity struck her as well as she listened.

"Go!" he shouted, and the line went dead.

It was the voice on the phone at the studio, she realized. She dropped the phone where she sat rather than hanging it up and shook Luke awake. She stumbled out of the bed and pulled on her jeans and t-shirt, throwing everything randomly into the gym bag.

"Get dressed," she demanded in a whisper to Luke, who was standing at the end of the bed staring at her, confused.

"Mom, what's going on?" he asked, frightened.

"Somebody bad is coming," she answered. "Now, just do what I say and no more questions."

Luke tied his shoes, and Elaina threw his Gameboy and headphones into his backpack when she heard the click of the dead bolt being turned at the door. She looked at the door and saw the dead bolt knob turning slowly to the right, and at the base of the door was a shadow of two feet spread wide apart. Fear welled up inside of her, and she looked to Luke and put her forefinger to her lips, motioning for him to be silent. He stared back at her, too frightened to say anything anyway and waited for her instructions. Only she didn't have any to give. There was no way out of the room other than the door that the intruder was now coming through.

The door swung open silently and a large, burly man of about forty stepped through, holding an abnormally long gun out in front of him. He shut the door behind him and took a step forward. Elaina recognized the extension screwed to the end of the gun, increasing its barrel length, as a silencer. She'd seen them only in the movies, but they must have been pretty accurate because it looked just like the ones on the big screen. She realized in an instant that there was only one reason the intruder would have that attached to his weapon—murder. He had come there to kill them, or at least to kill her, and she doubted he would let Luke live after witnessing his mother's murder. He was here to kill them, and as quietly as possible.

The man grinned as their eyes met, and Elaina did the only thing that came to her mind at the moment. She threw herself at the bedside table, knocking the lamp to the floor, the cord jerked from the wall socket and the lamp crashed to the ground, extinguishing the only light in the room. The room was plunged into darkness, and Luke screamed.

CHAPTER 13

14 December 2002

REID tossed his bag in the back of his dark blue Ford Explorer and threw his cell phone on the seat next to him on top of a family photo of himself, Elaina, and Luke. He needed to show it around and ask questions. He planned to follow the same route he thought Elaina would take to her parents' house. He was sure that's where she would go. She didn't have any other family, and he felt confident she wouldn't know what else to do.

At Ft. Clairemont, Simms typed the number into the computer that activated the chip that was buried under the skin in the back of Joel Carpenter's neck. Once activated, the program would locate Carpenter and track him wherever he went via satellite transmission. There was no place they couldn't track him. There was a small delay in the system, though. There always was when dealing with satellites, but it wouldn't be a problem. They would have Carpenter back home where he belonged in no time.

Tessier had ordered that all his subjects who were used for assignments have the chip surgically implanted to keep track of them. They were far too valuable not to.

Simms downloaded the information to the satellite link and waited for a reply.

* * *

Joel swatted at the back of his neck, driving down the road in the stolen white truck. An insect must have gotten into the cab with him because it felt like he just got bit. It must have been a small spider because it certainly wasn't mosquito season, and it had felt small, harmless. He pulled into the hotel parking lot he'd seen in a vision and spotted Elaina's black Jeep immediately. He had a bad feeling about this place for some reason. He parked the truck on the other side of the lot from the Jeep and went inside.

* * *

Elaina crawled across the floor with a sharp pain in her side from hitting the lamp and rolling to the floor. She heard the man stumbling around the room and Luke whimpering by the bed. *Luke, be quiet!* she thought, afraid that the man would locate him first by the sound. Elaina put her hands around the lamp and felt it. It was metal at the bottom and felt heavy. She tore the shade off of it and gripped it by the brass fixture, holding it upside down. She sat on her knees listening when suddenly she saw a flash of fire, momentarily lighting up a portion of the pitch-black room. She saw the man standing in front of her, gun in hand. The smell of the gunpowder nauseated her, but she managed to get to her feet, still gripping the lamp. Luke had shrieked when the gun went off, the sound he made almost louder than the soft "pew-w-w" that the gun made, muffled by its silencer. She was relieved to hear that he still whimpered in the corner.

She was completely blind. Her eyes had started to adjust, but the bright flash from the gun had rendered her sightless again. Elaina inched forward with the lamp clutched tightly in her hands, and suddenly she felt the warmth of a body pass beside her. She twisted her body to the side and raised the heavy lamp over her head and let it crash down, miraculously hitting its mark on the back of the man's head. The blow rocked her body, and her arms felt tingly. She heard the man fall forward on his face, just missing the bed. She screamed for Luke to get out and ran for the door. Swinging open the door, the dim light from the hallway illuminated the room softly. Elaina turned to see Luke huddled on the floor beside the bed, apparently too frightened to move. Her eyes moved to the motion-less man on the floor. She ran to Luke and pulled him up, dragging him to the door.

"Come on," she pleaded. "We have to go."

The man didn't move. *He must be unconscious*, she thought. Her eyes went to the bed where she had left her gym bag and Luke's backpack. Her wallet was in there and her car keys, but she would have to step over him to get it. She walked cautiously to the man and kicked him with the edge of her hiking boot. He didn't move. She took a step closer and reached, stretching her arm as far as it would go and hooked her finger under the strap of the gym bag. She curled her finger around it and pulled it into her arms with a thump. The man hadn't moved. She saw a drop of blood drip slowly down his brow toward the carpet, and a sick feeling filled her as she realized that she might have killed a man. She swallowed the lump in her throat and stretched out farther, resting one hand on the mattress, toward the backpack, feeling safer now. The sight of the blood, although making her ill, also relaxed her fears somewhat. She snatched up the pack and spun around, stepping over the man and heading for the door where Luke stood, staring blindly into the room.

"Come on," she said pulling him by the arm out of the room.

She heard the ding of the elevator as she stepped into the hall. She glanced toward it as the doors slid open. She turned in the opposite direction and ran, pulling Luke by the arm. They turned left down the hall, and she saw the green "Exit" sign over the door to the stairs. She shoved open the door, and they ran down the stairs to the ground floor. Elaina heard the heavy fire door slamming shut above them and pulled Luke faster.

"Luke, you have to concentrate," she told him. He had snapped out of his paralysis, but he cried softly, mumbling to himself, and was stumbling down the stairs. She had to keep lifting him up to keep him from falling. They reached the bottom floor. She pushed open the door, and they ran through the side exit of the hotel that led to the back lot where she had parked the Jeep.

She shoved Luke in through the driver's door and followed him in, scrambling for the ignition key. She started the Jeep and squealed out of the lot, just as the door leading out of the hotel swung open.

CHAPTER 14

Road Trip
15 December 2002

ELAINA drove, Luke sleeping in the seat next to her. A faint orange glow began to show on the eastern horizon beyond the red-rock valley, draped in snow. Elaina yawned and pulled over to the edge of the highway and stretched. She switched on the dome light, reached across Luke, and pulled a map from the glove compartment. It still wasn't light enough to read, yet. She hadn't seen anyone behind them for miles and was satisfied that no one was following them. Luke stirred from his sleep and sat up.

"What time is it? I'm hungry. Can we stop, now?" he asked, rubbing his eyes.

"It's six-fifteen. I don't see anything on this map anywhere around here, but there has to be a gas station or something." She pulled back onto the deserted highway, and they read each sign along the way. They had left

Colorado thirty minutes ago, and had passed only one small town along the way. Elaina wished she would have stopped there. The signs along the highway said that it was seventy-five miles to Taos. She didn't think she could make it that far. Her eyes felt like lead weights, and the white lane markings were hypnotizing her as they flew steadily at her. Finally, a sign announced gas and food in a town called Milton up ahead, population sixty-five. She glanced over at Luke; he was asleep again.

Elaina took the next exit and saw a small store on the edge of the road just ahead. It was the kind of store you expected to see in a small town. There was a dirt road with patches of dirty snow in front of it, and it curved around and up, over rocks and tree roots protruding through the snow, leading into a yard filled with old bikes and junk car parts that spread all the way from the road to the front porch of the store. The loose boards and cracked paint of the porch were home to an old hound curled up in a ball on a worn rug, oblivious to the man in the doorway, arms crossed over his chest. He seemed to be looking at Elaina. He was familiar, but she couldn't place him. He was tall, had dark wavy hair that hung almost to the top of his shoulders, and the beginning growth of a beard. He wore a flannel shirt and blue jeans. No jacket, even in this weather.

Elaina stepped out of the Jeep and reached into the back seat for her jacket. The sun began to appear over the red-rock valley, turning the whole world a deep orange, reflecting off the white snow, covering the expanse of untouched land. The temperature was still dropping, regardless of the sun's emergence, and she shivered in response in spite of her jacket.

Elaina glanced back at Luke sleeping in the Jeep and decided not to wake him. There was no point. The store obviously had no restaurant. She would get some gas, although she still had plenty. You couldn't be too careful crossing open country like this. Then she would buy some sandwiches or snacks, whatever they had, and Luke would eat them when he woke up. Maybe putting something in her stomach would wake her up. At least she couldn't fall asleep while she was eating. She walked up the path, and she could see that the man was still looking at her, possibly staring. She was sure she knew him from somewhere, and he seemed to know her as well. She could see that his eyes were a brilliant blue, even from a distance, and he was very handsome. Handsome or not, he was making her uncomfortable. Something about those eyes. She knew those eyes. She climbed the few rickety steps in dire need of paint.

Uncomfortable, she glanced away from the man and tried to walk around him, but the opening in the doorway was too narrow, and he made no attempt to step aside and let her pass. She glanced back at Luke, still sleeping in the Jeep, then back at the man. She started to walk past him, but there wasn't enough room, and her arm brushed against him. Suddenly, he reached out and grabbed her by the arms and held her tightly, cutting off her circulation. Startled, she let out a yell and struggled against him. The man clung to her with a grip that left white marks on her skin around his fingers. Without loosening his hold, he swayed forward, pulling her down with him as he doubled over. His bright blue eyes were glazed over, and his lips moved uselessly. He groaned as if in pain, and Elaina stared at him in shock. *What's happening? What's the matter with him?*

"Let go of me," she said, but her voice was so quiet she could barely hear it herself. She managed a little more volume the next time, saying, "You're hurting me!"

He continued to clutch her, obviously in pain, crying out. He slumped forward even farther. He was on his knees in front of her, as if engaging in some kind of bizarre proposal, and she leaned over the top of him struggling. She thought the man must be dying or something and didn't understand why he wouldn't let go of her when she remembered the file in Reid's briefcase. THE EZEKIEL PROJECT, SERGEANT JOEL CARPENTER, SUBJECT #33; she saw his face in the picture, clean cut and shaven in his military uniform, his brilliant blue eyes staring at the camera solemnly. It was him! This man was the man from the file— Joel! So Reid must have sent him. He had a strong hold on her, still, and she couldn't get away. But something was terribly wrong with him.

Joel clung to Elaina without realizing it as the world went dark and faded into a snowy forest.

Elaina is there, stumbling through the night, slipping on rocks and tripping over fallen logs, pulling Luke behind her. All around her an alarm is sounding, and searchlights are circling her from above. Approaching a rocky slope, she and Luke try to get their footing, but it is snowing, and they are moving too quickly. Luke slides on the slippery surface of the wet rock and because Elaina has a hold of his hand, they both go sliding down the rock. Hitting a branch, they begin rolling and sliding towards the bottom of the slope. Elaina hits the bottom. She skids to a stop at the base of the hill and the start of a road. Just as she is blinded by the headlights of a huge truck coming down the road, straight at her, Luke slides down behind her, slamming into her back, knocking her directly in front of it.

The shouting had awakened Luke in the Jeep, and he looked on in fear, as it appeared that a man was harming his mother. He sat up straight and watched in horror through the window.

Coming back to the present, Joel released Elaina's

arms and stood up unsteadily. Elaina was shaken and frightened. She backed away from Joel and steadied herself against the porch railing.

"What'd you do to me?" Her breathing was shallow and her face pale. "What was that?"

"I'm sorry, I—" Joel stammered.

"My husband sent you. You're him, aren't you? Carpenter?"

"You know who I am? How?" Elaina thought he looked shocked.

"Tell me what you did to me. Why was I in the forest with Luke?" Elaina ignored his question and asked her own, her eyes wide and frightened.

"You saw it?" Joel's breathing was still labored, and he was surprised at her statement. "That's unusual." He was puzzled. Somehow she'd seen what he'd seen. She'd shared his vision.

"Why are you following me?" she shouted, nearly hysterical.

"Technically, I was here first, so you must be following me." Joel's breathing had returned to normal, and he managed a small smile.

It seemed like an interminable amount of time had passed, but in reality it had only been a minute or so. The door burst open and an older man dressed in overalls came out onto the porch.

"You all right, Ma'am? Heard some shouting out here," the old man said, eyeing Joel carefully.

"Yeah, I'm all right, I guess," Elaina replied.

Joel stared back at her.

"I-I'm sorry," Joel said, and then he abruptly turned

and fled down the steps, following the path around the building toward the dirt lot behind the store. Elaina, remembering Luke, ran over to the Jeep and leaned in the window. He was awake and frightened.

"Come on. Let's get some food," she told him, and he hesitated before getting out of the vehicle.

He pointed to the building and said, "Who was that guy? What'd he want?"

"Nobody. Just some psycho. He's gone now." Elaina smiled at him, hoping she looked sincere, although she glanced around nervously to see if the man had really gone. Luke got out, and they both went into the store. Elaina looked all around her as she walked up the steps, but Joel was nowhere in sight. Still stunned, she ran her fingers through her hair, wondering what to do next. A battered white truck pulled out of the lot and sped down the road. Elaina remembered seeing it pass her along the road a couple of hours ago. She thought it was following her, but when it sped up and passed her, she decided she had been paranoid.

Inside, Elaina approached the man who had come to her aid out on the porch, and was now behind the counter. Luke wandered through the store looking at snack food.

"Do you know the man who was just here?" Elaina asked the old man.

"No, don't know him. He's just in here askin' 'bout a dark-haired girl. A small girl, he said, with a kid. Guess that'd be you, huh? Asked, had you been in here yet, like he's expecting ya and thought he mighta missed ya. You want me to call the police?"

Elaina shook her head and turned away. Picking up some trail mix, a couple of candy bars, and some Gatorade, she paid the man with cash, and she and Luke left the store.

Joel sat in the white truck, hidden behind some trees, on the frontage road next to the highway, waiting for Elaina and Luke. As Elaina pulled back onto I-25 south, Joel followed a distance behind them.

CHAPTER 15

New Mexico
15 December 2002

BACK on the road, Elaina frequently checked her rearview mirror, and every once in a while she saw the light from a distant vehicle behind her, but then it would fade and disappear again. After stopping in Taos, Elaina took a quick nap on the side of the road, but Luke who had slept most of the way, shook her awake complaining of hunger and boredom. Reluctantly, she agreed to stay for a while, and they ate lunch in a large arcade with a mini-race track. They spent several hours there, and Luke let off a little steam. Even though they had quit fighting, seven hours in the Jeep, some of it spent sleeping, was enough to drive them a little stir crazy. Besides, she felt safe there, blending into the crowd.

They left Taos about five o'clock, drove for a couple more hours, and stopped for dinner in Las Vegas, New Mexico. A small town, but it had good food. It was probably the last good meal for miles if she chose to go east. The next town was Santa Fe, and she knew she should change directions. She didn't think Reid would have taken this route, but the appearance of Joel Carpenter in Milton had proved her wrong. She needed to change directions, she decided.

It was getting increasingly difficult to see in the dark, so she leaned forward to turn on the dome light and have a look at the map.

"Luke, get the map out of the glove compartment and see if you can tell how much farther till we get to I-40. We need to get on before Santa Fe," she said.

Luke took out the map and looked over it. He had always loved navigating their trips in the past, but now he just went through the motions. *Still in shock*, she thought.

"You have to get back on I-25 south, just for a little ways, and then get on US-84 south-east," he said, examining the map.

She trusted his map reading skills and entered southbound I-25. She decided to tell him a little more about what was going on. If he didn't understand, he couldn't be as careful.

"I think something is going on that you need to know about." She wondered how much she should tell him and how. Luke looked back at her with curiosity and apprehension.

"Yesterday, I found a file in Dad's briefcase. The guy back there, it's about him. He's a sergeant in the army — he's part of Dad's research project. I think he sent him to follow us." Luke looked at Elaina with disbelief and anger.

"You're lying. Why would Dad send that guy to follow us?"

"Luke, I'm not lying. I would never make something up to hurt you." She paused, thinking how to continue. "I

think your dad might be mixed up in something dangerous, and I want us to be safe — so that's why I wanted to
leave so fast."

"You're just trying to turn me against him because I
love him and you don't."

"That's not true," Elaina said, and then decided that
maybe this wasn't a good time after all. *But when would it
be?* she thought. "Look, let's not talk about it right now."

Luke turned and looked out the window.

"We're going to Texas. You've never been to Texas,"
she said, changing the subject. Luke didn't respond and
continued to look out the window into the blackness.
Elaina looked forward again, giving up on conversation.

* * *

Joel was listening to an oldies station on the radio.
A song captured his ear, and he turned it up slightly.
He turned onto I-25 south and followed the same route
as Elaina and Luke. Joel took the gum out of his mouth,
wrapped it in paper, and replaced it with another, then
popped in a second one, the first not sufficient to rid him
of the bad taste in his mouth.

Elaina drove along the road, still checking her rearview mirror, and Luke sat next to her playing his Gameboy.
Yawning, Elaina flipped down her lighted visor mirror and
looked at her tired eyes. Flipping it back up, she pulled off
into a rest area where there was a camper and a semi parked,
their occupants sleeping. The temperature had dropped and
snow had begun to fall. She would be glad when they got
farther south, and sleeping in the car wouldn't be so cold.
Elaina parked the Jeep, turned off the motor and lights, and
leaned her head back against the seat to rest.

* * *

Reid was on his cell phone, driving down the road. Snow was lightly falling.

"Any word on Carpenter?" He listened briefly. "He can't hide forever; he needs the drug." Again he paused. "I'm on it. There's no doubt she's going to visit her mother just like she said. I'll make sure she doesn't get there."

Reid hung up the phone and threw it on top of the photograph on the seat. He picked up the picture and looked at it sadly.

"Sorry, Baby," he said aloud.

He didn't want to kill her. He really did love her even though she was a pain in the ass sometimes. But she had seen too much, and taking care of her and getting his son back was the only way to insure Luke's safety. If he took care of Elaina, they would know he was loyal and could keep his son under control. If they decided to send someone after Elaina, they would kill Luke, too. He knew it.

* * *

Elaina slept with her head against the driver's window. The windows fogged over, and the snow was beginning to build up on the edge of the windshield wipers. It was snowing heavily, now. Large heavy flakes fell silently, the occupants of the Jeep unaware of the dropping temperatures. Elaina dreamed she and Luke were riding her parents' horses through the Arizona desert, surrounded by small shrubs and Saguaro cacti, the orange-red sun going down in the distance. The wind was blowing through her hair, and the sun was warm on her face. She looked at Luke and they were laughing, but then she saw a fearful look come over his face as she watched him and he gazed past her, over her shoulder. The hairs on the back of her neck stood on end and prickled as she slowly turned her head to see what had frightened the boy. She knew what it was before she even turned around. She turned and saw Joel Carpenter sitting on top of a white stallion, the horse blowing out air through his nostrils and stomping his front feet on the ground. Joel, his ruggedly handsome face, spread into a grin, showing his perfect white teeth. Her heart skipped a beat, not because she was afraid of him, but because he was so good looking and because of the way he smiled at her. She smiled back and heard Luke scream, "Mom! Look out," just as Joel pulled a pistol out of his long waving coat and struck her across the face with it. But right before the blow hit, she could have sworn it was Reid's face she saw. Reid's smirking, arrogant grin, not the handsome smile of Joel Carpenter.

She woke up with a start, hearing a small tapping noise. She sat up and looked around. She was in the Jeep where they had been sleeping, and it was very cold. She would have to start the engine and run it for a while to warm it up. The tapping again. Groggily she looked around for the source of the noise. She wiped the fog from the front window and saw the small glow of light in front of the restroom and shower building about five hundred yards away. The semi that had been parked in front of her when she went to sleep was gone. She must have been sleeping deeply to have missed a semi starting its engine and driving away. She took the sleeve of her jacket and wiped the side window this time. The tapping came again, louder this time and coming from right next to her.

Still groggy and not thinking straight, she finished clearing the window and saw a face peering in at her through the dark. Startled, she jumped back from the window and let out a shriek. It was Joel Carpenter! She stared dumbly at him as he knocked on the window again, harder. His lips were moving, saying something, but Elaina was still foggy from sleep and couldn't get his meaning. Finally, she heard him as he shouted to her.

"Open the door! I want to talk to you! I'm not going to hurt you!"

Suddenly, Elaina was terrified; a delayed reaction startled her into motion. She turned to look at Luke, and he was gone! She twisted in her seat to check the back to see if he, perhaps, stretched out to be more comfortable. He was nowhere in sight. She looked at the passenger door, and it was unlocked. Quickly, she hit the lock button. Frantically, she began scanning the parking lot for Luke. The windows were still fogged over, and even where she had wiped them down, they were fogging up again. She wiped madly at the windows and searched with her eyes until she spotted him coming out of the restroom across the parking lot.

Elaina turned the key in the Jeep to start the motor. The cold engine wouldn't turn over. The starter strained, and Elaina prayed silently for it to start. She turned the key again. It just groaned and strained once again, sounding as if the battery might fail. *Please, don't let the battery go dead before it starts.* Elaina heard Joel's muffled shouting outside the Jeep. She looked up and saw Luke's startled expression as he began walking toward the Jeep, then hesitating, no doubt wondering what was happening. Elaina tried the ignition a third time, and it started. She put it into gear with a jerk and hit the gas all at the same time. The Jeep lurched forward, tires squealing.

As the vehicle moved forward, Joel grabbed onto the windshield and the handle of the door. He tried to get his footing on the narrow running board. He hung on for a few seconds before his feet began to slip. Elaina sped forward, glancing one second at Luke, then at Joel hanging onto the side of her Jeep. She jumped a curb, accidentally, but it did the trick, and Joel lost his grip, rolling to the pavement. He managed to get back up immediately and ran after her, still calling her by name.

Luke stood dumbfounded in front of the restroom and stared at his mother driving the Jeep toward him, recklessly. In her terror, she overcompensated for a slippery patch of ice and hit another curb, harder than the first, and went up on two wheels, momentarily out of control. With all four wheels back on the ground again, but still driving wildly, she drove over a small shrub and tore the muffler from the Jeep. Managing to bring the Jeep back onto dry pavement, she reached Luke and skidded to a stop. She reached over and unlocked the passenger door beside him.

"Get in!" she yelled. With Luke safely in the Jeep, she took off for the road, again squealing her tires. In the rear-view mirror, she saw Joel stop running and stare after her in the distance. She drove the smoking Jeep up the on-ramp to the highway and sped up as fast as the cold engine would go.

CHAPTER 16

Wilson's Corner
16 December 2002

THEY drove for miles in silence, too shocked to speak. Finally, Elaina looked over at Luke, who was also wide awake.

"Are you okay?" she asked.

"Yeah. That was him, wasn't it?" he asked, his voice trembling.

"Yeah."

"What does he want?"

"I'm not sure. I think he wants to stop me from telling anybody what I saw."

"About the file?"

"That. And something else." She paused, not knowing how much she should tell him. Then deciding that what he didn't know might hurt him, she said, "Luke, there's something I didn't want to tell you before. I saw your dad do something pretty bad."

"What?" Luke asked, a note of defensiveness in his voice.

"He killed a man. I know it's hard to believe, but I saw it—I was there, and he knows I saw it. And I think now he wants to kill me, too." Seeing his anger and disbelief, Elaina went on, "I wasn't even going to tell you about this, but I guess I have to."

"I don't believe you. You're lying!" he shouted, beginning to cry.

"Luke, I'm not lying. I promise you—he strangled a man, another officer. His name was Tom." Elaina began to cry as well.

"If Dad killed somebody, then they deserved it."

"He didn't deserve it," she said, shaking her head. "Nobody deserves that, Luke."

Luke didn't answer and stared straight ahead into the dark highway. Elaina checked the mirror again nervously.

"That's why going to Papa and Nana's isn't such a good idea anymore," Elaina said, wondering where they could go. She had very little cash, and she couldn't take the chance of using her credit card again. And now the Jeep was smoking. She didn't know how much farther it would take them.

"Where are we going?" Luke asked without taking his eyes from the road.

"I don't know, Honey," Elaina answered honestly. "For tonight, I guess, a motel. I'm going to get off the main highway, maybe head east." Reid would be expecting her to go south toward Arizona. He wouldn't think she would have the nerve to go somewhere where she knew absolutely no one to help her. She didn't know if she had the nerve either, but she would just have to find out.

"It's morning already, and I want to sleep—and I have to go to the bathroom again."

"All right," she said, pulling off the highway, taking a small junction east as the sun began to rise. "We'll stop at the first place we see." She could only hope that the man following her would think that she continued south on the highway.

"Look, there's a place," Luke pointed to a sign on the road. "The sign says, 'Wilson's Corner.' Can we stop there? It says they got HBO." Luke had already perked up. Elaina smiled, marveling at the resilience of eight year olds and the power of television.

"It should be all right. He'll probably think we're still going south on I-25."

Elaina took the next exit, pulling into Wilson's Corner, which turned out to be one giant truck stop. It was the only thing for miles. It seemed, indeed, that the truck stop *was* Wilson's Corner. A huge, neon-blinking oasis in the middle of nowhere, no town. Just a café, an attached motel, a convenience store, gas station, and a lounge with showers for truckers on the long haul. A pit stop in paradise before descending to a lower elevation and hitting the miles of New Mexico desert. It reminded Elaina of those casinos you pass about every fifty miles when you leave Las Vegas, with signs announcing that it was your "last chance for gaming," so you could get one more hit of slot-machine-heroin before escaping the high rolling demons.

The parking lot seemed completely filled as she scanned it for a place to park. It was mostly semis refueling or parking for the night while their drivers were inside showering, sleeping, eating, or refueling themselves with enough coffee and NoDoz to drive another thousand miles. She did find an empty spot in the dirt, past the paved lot on the café side of the building and quickly took it. At least she didn't have to worry about being in a dark, desolate area if this Joel Carpenter did manage to follow them there. There would be plenty of witnesses around if he tried anything. After parking, they made their way through the maze of trucks to the motel lobby to ask for a room.

Compared to the rest of the place, the lobby wasn't very crowded. There was an old man sitting in the corner, reading a newspaper, a little girl spinning the postcard rack, and a man with a woman and two suitcases handing his credit card to the lady behind the counter. The woman asked them to sign the receipt, separated the old fashioned carbon copy from the original, and handed them their copy, wishing them a good trip. They were apparently checking out. Elaina hoped that she would be able to pay for no more than one day, even though it was already morning and the check out time would probably be in only a few hours. She tried to avoid eye contact with everyone in the room while still appearing natural. She dug through her purse and counted the money she had left, even the change in her change purse. Thirty-three dollars and twenty-seven cents. She glanced at the sign in the window, SINGLE OCCUPANCY ROOMS, $39.00. She turned her back to the counter and bent down to whisper to Luke.

"How much money do you have?" she asked, hoping Reid had given him some in the morning before he left for school. He usually did whenever he was feeling particularly guilty.

"Why?"

"I need to borrow some—just till I can figure out how to get some more. Come on, give it up," she said.

He reached into his pack and pulled out a roll of ones and fives.

"Seventeen dollars," he said, handing over the money resentfully.

"Thanks. Wait for me outside."

"Why?"

"Just go and be quiet. I'll be out there in a minute, and don't talk to anybody."

Luke left reluctantly, and Elaina waited until he was all the way through the door before walking up to the counter. The counter lady was smiling and saying good-bye to the couple after ringing up a postcard for the little girl who seemed to belong to them. The counter lady turned her attention to Elaina and smiled.

"May I help you?" the middle-aged woman behind the counter asked politely.

"Yes. I'd like a single room just for today, please."

The dark haired woman's expression changed from one of friendliness to one of suspicion. "Check in time for tonight is one o'clock."

Elaina looked at her watch. It was five forty-five AM.

"I've been driving most of the night, and I'm very tired," Elaina explained.

"Of course, Dear," the woman's expression softened, "but will you be checking out by three?"

"I don't know," Elaina said, uncertainly. She had no idea what they would be doing. They needed to eat, and she would have a little over ten dollars left after she paid for the room.

"Well, then you'd better get the room for two nights."

Elaina saw where this was going. If she were going to check in now, she had to be out by three or pay for two days. That was fine. It would have to be. She thought they should be back on the road by then anyway. Even if she had money, she couldn't afford to stay in one place very long. If Reid and his men didn't find her pretty soon going south, they would begin to try other options. Elaina's heart sank at this realization. She couldn't run forever, not with a young boy who needed to be in school and have friends and sports and a home that was the same from one night to the next. And Reid would never stop looking, not with what she'd seen. The risk would be too great. Besides, he would never stop looking for Luke. But she didn't have time to worry about that far into the future right now. She had to think about today, and today she needed some rest.

"Three's fine. Just a single for today, please," she told the woman.

"A single?" the woman asked curiously. "Didn't you have a little boy with you?" she asked looking around the small lobby.

"No, no," she lied badly. "That boy wasn't with me." Elaina prayed silently that Luke would choose to obey her for once and stay out of sight until she came out to get him. She couldn't afford to pay for a double and get them something to eat. At least she still had half a tank of gas. That was something.

"Your credit card, please," the woman asked.

"I'll pay cash," Elaina replied and pushed the wad of bills toward her. "Is there tax?" she asked.

"Tax is included in the thirty-nine dollars, but we need to run your card as a security deposit. You can pay cash when you check out. We won't put anything on the card unless you decide you want to leave without going through the bother of checking out. Then we charge the card automatically. It's for your convenience."

Elaina's heart hammered, and she considered giving her the card for a moment.

"I don't have a credit card," she said. "I cut them all up. You know, so I wouldn't spend so much. Isn't it possible to pay in advance?" Elaina begged.

"We'll need a ten dollar phone deposit, and you won't be able to call long distance without a calling card," she replied coldly. Elaina counted out ten more dollars and handed them across the counter. *So much for eating*, she thought. One dollar and twenty-seven cents left. Maybe there was a vending machine somewhere.

"You'll get the ten back if you don't make any calls," she told Elaina. "Your name, please."

"Halle Berry — more," she replied dumbly. It was the first thing that popped into her mind. She had just watched a movie starring Halle Berry a couple of nights ago, and when she realized that the woman might think it odd that she had the same unusual name of the famous Academy Award winning actor, she lamely added "more," turning into yet a different famous name.

"That's Hal E. Barrymore," she explained. "Hal is short for Halaina. H-a-l-a-i-n-a," she spelled it out for the woman who typed it into the computer. No book register like you would expect from a small place like this. She realized that after all that, she'd ended up giving a first name very similar to her own. "My mom wanted to be different," she explained lamely. She should probably just quit while she was behind, she told herself, but the woman didn't say anything, just kept typing and didn't even seem interested anymore. Elaina guessed that she probably had people come through with aliases all the time. She could only hope that her blunders would not make her stick out in the woman's mind if she were ever to be questioned.

Outside she was relieved to find Luke sitting on the curb in front of the café next door to the lobby.

"Come on," she said, leading him to their room. "Let's get some sleep and then try out the restaurant — have some real food." She decided she would try to charge it to her room, if they did that in a place like this. It wasn't exactly a Holiday Inn. But they had to eat, and if they wouldn't let her charge it, they would just have to make a run for it. *Strange how quickly a person can turn criminal*, she thought. She had to think of a safe way to get some more money. That was her last thought before drifting off to sleep on the bed next to Luke.

* * *

Joel fell asleep in a chair watching Elaina's room, waiting for her to come out. His room was directly across the walkway from hers. He'd requested it after seeing which room Elaina and Luke entered. He'd gotten lucky, and it was unoccupied. He had pulled the chair in front of the window to watch, but exhaustion overwhelmed him, and he gave in. Joel never slept soundly, but this was the best sleep he'd had in a long time. The sedative they'd been giving him in the research hospital must have had an opposite effect on him, he thought as he drifted slowly away.

As usual, he dreamed of Elaina, but this time it wasn't a premonition, at least it didn't seem like one.

He gazes at her beautiful face over a candlelight dinner in a cozy Victorian room in front of a roaring fire. They talk and she laughs, a silky, throaty laugh, and it drives him crazy. He leans closer to her and touches her face, softly with the back of his hand.

Her skin is like smooth milk, with a hint of chocolate. Her dark eyes melt him as he stares deeply into them, trying to see who she really is. Windows to the soul and all that. In them all he can see is himself. How she sees him, full of love and admiration.

He awoke with a start as he heard voices and saw the shadows of people crossing the walk in front him. What a sap! Was he getting that romantic in his old age? He was all of thirty-one years old, but he felt very old. A millennium if he was a day, and here he was having romantic fantasies about a woman he'd only met for a few brief seconds when he'd managed to scare her half to death. He was ashamed of himself. An army soldier should be having sexual fantasies, not love fantasies. But there had been a lot of sexual tension in the dream, hadn't there? He noticed the uncomfortable proof of that as he sat up straight in the chair. Now he really felt old. Waking up with an erection might be something that the young often did, but getting hard over an innocent little dinner with someone he'd barely met was more akin to dirty old men in nursing homes, he thought.

Joel looked at the bedside clock in the small motel room, one o'clock. He had no idea if Elaina and her son had left the room, but he assumed that they would be hungry and ready for lunch soon, if they hadn't eaten already. He got up and took a cold shower, trying to erase the memories of the dream. He dried off and rubbed his beard. It was getting longer now. He thought about shaving it, but he'd have to go down to the store and get a razor. Besides, did it really matter if he shaved or not? A spasm of pain shot through his head and he reeled forward, clutching the sink for balance. In an instant he would be convulsing again. Why'd did it always have to be in front of the mirror, so he had to see how pathetic he was? Gathering his strength, he went into the bedroom to get his medication.

* * *

Elaina blow-dried her hair with the built-in unit hanging on the bathroom wall. She had changed back into the jeans and top she had worn that morning and repacked her dance leotard and sweats in her small gym bag. She shut off the drier, hung it up, and ran a brush through her shiny dark hair while Luke watched cartoons on the bed. Luke didn't have a change of clothes but removed his outer flannel shirt and now wore only the Colorado Avalanche t-shirt. He pulled his Avalanche cap out of his backpack and put it on backwards.

"Hurry up, Mom. I'm hungry," he called from the bedroom.

"Pack up your stuff, please," she said. "We might be leaving in a hurry," she said, thinking about the impression stealing lunch was about to make on her young son.

* * *

Reid drove south on I-25 when the ring of his cell phone brought him out of his fantasy of accepting the Nobel Peace Prize for Science in front of thousands of admirers gathering to honor him.

"What do you got?" he growled into his cell phone. He listened, annoyed, apparently not liking the news on the other end. "Put somebody on her mother's house. Keep watching the credit card activity and track her cellular." He paused, listening. "I don't need anybody else on this; I got it." This time whatever the person on the other line said made him very angry, and he raised his voice. "Look, my son's with her—do you get that? I can't have somebody screwing this up. Give me twenty-four hours." Reid snapped the phone shut and tossed it on the seat next to him.

* * *

Elaina checked to make sure the door to their motel room was locked before she and Luke walked toward the crowded café. It had stopped snowing and had warmed up a little, but it was still too cold to be without a coat.

"Where's your coat, Luke?" she asked a little more sharply than she meant to.

"We're only walking from the room to the restaurant."

She glanced down at her watch, one-twenty. Hopefully the lunch rush would be almost over. And it had died down a bit, although it was still crowded. Earlier it had been standing room only. Now there was one empty booth facing the door. The café had that old time diner feel with red vinyl chairs, Formica top tables, and Coca Cola napkin dispensers, except that everything was new and in perfect condition. They had to be replicas. In fact, the whole place seemed recently built. An oasis in the middle of nowhere would probably be quite a money-maker, even without the slots. Fifties music poured out of a shiny jukebox replicant that played CD's instead of forty-fives. Elaina and Luke headed for the empty booth quickly before someone else came in and got to it first. The air smelled of cheeseburgers and onions, heavenly to Elaina after nothing but Twinkies and trail mix for hours.

She sat down facing the door, opposite Luke, and picked up the menu wedged between the napkin dispenser and the ketchup and mustard bottles. She briefly scanned the menu, knowing exactly what she wanted already. She glanced up at Luke to see if he knew what he was going to have when she saw Joel Carpenter sitting one booth over, openly staring at her. Her stomach tightened in a knot of fear, and she tried to say something to Luke, to warn him that they couldn't stay. They had to leave, get out now, but paralysis had set in completely, and she could only return the stare. Luke noticed her strange expression and lowered the menu from his face.

"What's the matter, Mom?"

Before she could respond, if she had been able to respond, Joel stood and strolled over to their table and sat down next to Luke, across from Elaina. Now it was Luke's turn to be paralyzed as he sat shocked and staring at Joel Carpenter sitting next to him on the red vinyl bench.

CHAPTER 17

Confrontation

ELAINA was not only paralyzed, but speechless as well, as she regarded Joel Carpenter on the seat in front of her, right next to her son. But her mind was able to move, flying from one scenario to another, mostly about how Joel would manage to kill them and walk away without drawing any attention to himself, right in front of all these people. Joel looked at her with a curious intensity that looked more like concern than someone who was about to threaten or kill them. Of course, this was a public place, and he was probably trying to be inconspicuous. But the look was more than concern; it was like worry. She uttered a small gasp when Joel suddenly leaned forward and folded his hands on the table in front of him.

"Elaina Tessier." It was more a statement than a question. "Why are you running from me?"

Elaina swallowed hard, and as if his soft, deep voice

magically cured her paralysis, she lifted her shaking hand to run her fingers through her hair, and then changed her mind, putting her hands on her lap instead. Her voice sounded hoarse as she said quietly, "Why are you following me?"

"I'm trying to help you," he said in that quiet but resonant tone.

"My husband sent you, didn't he?" Her voice cracked in her throat, and she sounded different to herself, like she was outside of her body, eavesdropping on someone else's conversation.

A young waitress with dyed black hair, a pasty white face, and black painted nails brought a tray with three glasses of water and set them down one by one in front of them. She pulled out her notepad and stared at Elaina, seemingly too bored to speak. When Elaina didn't respond, she looked at Joel.

"Give us a few minutes, please," he told her, and she turned with a roll of her eyes as if everyone were wasting her precious time and sauntered back to the kitchen.

"No, he didn't send me. I am from the Department of Scientific Research, though." He looked down at the table thoughtfully, and then spoke in such a quiet tone that she had to lean forward to catch what he was saying. "I'm just a research subject."

"You're the one in the file." Elaina remembered the pages of diagnoses and test results, the lists of medications, the description of his abilities. She wondered how much of it was true. She didn't really believe that people had the ability to move objects with their minds, to tell the future, or view places outside their bodies, although she felt like she was doing the latter.

Joel looked up surprised. "You've seen my file? That explains why he wants to kill you," he said, forgetting how he had rehearsed giving her the bad news, that was if she didn't already know.

"No," she said, "that's not all I've seen."

Joel leaned back in the chair, pulling a pack of gum out of his pocket. He offered the pack first to Elaina, and she shook her head, then to Luke, who just stared at him dumbly.

"What have you seen?" he asked, putting two pieces of the gum into his mouth.

"You first," she said, not sure if she wanted to hear what he had to say, but something made her want to listen to him. *He seemed* . . . she tried to think how he seemed . . . *kind*, she supposed, but that was crazy. If Reid didn't send him, then why was he following her, scaring her in the middle of the night, rapping at her window? And then it struck her. He was the voice on the phone back at her studio. Before she could ask him about that, he surprised her with his answer.

"I see you, Elaina, in my mind," he said quietly. Was that compassion she heard in his voice? No, something different but like that, she thought. His comment threw her off guard and a slow fear crept over her. He knew her name, and what did he mean he saw her? Was he crazy? Or did he mean psychically? Either way, a chill went up her spine.

"What is this?" she asked, speaking barely over a whisper. He didn't answer right away, and Elaina searched his eyes for his meaning. Luke looked at his mother looking at Joel, then turned his gaze back to Joel again.

"It's a project your husband started a long time ago. The Ezekiel Project, named for a book of prophecy in the bible." He was talking in his normal, deep musical tone that he used before.

Elaina nodded. This was all too familiar to her. There was a time when Reid talked of nothing else. He had always said that "psychic phenomenon and precognition had been documented throughout the history of mankind, and was even written about in the bible."

"Prophecy," Elaina agreed, "about coming war and destruction for Israel. Reid talked about it a lot." She relaxed back against the chair. Somehow, he was putting her at ease, and she wasn't sure how. "He was obsessed with the idea that psychic abilities existed all throughout history. That's what the project is about—psychic abilities?"

Joel nodded and went on, "Experiments on Gulf War vets, testing their psychic abilities."

"What kind of psychic abilities?" she asked, already knowing the answer, but wanting to hear about it from him.

"Extra sensory perception—mind reading, telekinesis, precognition, remote viewing."

"Reid's always been obsessed with psychic phenomenon, but why does the military care?"

Joel picked up the saltshaker and turned it over in his hand, staring at it while he spoke.

"Its use as a weapon has great potential. Foretelling the future has its obvious strategic advantages. Telekinesis would be a powerful tool in covert operations, as would remote viewing. Mind control is probably the most important to them. It could be used to program the perfect killing machine, soldiers who don't question orders."

For some reason Elaina's thoughts went to the man in the mall, the bum who had accosted her, threatening her. The one who, according to Tom Pierce, was most likely on an errand for Reid, possibly just keeping tabs on her.

"Soldiers," he continued, "who won't be able to question the morality of an order. And then there is the potential political use of mind control." He didn't elaborate on that, and Elaina wondered what exactly was the "potential" for political use.

"That's not possible," she said, shaking her head with disbelief. "How do you expect me to believe all this? Why are you telling me this? Aren't you just as involved as my husband?"

"More so. I'm a test subject, an unwilling one. I want the research stopped. But that's not why I'm telling you this. There is no way to stop the project."

"Then why?" His intense gaze was making her feel uncomfortable and frightened again.

"I want you out of my head." Joel's gaze was so compelling that she couldn't turn her eyes away, even though she wanted to look over at Luke and see how he was taking all this.

"I see Tessier trying to kill you. I see you and Luke in danger. I want to help you — I," he faltered, "need to." He leaned forward and pulled a little yellow piece of paper out of his pocket and placed it in her hand. As his hand brushed hers, she pulled away sharply, yet it had felt . . . exciting — or something, she wasn't quite sure.

"Think about it," he said, and she took the paper, staring up at him silently as he abruptly got up from the bench and left through the front door.

She looked down at the paper after he had left and read it. It said, "Meet me in the game room in an hour."

"Do you believe him?" Luke broke his silence for the first time. It startled Elaina, and she looked at Luke shakily, trying her best to smile.

"No — no, of course not — I don't know." She shook her head and looked down at the yellow sheet of paper with the neatly printed letters. "I don't know who to trust anymore. I don't even trust myself, my own judgment."

Joel went to the gift shop attached to the motel side of the building and bought a blue denim jacket with brown sleeves, NEW MEXICO printed on the back in the colors of the sunset, a couple of t-shirts, and several packs of industrial strength breath-freshening gum, Eclipse. It was the best at removing the aftertaste the Anasymine caused. He used Sheldon's credit card to pay. He knew they would trace it, but if things worked out, it would be too late. Besides, he thought he should get some money while he could. He had to give the credit card number to the front desk clerk to get a room anyway, and he had registered under the name of Sheldon.

He was planning on leaving at three, checkout, even though he'd paid for two days. He hoped he wasn't leading Tessier to Elaina, but she needed to know what she was up against. He was relieved that it seemed like she had already given up the idea of going to her parents' in Arizona. He couldn't remember how he'd known that, but he assumed he'd seen it in a vision. Now, he would have to talk Elaina and Luke into going with him. They would turn around and head north again, through a different route, and throw Tessier's men off. He went to the ATM machine in the corner of the store and withdrew three hundred dollars. He didn't want to take too much because he didn't know how much was available on the card. He figured that the only reason it had not been cancelled was because they wanted to track him with it. Even with the card, they wouldn't be able to get the information in less than a few hours, maybe longer. He left the store and was glad he bought the jacket because it had started snowing again and the temperature was dropping fast. He put on the jacket and walked down the path back toward his room, passing a bum sitting up against the wall of the building.

"Loose change?" the bum asked, his hand outstretched as Joel walked by. Joel stopped in front of him and leaned down, placing Sheldon's credit card and his room key in his hand. When Tessier's men showed up, they would find the harmless bum in his room, registered to Sheldon, and the credit card. He would tell them where he had gotten it, and by that time Joel would be long gone, hopefully with Elaina and Luke. They would have no reason to hurt the bum, and hopefully he would be able to get dinner and a warm night's sleep out of the bargain.

"Room twelve. I'm leaving early, and you can have my room for tonight. Get yourself some dinner on the card." He smiled at the shocked bum who could only nod his thanks. Joel let himself in the room with the second card key and gathered up his things when another vision hit him hard, knocking him to his knees, spilling his bag of things on the carpeted floor.

He sees a blue Ford Explorer pull into the lot and park a few spaces down from Elaina's Jeep; it is Reid Tessier. Stepping out of the vehicle, Tessier's gaze searches the area for Elaina and Luke. Reaching into his coat pocket, Tessier pulls out a silver semi-automatic pistol and checks it, pulling the slide back and replacing it, then pocketing it before heading towards the motel.

Joel came out of his vision, the scene fading back into the dark motel room. Shaking, he gathered his things and put them back in his paper bag and got unsteadily to his feet. He stumbled to the bathroom and ripped off his jacket, splashed his face with water, and prepared his injection. Afterward, breathing heavily, he stumbled back to the front room and picked up his things, glancing quickly at the bedside clock before leaving.

The shrill ring of the phone startled Luke and Elaina when they entered their room. They looked at each other in surprise.

"It must be Joel Carpenter or somebody from the motel office. Nobody else knows we're here," she said, hoping that were true. She picked up the receiver hesitantly.

"Hello?"

"Hi, Baby," Reid said, in his most apologetic and pitiable voice. "It's me."

Her heart rolled headlong into the pit of her stomach, and she couldn't respond immediately. She sat listening into the earpiece, staring at Luke.

"Elaina? Are you there, Baby?"

"How did you know where to find me?" she asked quietly, barely breathing.

"I knew you were going to your mother's. You had to stop somewhere on the way." He sounded so calm and reasonable.

"This is not on the way," she replied, giving him no out.

"Elaina, I needed to explain things to you. I know what it must've looked like to you back there."

"I know what I saw," she blurted out, knowing that she should pretend to believe him but unable to. "You can't explain that away!"

"Elaina, it was an accident. Tom was angry; he's against the project for personal reasons, and he attacked me. I was just defending myself. He's threatened me before. He said he'd do anything to stop the research."

"Then why did you send someone to follow me — someone from the project?"

Reid hesitated for a moment, confused. Had they sent someone after all, even though they said he could handle it himself?

"I don't know what you mean. I don't have anyone following you."

"Does Joel Carpenter ring a bell? How else could you know where I am?"

"Carpenter is following you?" he said quietly, and she suddenly instinctively knew she had made a mistake mentioning Joel's presence. "What are you talking about?"

"You didn't send Joel Carpenter to find me?" Now she wondered if maybe Joel had been telling the truth, in which case she'd done the worst possible thing she could have done by telling him he was here. "And the other guy—the one with the silencer on his gun? Was it the same guy that grabbed me in the mall?"

Reid shook his head as if he couldn't comprehend anything she was saying.

"Elaina, Joel Carpenter is a severely mentally unbalanced patient that escaped from the research hospital. He's suffering severe psychosis from his exposure to toxins in the Gulf War. If he's following you, he must have somehow found out that you're my wife, and he's gotten it into his head to target you for some kind of vendetta against the army or something. Who knows what he's thinking? Just stay away from him."

This was close enough to the truth to sound convincing, the psychosis, the Gulf War Syndrome, toxins, all things she had either read in Joel's file or overheard Reid and Tom arguing about in her kitchen. But then there was that. There was nothing he could say that would convince her that he had killed Tom in self-defense. She had been there, and she knew what happened. Tom had spoken the truth and was going to tell someone, and Reid didn't want anyone finding out about his little secrets. Top-secret government project or not, Reid had other things to hide, things that the government might not know anything about. Maybe the people working with him didn't know, and he wanted to keep it that way. But that didn't mean that Joel Carpenter wasn't psychotic and hadn't followed her there to get revenge on the government who had caused his illness. Reid had been surprised to hear that he had followed Elaina. He must have believed that Joel had escaped for other reasons, and she didn't think Reid knew about Joel's supposed visions of her and Luke. At any rate, she would have to convince Reid that she believed him and accepted his story, or she felt confident that he would send someone else after her, like the guy with the gun at the Colorado Springs hotel.

"He escaped yesterday? He's the one in your file," she said carefully, trying to sound skeptical. If she accepted his story too easily, he would see right through it. She had had a lot of years to find out how Reid's mind worked and to learn the best way to survive around him.

"That's what this project is about. Trying to solve these mental and physical problems of the vets from the Gulf. Honey, you're in a lot of danger if Carpenter is there. I'm going to come and get you and Luke."

"Oh, no. I'll be okay and anyway, Luke isn't with me," she lied. She knew she was taking a big risk with this one, but if he believed Luke wasn't with her, she felt he would be less inclined to look for her, especially if he believed her. Luke looked at her angrily, and she pleaded silently for him to stay quiet. He sat down and sulked in the corner, but he didn't make a sound.

"I dropped him off at Val's. They went to the mountains for a few days. Luke will love it. I didn't know what to do after I left the house. I was afraid, so I took him to Val's and told her that I had a family emergency. They were going to the mountains, and she said Nathan would love to have Luke come, too."

"You wouldn't be trying to fool me, would you, Baby?" he asked, his voice a smooth drawl that sounded even more menacing than if he had raised it angrily. It was the way he always sounded when he drank Scotch. No ice. "Give it to me straight up, Baby," he'd say, and then he would give it to her straight up after the third or fourth drink. The blood drained from her face as she stammered an answer.

"N-no, of course not." Her grip tightened on the phone until her knuckles turned white and something snapped inside her. She wasn't going to let him do this to her any-more. She needed a little ice in her veins, as her father always said. "Lainie, you're too sensitive. What you need is some ice in those skinny little veins."

"Good. I'm glad he's safe," he said in that smooth-as-Scotch voice, and he didn't fool her any more than she fooled him. She knew he didn't buy her story. "But I'm still worried about you. I'll pick you up in your room. Number twenty-three, right? I'm outside in the parking lot, so I'll just be a moment."

What? Had she heard correctly? *He couldn't be here already. How?* She almost dropped the phone. The room went fuzzy and the walls were moving. She closed her eyes and tried to calm her voice.

"Okay. See you in a minute," she managed and hung up the phone without dropping it.

CHAPTER 18

16 December 2002

ELAINA began throwing things frantically into her gym bag—her purse, sweats, makeup, Luke's button down shirt that he'd taken off along with a leftover candy bar she'd bought the day before. Grabbing Luke's backpack, she headed for the door.

"Let's go, now!" she said loudly, and when he didn't move immediately, she grabbed him by the arm and pulled.

"Dad's here? I want to see him. I want to ask if all this is true about him."

"No," she said, sharply hanging onto his arm, "you just do what I tell you. Do you understand?" She saw the white marks she was leaving on his arm, and she abruptly let go. "I'm sorry, Honey. Please, just get your coat on."

Luke put on his coat, reluctantly wriggled into his backpack, adjusted his Avs cap on his head, and followed

Elaina to the door. Relieved that he was cooperating, Elaina swung open the door and slammed straight into the chest of Joel Carpenter. She almost screamed, but she was so startled when he grabbed her by the arms just as he'd done in Milton, that she stifled it.

"Let's go. Tessier's in the parking lot. We'll take my truck. It's parked out back, and he's next to your Jeep over in the dirt."

Joel released one of her arms and turned, pulling her along with the other. Elaina resisted, and he stopped and looked at her.

"We have to go now. I'm not kidding; he's here."

She hesitated, still not sure if she could trust him, and then decided she had no choice. "All right." She turned to Luke. "Let's go."

Elaina followed Joel out the door, and suddenly Luke bolted and ran the opposite direction toward the semis. He disappeared amid the network of trucks, and Elaina shouted after him.

"Luke, no! Come back!" she screamed.

Elaina chased after him through the obstacle course of eighteen-wheelers, many of the engines running loudly.

"Luke! Luke!"

Losing sight of him again, she screamed at the top of her lungs, but her voice was lost in the cacophony of running engines, and her throat grew sore, not only from screaming, but from the inhalation of diesel fumes surrounding her. It grew darker between the trucks; the huge vehicles shaded the area, and the snow continued to fall. She ran along the length of one truck, turned right at the next, then left, unable to find her way out of the maze of semis. At every turn was another row of trucks. She was like a child, lost at the state fair, turning this way and that, not knowing which way she had already been, her fear compounded because she was not the child. It was her child out there in danger, and she could do nothing to prevent it. Finally, there was an opening of light at the end of one semi — headlights from a smaller vehicle. Running headlong through the opening, she ran directly into Reid, driving his Ford Explorer straight at her, Luke in the front seat. She ran to the side of it and beat at the window with her fists, screaming.

"Luke! Luke! Get out of the car! Reid, let him go." Her screaming deteriorated into desperate sobs.

Reid backed up the Explorer and headed right at her again, obviously trying to run her down. She could see Luke screaming in the car. She didn't hear Joel coming up behind her as he pulled her out of the path of the oncoming vehicle, just in time. Attracting a crowd, Reid threw the car into reverse and peeled out of the parking lot, leaving the area with Luke still in the car. Joel grabbed Elaina by the arm. Elaina cried hysterically, staring after the Explorer. Joel pulled her away from the crowd forming around them, some staring, others asking if she needed an ambulance.

"Come on. We'll take my truck — he'll be looking for your Jeep," he said, still coaxing her from her position. Elaina saw Luke's Avalanche cap that he'd been wearing on the pavement. It must have fallen off while he was running. She bent to pick it up as tears rolled down her face. Carrying Luke's cap, she allowed herself to be led to Joel's truck.

When they reached the truck and got inside, Joel reached under the steering column and touched the stripped wires together to start the motor. Elaina stared at him in disbelief.

"You stole it?" she asked incredulously.

"They don't exactly let us keep cars at the research facility when we're being experimented on against our wills," he replied sarcastically. Immediately he regretted using that tone. She'd been through enough, and he didn't have to lose his patience that quickly.

"What if we get pulled over?" she asked.

"We won't. We'll dump it in the next town and pick up something else."

"Hurry," she said, looking toward the road, "we're never going to catch up with them."

Joel pulled out of the parking lot and raced down the street in the direction Reid had gone.

"Don't worry; he won't hurt him. I know it." He said this with the conviction of someone who knew Reid very well, and she looked at him curiously.

"How do you know? I've seen him do things that I never thought he was capable of."

Joel paused for a moment before replying, and then said, "Sometimes I just know things. I see things — without really seeing them."

Elaina stared at him cynically. *Oh yeah, that psychic shit again.* She was really tired of the subject. They entered the highway going west, back the way they had come, and drove twenty miles an hour over the limit. Luckily, they saw no squad cars along the way. After a few minutes they saw Reid's Explorer in the distance, but a Greyhound bus got in between them, cutting off their line of sight completely.

"Don't let that bus get in between us!" she shouted at him.

Joel looked at her with irritation.

"It's already between us." Joel moved slightly over to the left into oncoming traffic to see around the bus, but before he could see anything, a large truck appeared, heading east on the highway straight at them. Joel switched immediately back to the west bound lane. The truck whizzed by.

"I can't get over. Shit! I can't see anything," he exclaimed.

"You mean you can't see him without seeing him!" she shouted sarcastically. "Do something! Go around him on the right." Elaina pointed to the dirt shoulder, and Joel looked at her as if she had grown another head and three eyeballs.

"Do you want to die? That shoulder is soft dirt and not wide enough to get by anyway!" Joel said, exasperated. He continued to move over to the left, hoping to speed around the bus. He was barely gaining speed, side by side with the bus when the truck began to whine. He pressed the gas pedal to the floorboards, but the truck refused to go any faster, and the engine whined louder. He looked at the tachometer on the dashboard. It read five thousand RPM's, and the truck still would not shift into the next gear. Joel looked up from the tachometer in time to see the car heading straight at them.

"Dios mio, speed up!" Elaina shouted.

"I can't! It won't shift!" he shouted back to her.

Joel leaned on the horn, and the bus driver finally noticed him and slowed down. They cut in, just in time. Reid was still nowhere in sight.

"He must have gotten off while the bus was in the way." She looked out the back window. "Go back."

"How do you know he got off? If he didn't, we'll never catch up with him, getting off and getting back on again."

"What do you suggest?" He did have a point, but she couldn't think of what to do.

Joel slowed the car and pulled onto the shoulder, putting the truck in park. Elaina stared at him, appalled.

"What are you doing? Don't stop!"

"Give me his cap."

"What?" She looked at him, confused.

"His cap. Let me see it," he replied patiently, ignoring her skeptical expression.

Elaina handed him the cap, and Joel held it in his hands, turning it over and running his fingers lightly over the brim with the embroidered letter A for Avalanche. Joel sat back against the seat as the vision started, gripping the cap tighter.

The cab of the truck disappears and dissolves into the front seat of the blue Ford Explorer. He sees Luke in the passenger seat, and Reid Tessier is driving down the road at an extremely high speed. Luke looks very frightened. Slowing down to make a turn, Reid pulls into the gate of an army post. It is broad daylight. The sign at the gate reads, FORT POWELL, UNITED STATES ARMY. Reid salutes the guard as they are waved in.

The Explorer faded away, and Joel was back in the cab of the truck again on the side of the road. Joel jerked his head up suddenly. Sweat was beading on his forehead, but he didn't seem to be terribly shaken. The vision had been short and did not weaken him much. He handed the cap back to Elaina.

"He's taking him to Ft. Powell. That's in Spradley, Colorado, a little south of Breckenridge. He's heading north.

"How do you know?" she asked him doubtfully.

"I saw it," he replied nonchalantly.

"You saw it?" Then realizing what he meant, she said, "Like I saw it at the store in Milton?"

"Yeah, like that," Joel replied.

"You really do see the future?" she asked, and Joel nodded his head sadly.

CHAPTER 19

Night
16 December 2002

REID drove north on I-25 at a high speed while Luke cried softly in the seat next to him. Reid was ashamed of his son. His son. Who would have thought he would be such a sissy boy? It was a good thing he'd gotten the kid away from his mother before he'd started wearing dresses, he thought.

"You tried to hit her, didn't you?" Luke accused his father with tears running down his face. "Mom was telling the truth, wasn't she, Dad?"

"What'd she tell you?" he asked furiously.

"She said you wanted to kill her, and you killed somebody else already." He wiped his face on his sleeve.

"She's lying. She's trying to turn you against me."

"But you tried to run her over back there."

"I was just trying to scare Carpenter, the man she's with. He's dangerous, Son."

"But what about Mom? She's with him," he asked, thinking that if he was trying to scare Joel, then why aim the car at his mom.

"There's someone else looking for him. When they catch him, she'll be okay," he tried to make his voice sound light and reassuring, but instead it sounded to Luke like his teacher, Mrs. Cox, trying to get the class to be quiet when the principal, Mr. Farrington was in the room. She never sounded like that when Mr. Farrington wasn't in the room.

Reid stopped at a motel in Arrowhead, New Mexico at about nine-thirty that night. As Reid and Luke found their room, they were very short tempered with each other. Luke wasn't cooperating with Reid's plans very well, constantly arguing and complaining about everything. Luke didn't usually act this way with his father; he ordinarily saved this behavior for his mother.

"Let's get something to eat," Reid said, as they entered the small room. "Then you'll feel better."

"I'm not hungry. I want to call Mom," he said disconsolately.

"She's okay; I told you," Reid raised his voice, unable to contain it any longer. "Besides, there's no way for you to get a hold of her now. I'm sure they're gone by now."

"You can call her cell phone," he replied, making Reid even angrier.

"No. If we call, it will just make things worse with the man she's with." He took a deep breath and tried to sound logical instead of angry. "We don't want to make him angry with Mom, right?"

"Did you kill somebody?" Luke asked suddenly, startling Reid.

"I told you it was an accident, Son. He attacked me; I was just defending myself," he answered. He was going to kill that bitch for putting these ideas into his head, even if they were true. Luke was too young to understand the enormity of the situation.

Up until now, Reid had felt bad about the whole situation with Elaina. After all, he had been in love with her at one time. But that was before she started disagreeing with everything he said, contradicting him. She was turning into a nag, just like they always said wives did when the honeymoon was over. Elaina had become harder and harder to control, and now she had run off with his son! And infected him with her version of the truth. He couldn't trust her anymore. He could never trust her again. He had to let them take care of her.

At least he wouldn't have to do it. He still cared that much. He might feel sorry for her at the last minute or something and go easy on her. He had always been too easy on her. Like buying the dance studio for her when she'd lost the baby she was carrying. Why had he thought that was his fault? She'd asked for what she'd got. She pushed him. She was always pushing him. And now she'd taught her son to push, too.

Well, he might have to do something unpleasant, as much as he didn't like the idea, to get Luke back under control. He'd been under his mother's influence far too long. He needed Luke on his side, especially with what he already knew. If not, there were people that wouldn't like it—people with more say than he had, and they would make the decision of whether or not Luke would have to be taken care of. Reid couldn't let it get to that point.

He looked over at Luke with his headphones, playing his Gameboy. *Yeah, this has gone on long enough,* he thought, *the boy will have to learn a lesson. School's in session*, he thought as he pulled his belt from the loops on his pants.

* * *

On the verge of exhaustion, Elaina and Joel pulled into a motel in Canōn City several miles south of Ft. Powell. She had had very little sleep back at Wilson's Corner, and Joel had none, unless he counted the few minutes in the chair when he'd been watching Elaina's room. Now it was nearing eleven, and they had made it all the way back to Colorado, deciding to spend the night. Joel had no idea where Luke and Reid were at the moment, but he kept assuring Elaina that he was on his way to Ft. Powell, and that they were making good time.

"He'll have to stop and eat, especially with Luke," he told Elaina when she protested the stop. "Besides, he needs rest if he drove straight through to Wilson's Corner without stopping. He should be pretty tired by now.

Elaina reluctantly agreed to stop as long he agreed to leave before the sun came up. She waited in the truck, and let Joel get them a room with the cash he'd gotten from Sheldon's card. He guessed that the bum wouldn't have any trouble with the card unless he happened to head north with it, and that was unlikely unless Sheldon happened to have enough available credit to buy a car.

Joel exited the motel office with the key to a small, ground level room close to his truck. Elaina stepped out of the truck with her gym bag and handed Joel his paper one. As they entered the room, Elaina hoped she hadn't made a mistake in trusting Joel. She was trusting not only her own life to him, but also Luke's. She looked around the tiny room that hadn't been redecorated since the seventies. Gold shag carpeting, yellow, smoke-stained curtains, and a fuzzy black coverlet on the lumpy double bed, the only bed in the room. There wasn't even a sofa in the room, not that there would have been room for one anyway. There was no other furniture with the exception of one relatively decent leather chair, a nightstand, and a small battered writing desk.

"It's clean," Joel said optimistically.

"There's only one bed," Elaina noted.

Joel nodded. "I'll sleep on the floor." He set his paper bag of things on the writing desk, and Elaina turned toward him, her expression softening.

"No. There's no reason for that. We can share the bed. It's not a big deal. We both need a decent night's sleep. But what if Reid and Luke drive all night?" She brought it up again. Joel came over and put his hands on her upper arms and gave them a gentle squeeze. He seemed to be touching her on a regular basis, she thought, but this grip felt much better than the first, much better. In fact it felt downright good. It was nice to have the comfort of another human being, she realized. And there was something about him that persuaded her to trust him.

"He won't hurt him. Luke will be fine. Reid is after you—and me, but Luke isn't in any danger," he reassured her in that deep baritone of his. But she couldn't help worrying.

"Only if Luke believes the lies he's telling him. Because if Luke confronts him, at all hostilely, Reid will lose it. He can't stand to be questioned or told he's wrong. He'll get violent. I know him," she said, remembering the many times he'd told her not to question him, with his fists.

Joel's eyes narrowed, and he wondered what exactly Elaina meant by that.

"Was he violent with you? I mean, before all this?" he asked soberly.

Elaina turned her face away from Joel, embarrassed by his insight. It was fairly obvious, she supposed. She had a slight bruise over one eye, and her cheek was still a little swollen. She nodded her head, finally meeting his eyes. He took her chin gently in his hand, lifting her face to look at her more closely. For some reason she didn't resist.

"You don't need to feel ashamed. You haven't done anything wrong," he said quietly, but still with that somber quality.

Elaina looked into Joel's bright blue eyes; those amazing eyes made her feel lost and found at the same time. It was this damn situation, she thought, making her needy. She licked her lips nervously, a habit she had just acquired. It only seemed to appear in Joel's presence. The touch of his hand on her face made her feel all tingly. He was stirring up feelings that she had not felt in a very long time, except when she read those cheap romance novels that she rarely indulged in. They made her think of things she would never have, so she usually avoided them.

Startled by her attraction to him, she pulled away from his touch, turning to face the other direction. Not wanting to offend him, she pretended to be interested in finding a place for her bag and getting settled in for the night. Maybe sleeping in the bed wasn't such a good idea. She trusted him, but she didn't know if she could trust herself anymore. How could she be thinking of sex at a time like this, when her son was missing? Maybe that was why she was having these feelings. Her emotions were worn ragged; she was sensitive, vulnerable, and this beautiful stranger was trying to help her. At least he seemed like he was. She didn't know what to trust anymore. Still, it had seemed natural to confide in him about Reid. She'd never talked to anybody about him before, not even to her mother. Especially not to her mother, and now it all came pouring out.

"He wasn't like that when I first met him." She felt she needed to justify her madness a little. "He changed with the job, when we came here, and he started working all the time."

"Where'd you meet him?" Joel seemed genuinely interested.

"I worked at Ft. Huachuca, part-time in the summers. Reid was stationed there. He was working on developing anti-toxins for chemical and biological agents. They needed his expertise. Back then that was his specialty," she explained. She smiled when she remembered. "I was so impressed with him—he was brilliant, a scientist, and he was doing something to help people. Not making weapons, but disabling them in a way."

Joel listened intently, imagining how Elaina was back then, naïve and wanting to believe in Reid. She paced around the room as she talked, and Joel's eyes followed her around, resting on her as she finally sat down on the bed.

"He was older than guys I was used to. He seemed mature and smart—like he had a purpose in his life. It turned out to be more like an obsession. He wanted to make a great discovery and be famous." She laughed then, thinking that at least he had proved one thing. "He always believed in psychic phenomenon, even when everybody else thought he was crazy. He said he knew it was real—that there were parts of our brains nobody understood or even knew existed." She stood up again, restless, and began pacing. "When he was a kid, he dreamed that his brother got shot. Then a few days later his brother was killed in a hunting accident. His brother's friend dropped his rifle, and it went off. Reid always blamed himself for not making everyone believe that the dream was real. But I always got the impression that it was the fact that they didn't believe him that hurt him more than his brother actually dying." She sat down on the bed again. "Anyway, he vowed he would prove that such a thing existed, but as far as I know, he never had any more experiences with it personally."

"Sometimes a strong connection with someone creates a situation where a one-time psychic experience can happen," Joel said. He had never imagined this side of Reid.

"He was heavy into biblical prophecy, too. He said that there was a history of psychic abilities dating back at least three thousand years." She felt pity for Reid as she spoke. "People made fun of him a lot. People he used to respect. That hurt him—he changed. He started taking everything out on me. Nothing I did was good enough. Everything I did was wrong. Kind of like my parents." Elaina unzipped her gym bag, wanting something to do with her hands, but Joel never took his eyes off of her.

"Oh, there was always something missing in him. I see that now. He was always more selfish than other people, but then it was like people didn't matter at all anymore."

"Then he started getting violent?" Joel asked, and she nodded.

"Yeah. At first he would just say horrible things to me. Call me names and tell me I was stupid. Then he started throwing things at me and slapping me. Then when Luke was about five, we moved to Spring Forest, and he got worse. I was pregnant. I wasn't feeling very well, and he got tired of it. He lost his temper and threw me down the stairs. I lost the baby. I don't think I ever forgave him. He bought me the dance studio, and I lost myself in that. I wanted to lose myself."

Joel frowned and walked over to the bed and sat down next to her, putting his hand on her knee.

"I know he's under a lot of stress, and I keep thinking I should be able to help him through it, but no matter what I do, it doesn't get any better.

"You can't do anything to make it better, only he can. It's his problem. It's not your fault he's under stress. He put himself there. They're the choices that he made. He's probably having trouble living with those choices right about now." Joel hesitated a moment, thinking. "I don't know though—I don't think he does. He doesn't think about other people or the consequences of his actions. He's one of those narcissistic personalities, I guess." Joel stood up and walked to the window, pulling back the blinds and looking out.

Realizing she'd dumped so much on a virtual stranger, Elaina tried to think of how to apologize. "I'm sorry. I didn't mean to go on like that after everything he's done to you—I mean you probably don't care about what made him who he is," Elaina apologized.

"People ultimately make themselves who they are—things happen. It's how you choose to deal with them that makes you who you are. If you want to be something different, act different."

Elaina smiled. "You make it sound so easy."

"Nothing's easy, at least it seems that way. So you don't need to make it any harder," he said gently.

"You think I'm a masochist? Is that it?" she asked defensively.

Joel walked over to her and stood in front of her. He reached over and removed a strand of hair from her forehead, revealing the cut Reid had made. "Maybe you think you deserve the pain you get, so you endure it."

Elaina turned her head and looked out the window. "I knew I had to do something because I couldn't let Luke see that."

"It takes a lot of courage to get out of a situation like that."

"Courage? Not me. I stayed because I was afraid, afraid of what would happen, and now that I'm leaving, it's out of fear, not courage."

"Doing something when you're afraid is courage," he told her, turning her around to face him again. "So that's why you left? Not because of anything to do with the project?" he asked.

"No. It wasn't because of the project, either—at least not directly. I saw something, and that's why Reid wants to kill me."

"The file. You know who's behind it?" he asked.

"No. I barely glanced at the file. I read about you and that was it. I was just going to take Luke to visit my parents for awhile to think things through, and when I got home to pack, I saw Reid with Tom Pierce, a colonel who Reid's been working with since Ft. Huachuca." Her emotions were taking control again and her voice broke. "He killed him, Joel." Elaina covered her mouth as if she were seeing it all over again. "He strangled him in the kitchen because he was going to let out some secret that Reid and somebody else caused the whole thing intentionally. He saw me there, watching. I ran away, got Luke, and left."

Joel was confused. *Caused what exactly, the project?*

"Killed Pierce? But why? Pierce knew about the testing and the drug and everything—he's been there since the beginning. He's just as guilty."

"No. The drug—it's untested, and Pierce was going to

tell somebody named Speare—and that Reid engineered the attack, so that you and the others would get the disease."

"What are you talking about? What disease?" he asked, confused.

"Gulf War Syndrome. Reid gave it to you."

Joel's face paled. His heart hammered against his chest with such ferocity that he thought it would fail right then and there. That couldn't be. He had accepted the fact that he was a guinea pig for army research, and that he had contracted the debilitating disease of Gulf War Syndrome as he fought in service of his country, but Tessier engineering the attack? He wasn't ready to know that his government had had any part of exposing him and his men to deadly toxins, deliberately.

"That's not possible," he said stunned. He sank back to the bed and sat motionless. "That can't be. How?" he said, though he didn't, even for a moment, doubt her words. They rang with a truth that couldn't be denied.

Seeing Joel sitting there so obviously upset, she wished she hadn't said anything, but she thought he would want to know. It was time the truth came out. She sat down next to him and put her hand over his.

"Tom said that Reid and somebody else ordered a group of soldiers into the area where they were going to bomb a biological weapons plant, and that the soldiers were immunized against the biological weapons, so that they wouldn't die, but they would get sick, and they would have the abilities. He said Reid made sure they wouldn't get treatment for Gulf War Syndrome because it inhibited the abilities."

Joel was shaking with fury. He stood and stumbled over to the window, looking out at nothing in particular. He just didn't want to face her right now. His back turned, he shook his head.

"I should have known. All this time I thought they were taking advantage of our sickness, exploiting us, but I never imagined that they would've given us the disease on purpose." He turned around suddenly. "Somebody else had to be involved, somebody higher up, maybe even a politician."

"Tell me what happened to you since the war," Elaina asked.

Joel wandered over to the chair and sat down.

"In the war I was stationed in Saudi, Arabia. We heard about the toxin, Sarin, that the Iraqis were supposedly planning to use against us. So we were immunized — they gave us all shots that were supposed to protect us, although some people who took the shots and were never exposed to Sarin got sick too." Elaina stretched out on the bed face down, chin resting in her hands, listening with fascination to his story.

"Then right before the end of my deployment, my platoon was ordered into Iraq to inspect a weapons plant. We were to secure it and make sure it wasn't operational." Joel remembered, and he saw it all in his mind as if he were actually there again.

Helicopters are dropping paratroopers to the ground. Soldiers surround a weapons plant and have machine guns ready, but no one is detected in the area. Suddenly, American planes fly overhead. They swoop in and start bombing the plant. The soldiers scatter and run, taking cover behind the Jeeps and Iraqi vehicles in the area. Soon the sky is filled with gas and smoke. Many of the soldiers are falling to the ground and choking. Choking and coughing, straining for air, their eyes bulging, ready to burst. Standard issue gas masks are being pulled out of a supply bag across the way by one of the paratroopers, but they're too far away. Those nearby are grabbing them and putting them on, but they are so far away, and we can't make it that far. Even the ones that do are struggling with the bag and the masks, trying desperately to attach them and many cannot. They can't figure them out. Without air getting to their brains, they can't think. I take my shirt off and wrap it around my head, trying to block the gas, but of course, it can't filter out the toxins. I try not to breathe as I run, tripping over bodies. I fall to the ground, tripping over Marty, my friend. He's holding his mask in his hands, and he is already dead. He couldn't get it on in time. He was close to the blast and must have gotten a more concentrated amount of Sarin. Marty stares up at me with blank, dead eyes, just holding on to that mask, and I take it from him. I take it. His fingers are already stiffening, and I force it out of his hands. I imagine for a moment that he isn't dead, and that he is holding on to it. And I think I will take it anyway. I do take it. But he is dead, and he doesn't need it anymore; he doesn't need it. I put it on. I fasten it and breathe the air, and it feels so good, and he doesn't need it anymore.

"He didn't need it anymore," he said aloud.

"What? Who?" she asked, and he realized that he'd been seeing it all, but not saying it.

"We parachuted into the area and made it in undetected. But before we could get inside, some American planes flew over and blew the hell out of it. The sky filled up with gas instantly, and we couldn't breathe. We knew it was Sarin. It was so thick, and we were so close — seven of my men died, including Marty, my friend. Even though they were immunized, they died. We were just too close, and there was a hundred times more gas released than would have been necessary to kill us. But we had been immunized, and we were lucky 'cause it was windy that day. But the immunizations just made those who were dying suffer longer. The rest of us who were exposed were taken to a quarantine military hospital and made to go through decontamination. Then they flew us to the base in Saudi where they kept us in isolation in the hospital while we recovered. When we went back stateside, they sent us to Virginia, and eventually we were released to work in the research facility on the post. They monitored us weekly, and we weren't allowed off the post under any circumstances. After two years, they sent us to Ft. Clairemont supposedly to try a new treatment, a miracle drug created by Colonel Reid Tessier. By then most of us were having pretty bad symptoms—sleep disorders, neurological problems, memory loss, and headaches. We were given the experimental drug and were told that it was a treatment for Gulf War Syndrome. Anasymine, they eventually named it."

Elaina sat up. She couldn't believe all that he'd been through and because of Reid.

"But what about your families? Couldn't they help?" she asked.

"Many of us didn't have families, anyway. We found out later that the ones who did—their families were told we were casualties of war." Joel got up from the chair and poured himself a glass of water from the bathroom sink and returned, sitting back down in the chair.

"By then, people all over the country were being diagnosed with Gulf War Syndrome, but only we were held hostage—just the platoon from that one day, and a few from an earlier incident about a month before—but they were given a different treatment, Myotrophin, which seemed to help them quite a bit. But that didn't make the doctors at Ft. Clairemont happy. It turned out they didn't want us to get better. They wanted something else. Shortly after we were given the Anasymine, the exercises began. Paranormal testing—telekinesis, mind reading, mind control, remote viewing, and precognition. Anasymine turned out to have nothing to do with making us feel better, but was instead a neurological discovery by your husband, that actually caused new pathways in the brain to grow and develop, allowing the brain to use previously unused portions of the brain. Portions of the brain that controlled psychic abilities."

"Reid did all that?" she asked, amazed and appalled.

"Yes. And more. It turned out that Anasymine was highly addictive and caused side effects such as psychosis and seizures. Too much electrical stimulus in the brain. But they didn't stop. They liked that it was addictive because it gave them a way to control us when, otherwise, we would've been too powerful for them. The psychosis disturbed them, and that's what Colonel Tessier, Dr. Andrzejczak, and Dr. Simms have been working on solving most recently." He reached over the desk, picked up his paper bag, pulled out a bottle of Anasymine, and showed it to her.

"The implications as a weapon were what drove most of the research, but now I think Colonel Tessier, based on what you've told me, would do anything to get credit for his discoveries. It must be very difficult for him, after being ridiculed by his colleagues, to sit on a discovery of this magnitude—a drug which grows new pathways in the brain—it would be Nobel Peace Prize material—it could be used in all sorts of diseases from mild retardation to Parkinson's and Alzheimer's. I have heard that the effects are permanent. Maybe if it had been carefully given, addiction could have been prevented. And the psychosis side effects seem to be from extended use."

"I can't believe that Reid is capable of all this," she said, although she thought she could believe it if she gave it a minute to sink in. "Or that he could keep it all a secret for so long." That was harder to understand. Did he have free reign over the Department of Scientific Research? Not likely. And how did he keep the discovery of this drug from leaking to the public? "I guess I never really knew him at all," she said embarrassed again. "I'm sorry all this happened to you."

"I'd pretty much given up on trying to stop him, or trying to get out myself until I started getting premonitions about you. I started seeing you in my dreams and visions. I didn't know who you were until one day when I was in Tessier's office, and I saw your picture with Luke on his desk." He pulled the photo out of his bag and went over to her, showing her.

Elaina picked up the photo, and her eyes teared up.

"I couldn't believe you were real, and then I knew that what I saw in those visions was also real. I knew I had to help you. I couldn't let him hurt you — then after I knew who you were, my visions got clearer. I knew that it was Tessier trying to kill you, but I didn't know why." He stopped and looked up at her. "I knew if he wanted to kill you, you must be good." He smiled, and then grew uncomfortable, feeling like he'd said too much.

"Tessier keeps everything in his office, all his papers in his safe, and everything backed up on disk in his computer. How did you get a hold of the file?" he asked, changing the subject.

"He had it at home in his briefcase. I only saw the part about you, nothing about politicians or high ranking officers, and definitely nothing about ordering weapons plants bombed," Elaina answered. She was still absorbing all of this, but Joel had to be telling the truth. Everything he said matched up with what she'd read and overheard. She was past being suspicious of him anyway. She knew she could trust him.

"If there was any way to get a hold of those orders, find out who ordered them, and get some of the information on the project in general, we could use it as a bargaining tool to get your son back."

Elaina sat up straight and smiled. She remembered dropping the files. Some went under the chair, and she had kicked them under the bed, so she could have a look later to see what was so important about them. At least that made sense. Why else would she have kicked them under the bed? She hadn't really thought about it until now, and now it seemed like she had never intended on going back and reading them, not when Reid was so mad about it. Something had told her to kick them under, an inner voice or something. Hell, maybe she was turning psychic now, too. Or maybe she subconsciously thought she would need something to use against him at some point. Maybe just to have some influence, so that he would let her leave and take Luke with her. It was no use analyzing it; the important thing was that she did it. Now she could only hope that they were still there.

"I kicked some of the papers from the file under the bed. I'm not sure what's in them because I didn't read the whole thing. They probably wouldn't still be there. I'm sure Reid would have found them by now if he suspects me of turning against him, which of course, he does."

"It might be our only chance of getting Luke back, and we could use it as leverage to get him to leave you alone — although blackmail isn't the safest way to get someone off your back."

He made a point. What would stop Reid from killing her after he got the file back? If she could get the file back. They could worry about that after they got Luke. That was the most important thing.

Joel reached into his pocket and pulled out his pack of Eclipse, popping two pieces into his mouth. He offered the pack to Elaina, and she shook her head.

"You chew a lot of gum," she remarked. That was pretty rude, she thought, but the idea just came to her, and she wasn't very good at keeping her ideas quiet. That had gotten her in a lot of trouble with Reid.

"It's the medication—it gives me a bad taste in my mouth," he replied.

"Oh," Elaina replied lamely and wondered if she had offended him. She decided to return to the subject. "I think we have to go back and see if it's there."

"That's very risky. You know they'll be watching the house to see if you go back there."

"Joel, I don't know if I can do this. Leaving Reid is hard enough, but fighting him? And the government—what about them? It's a little over my head," she said.

Joel reached out and touched her face with the back of his hand. The touch was light and compassionate, but it stirred a deeper feeling in Elaina. More than desire. She felt something there that she could not quite put her finger on, and she liked it.

"You have everything you need to do whatever you have to do—except the faith to believe you can do it. You're strong—you're a mother. There's nothing stronger than a mother protecting her young." Joel's smile warmed her heart more than his words could. It was sincere and caring. She wondered how a perfect stranger could seem to have more kindness and concern for her than anyone she had ever known.

Joel took her hand and held it in his. Suddenly, he gripped her hand tightly, and he sagged over in pain, the room fading into another vision.

"What is it? Are you all right?" Elaina didn't know what to do, if there was any way to help, or if she had to let him just go through it. She wondered if she would see the vision with him like she did at the store. But there was no doubt that he was immersed in a psychic episode.

*Joel is back in the same warehouse where he was in his ear-
lier vision. He walks through the dark warehouse with the army
vehicles, pulled engines, and boxes of files. The dim light from
the swinging overhead lamp is the only source of illumination.
Had he noticed that before? He isn't sure. It is very dark outside. He can see the darkness through a small, dirty window.
Reid is pointing a gun at Elaina. Luke is standing behind Reid.*

*"No! Luke, run! Run!" Elaina shouts frantically at Luke.
The warehouse begins to fade away, and the motel room begins
to come back into focus as he hears a shot ring out, but can't tell
who, if anyone, has been shot.*

Joel fell to his knees convulsing. His head lolled back,
and he seemed worse than before to Elaina. She rushed
over to his side and knelt down next to him. She lifted his
head in her hands as he opened his eyes.

"Are you okay?" Elaina asked.

"Yes," he struggled to sit up.

"Did you see something? Is he coming after us?" she
asked, of course, meaning Reid.

Joel leaned back, his head on the bed and tried to
speak, but he began to seize.

"Oh my God, Joel."

He pointed toward the desk, motioning for her to get
his medication, but he was shaking so badly that it took
her a minute to figure out what he wanted. She finally
understood and ran to get it.

Elaina brought the bottle of Anasymine to him, but he
shook his head.

"I need a needle," he managed. She fumbled through
the bag until she pulled out a syringe sealed in plastic. She
gave the bottle to Joel, opened the syringe, and handed
it to him. Barely able to sit up, even though his seizures

had subsided a little, he grasped the bottle and opened it. He was still shaking badly enough that Elaina had to help guide his hand, aiming the syringe to the mouth of the bottle, and poking it inside. He filled the syringe, removed it from the bottle, and then held it up, flicking it with his fingernail to bring the deadly air bubbles to the surface. He then shot a tiny stream of the liquid from the needle, removing the air. He rolled up his sleeve, clenching and unclenching his fist a few times before inserting the needle into a vein that was already marked with many previous puncture wounds. He looked like a heroin addict shooting up, and any police officer seeing his pincushion arm would assume he was a junkie. He was a junkie, Elaina guessed, just not the usual type, and not from his own weakness, but from someone else's moral disadvantage. She had a hard time looking at him like that, reconciling the man she was beginning to know with this image of the desperate junkie. It just didn't seem to fit with that good-guy soldier quality he had. He leaned back, breathing a sigh of relief as the drug took effect.

"Maybe you shouldn't keep taking it, now that you're out. You could get off of it, couldn't you? Isn't it making you sicker?" she asked, concerned but afraid that she would seem condescending or judgmental. He didn't seem to take it that way.

"I have to have it, now. My brain is dependent on it—physically, to handle the premonitions and the telekinesis." He looked up at her gently, appreciating her concern. It had been a long time since someone had been concerned about him, not just as a test subject. "I'm dying anyway," he said without sounding terribly upset about it. It upset Elaina, though, to hear him just giving up like that. Like there was nothing that could possibly be done to stop it, and even if there wasn't anything they could do, he had to keep trying, have hope. But it seemed, Joel was a long way past hope.

"No," she said, refusing to be resigned to the fact just like that. "Joel, we're going to stop this from happening. When we get Luke back and tell what we know, they'll shut it down. They'll have to help you."

"It's too late for me, Elaina. My entire brain neurology is different, and the medication helps to even out my brain chemistry, so it helps my seizures. Two of the other subjects in my unit have just died. I'd probably die without it sooner than if I stopped taking it at this point."

"I thought you said it caused the seizures," she asked, confused.

"It does, but it's the dependence on the drug and not having it that causes the seizures, so stopping the medication would make them worse."

Joel got up and stretched out on the bed, careful to take up only one side, resting his head back on the pillow. Elaina lay down beside him. It seemed natural to lie down next to him, not the slightest bit uncomfortable.

"Besides without the medication, my visions wouldn't be as clear, and we might not find Luke as easily," he reasoned.

Elaina reached over and touched his cheek. He was too good to be true. Was he really risking his life just to help her and Luke, knowing that using his powers was actually making him weaker and requiring him to take more of the medication? Of course, what did he have to lose? Was death really inevitable? If he were that valuable to the military, they would find a way to help him. But living out his life as an experiment, or worse, as a weapon, probably didn't appeal to him much either. Still, this seemed like a big sacrifice for him to make, and she found herself becoming suspicious again. *Nobody is this good*, she thought. *What's the catch?*

"But it makes you so weak after the visions," she said, turning her hand over and placing it on his forehead. "You're pale and cold."

Elaina got off the bed and motioned for him to get up. He sat up but didn't look too willing to get off the bed.

"Get up for a minute," she said.

He did, and she pulled the coverlet down.

"Okay, lie down."

He obeyed, and she pulled off his boots, covering him with the blanket. She took off her own shoes and climbed in beside him.

"Are you warm now?" she asked, her head propped up on her hand.

Joel rolled onto his side and looked at her, nodding his head.

"Yes, thank you," he said. He wasn't used to being treated like this. Elaina seemed like an angel to him. He never thought he would have the pleasure of being taken care of by an angel, at least on this side of the grave.

"If you think it's too late to get better, why are you doing this? You don't even know me," she said.

Joel smiled wistfully at her and moved her hair away from her eyes.

"I do know you, Elaina. You've been with me for a very long time. I see you in my dreams and in my visions. I've always known I would meet you, and we would do something important together." He paused, thinking. "Don't you believe in destiny, Elaina?" he asked, his eyes so intense, like the day when she first met him, and like the picture in Reid's file. They were luminously blue, and it seemed like they were seeing right through her, but they weren't unkind, just intelligent and old—knowing eyes. He had seen too much in his life—literally. She stared up at him and moistened her lips with her tongue, unable to pull her eyes from his or even to blink.

Why did he say those weird, mysterious, romantic things to her? Her heart slammed inside her chest, and she felt a surge of emotion she couldn't comprehend. How could he do this to her? He came storming into her life, just as she was finally getting rid of one bad relationship, the only one she'd ever really been in. And he made her start feeling things she didn't want to feel, just like that, and then announced that he was dying. The realization hit hard. She was starting to fall for this stranger, this very strange stranger. She had no idea if she could really trust him, but she did. This was crazy. She knew she was going to get hurt, and this time she didn't know if she could survive it, but she also knew that there was nothing she could do about it.

"I never have before, before now—believed in destiny. I've never met anyone like you," she said, realizing that she was believing in a lot of things that she had never believed in before. "Thank you—and thank you for helping me find Luke."

Joel moved closer to her, wrapping his arms around her.

"Thank you for letting me and believing me." He rolled onto his back, but still held Elaina in the crook of his arm, her head resting on his shoulder.

"What was that you said about your parents? That nothing you did was right?" he asked.

"My father is very critical and strict, and my mother—

she's very loving, but she's strong. She thinks she knows how I should do everything, and it's always been different from what I think. The thing is, if I disagree, I feel like I can't tell her, or she'll think less of me. I can't imagine what she'd say about what I'm doing now." She looked sideways at Joel. "She's very old fashioned about sticking with your man and doing whatever he says."

"Surely she wouldn't expect that from you in this case," he said. He turned sideways and smiled at her. "How do you know she wouldn't be proud of you?" he asked.

"Anything's possible." She smiled back at him. They moved closer together, falling asleep in each other's arms while a man named Harris, a hitman sent by someone in the Department of Scientific Research, talked on his cell phone just outside the motel lobby where Elaina and Joel slept.

CHAPTER 20

17 December 2002

JOEL slept fitfully in Elaina's arms, but for the most part, she slept soundly despite his mumbling and turning in the bed. Outside, Harris sat in his white Oldsmobile, watching the motel and talking on his cell phone.

"Yeah, it's Harris. I'm pretty sure they're here. The clerk recognized Carpenter, but he didn't see any woman." He paused and then spoke again.

"He probably got the room, and then she met him there," he said, and then listened some more.

"No," he answered, "he wouldn't give a room number, and this place is pretty crowded. There are people all over the lobby. I couldn't push. I'll just watch until they come out. They probably won't leave till early in the morning, and I'm watching the truck he's driving. Don't worry. They can't get out of here without me seeing them," he said, pressing "End" on his phone, then shoving it in the pocket of his long gray coat.

Joel's sleeping became more and more disturbed as he dreamed. He woke Elaina with his murmuring, mentioning her name over and over in his sleep.

"Laina, Ela — get out of — hurry, Laina," he mumbled, and she sat up stroking his hair, worried about him. He couldn't even really rest when he slept, she thought sadly. She also worried about what he might be seeing in those dreams.

Outside, just before dawn, Harris slept in his Oldsmobile, snoring loudly, completely unaware of Joel and Elaina leaving the motel. Joel had woken from his vision and immediately insisted that they leave. Someone was coming, but he wasn't sure who, and Luke was not with them. They needed to go now.

They packed up their meager belongings and left the motel, never noticing the white Oldsmobile at all, probably because their attention had been focused on the squad car and the police officer looking over Joel's truck in the parking lot. Quickly changing direction, Elaina and Joel walked the opposite direction in search of a new vehicle. Out of sight of the policeman, they ran through the lot and crawled under a fence and into the lot of a twenty-four hour restaurant. Elaina followed Joel through the lot as he checked each door, looking for one that was unlocked. The first unlocked car was an old blue Chevy Blazer. Joel got in the driver's seat and pulled the wires out from under the steering column while Elaina got in on the passenger's side. Joel quickly stripped the wires with his pocketknife and started the car. They took off while Harris slept soundly in his car.

Joel and Elaina headed north toward Spradley in the stolen Chevy Blazer.

"I have an idea. I know someone who might be able to help us. My superior officer in Desert Storm, Colonel Mark Sorenson; he's a general now. I've heard he's stationed at Ft. Powell. We can try and talk to him before we see Reid. Maybe he can expose the whole project. He's high enough to get some attention. He could get to this General Speare you mentioned."

"You're assuming that Speare doesn't know all about this, and that the government is not okay with everything that the Department of Scientific Research is doing. If they are all in on it, then going to him would be a big mistake," Elaina reasoned.

"If that was true, Tessier would've had no reason to kill Tom Pierce. Pierce seemed to think that Speare had no knowledge of what was going on. It's all we really have to go on," he answered.

"We still need some evidence. We're going to have to go back to Spring Forest first, to see if we can get the pages from the file," Elaina insisted.

"All right. It's a huge risk, and you don't even know if the file contained anything helpful to us. But you're right. Even General Sorenson wouldn't risk going against another general or even a colonel without some evidence. He'd have no reason to." He paused, thinking. "We'll go to your house in Spring Forest, get the papers, and then go to Sorenson—if that doesn't work, we'll go straight to Reid and make the deal."

* * *

It was cold and snowy in Spring Forest, although it wasn't snowing at the moment. It was bright and sunny, the snow on the ground reflecting the light, making it brighter than it normally was in the afternoon. It didn't make it warmer, however, and the Blazer's heater was broken. *Thieves can't be choosers though*, Elaina thought.

They turned the corner, cautiously entering the side street adjoining the one where Elaina's house sat. An unmarked black van sat parked a few houses down from hers. Inside the van, two men sat watching her house, drinking steaming coffee. The coffee looked good, and she could almost smell it, watching the steam rise from the foam cups.

"There—see the van. They've got at least one surveillance vehicle on the house. Probably one in the back as well," Joel pointed out.

"What are we going to do? There's no way I can get in there without being seen," Elaina said. "We knew they'd be here. How did we think we could get in there?" she asked, frustrated.

She looked over at Joel who had been driving. He was rummaging through his paper bag. He pulled out his medication and was preparing it.

"What are you doing? It's not time, yet," she said, pulling on his arm. "It's only been two hours since you had some."

I'm going to try something I've only done a couple of times," he replied without looking up. He continued to prepare the injection, then rolled up his sleeve and shot up. "We'll park one block over. It's mind control. I'll make them see the empty house with no one around while you go in. I can only hold the image for a few minutes, so get in fast. Then come out at," he looked up at the dashboard clock; it said one fifty-seven, "exactly ten after, done or not, so I can give them the image again. Got it?"

Elaina stared at him as if he had gone insane.

"That's your plan? You're sure you can make them see

the house just as it is now, without seeing me going in and coming out? How do you know if it's working?" she asked, not believing she was even thinking about doing this.

"Don't worry. I can make them see what I want; I just can't do it for very long, so stick to the plan and stay away from the windows. If you're through early, don't come out until ten after," he said, but his voice didn't sound as confident as his words.

Joel backed the Blazer farther up the street and parked, the house just barely visible. Elaina turned to him, concerned.

"What about you? What if this really weakens you?"

"I'll be okay. That's why I took the drug now. I'll just be sitting here in the car. You might have to drive though—I'll move over to the passenger seat when you get out. When you get back, drive straight for Ft. Powell." He put his hand on hers reassuringly.

"Be careful," he said.

She nodded and synchronized her watch to the Blazer's clock, opened the door, and got out. She headed across the street to where it adjoined the street where she lived. She walked on the side opposite her house. She was so afraid that her knees felt weak, and her heart slammed out an irregular rhythm in her chest. She couldn't believe she was attempting something so foolish. Surely, the men assigned to watch the house had instructions to kill her. Maybe even interrogate her first, which probably involved some kind of torture. They would want to know to whom she had spoken.

Suddenly, she wondered if her parents and her friends were in danger. They probably were. Reid would think her incapable of doing anything on her own, and he would assume that she sought out help or advice from her loved ones. Now she worried for them as well as herself. She knew she had no choice but to go through with it. Luke's life was at stake, and Reid would never stop looking for her. Her friends and family would always be in danger unless she stopped him. And then there was Joel. She had to help him get better, find a cure. And all those other veterans that were living as test subjects in the research facility. She couldn't believe that she was responsible for so many people when she had never even been able to help herself or get her own life under control. Now, whether they knew it or not, a lot of people were depending on her to stop Reid and the whole Department of Scientific Research, for that matter. The thought was a little overwhelming, but it soon left her head as she neared the van.

She was at the point now that she needed to cross directly in front of the two men watching the house. Elaina glanced back at Joel. He was staring directly at the house in fierce concentration. She had to go now before holding the image became too much for him. Her heart thudded against her chest, and sweat beaded on her forehead despite the cold December air. She stared at the men drinking their coffee as she stepped shaking into the street. Her legs wobbled and threatened to spill her as she carried herself to the house. The two men never looked at her at all. They seemed to stare right through her, occasionally looking at each other and laughing, obviously engrossed in conversation. She couldn't believe it. She was right in front of them, almost to the driveway of her house, and they were oblivious of her presence completely! This gave her confidence, and she rushed the last few yards to the house, shakily inserting the key in the front door lock. She went in.

Elaina punched in the alarm code, praying that Reid hadn't change it, and for one horrible second she thought he did, but she had skipped a number in her rush to turn it off. She re-keyed the code, and the beeping stopped. Elaina sidestepped the kitchen where the murder happened, purposefully avoiding it, and then ran up the stairs to her bedroom. The bedroom was ransacked — her drawers pulled out, clothing strewn all over, and the chairs turned upside down. Going straight to the bed, she got down on her hands and knees and looked underneath. The loose papers were lying helter-skelter under the bed. She couldn't believe it! They were still there! How Reid could have missed them right under the edge of the bed was beyond her comprehension. He had apparently been looking for them and very much wanted to find them. She couldn't think of anything else that he would have been looking for, and even if he had been looking for something else, he would have picked these up, had he seen them.

"Thank you, thank you," she breathed excitedly and scooped up the papers. *Somebody's on my side*, she thought happily. Getting to her feet, she checked the time, five after. Glancing around the room she saw the safe and tried the combination, 09-07-57. It was Reid's birthday, a lame combination, but Reid had the world's worst memory and wasn't capable of remembering much more than his own birthday. She had tried to get him to change it to something less obvious, and he had said that if someone went to the trouble of finding out his birthday, then they were going to find a way into the safe no matter what the combination was anyway. Besides, he kept the most important things with him all the time, he said. The safe was empty.

She didn't have much time, but she thought this would be her only chance to come back to the house, and she should take advantage of it. She grabbed a pair of jeans off the floor, a pair of panties and a bra from one of the open drawers, and a fresh shirt from the closet. Carrying the clothes and the papers she had come for, she ran down the stairs and opened a drawer in the telephone desk in the foyer. She rummaged through it and found what she was looking for underneath the phone book, an envelope. She opened the envelope and pulled out several twenty-dollar bills. *Emergency cash*, she thought, *this is definitely an emergency*. She checked her watch again, and it was nine minutes after. She took a deep breath and backed away from the window, noticing that the drapes were open. She backed up to the edge of the kitchen, curiosity getting the better of her. She could no longer resist looking into the kitchen. It was perfectly clean and normal. No sign of a body, not even a sign of a struggle. She didn't know what she had expected. Of course, Reid would not have left the body there to be discovered, rotting and smelling until the neighbors complained. Still, seeing the room made a shiver run down her spine. She checked her watch one last time and saw that it was ten after two. She took a deep breath and prayed silently to give Joel the strength he needed to blind the men in the van of her presence. She knew the first time would have drained him, and she feared that he might be too weak to pull it off again.

She held her breath and opened the door, stepping out onto the porch. Luckily, there were no neighbors home during the day on her street. Everyone worked and had their children in either school or daycare. If anyone tried to talk to her, she would have to ignore them and keep going. Any delay would be unforgivable. Even though the men showed no signs of seeing her, she still ducked behind the bushes and sprinted from tree to tree until she crossed the street, bursting into a full run toward the Blazer. The men in the van continued to sip coffee, refilling it from a large thermos, occasionally laughing, not noticing anything strange in front of the Tessier home.

Elaina jumped into the driver's seat of the Blazer with a smile. Joel lay back in the passenger seat, slumped against the window, but he attempted a smile as she reached over and gave him a hug.

"That was amazing! I got it! They didn't even look at me!" She hugged him happily. He didn't hug her back, and she realized when she saw his faint smile that he must be exhausted and possibly even in pain. "Oh, are you all right? Are you in pain?" she asked, and he shook his head unconvincingly.

"I'm okay. Let's just go." He slumped back into the seat and shut his eyes. Sweat dripped down the edge of his hairline and a couple of tremors went through him, but he didn't seem to be in any pain, and he wasn't convulsing.

Elaina threw the clothing in the back and put the papers on Joel's lap. She turned the Blazer around carefully, so as not to attract any attention. Joel opened his eyes and picked up the papers. Still resting his head against the backrest, he scanned them for names.

"It's not here. It's still good, but it's not enough. No names, but lots of references to the drug and dosages, as well as the tests. But we need names." He folded the papers carefully and stuffed them into Elaina's gym bag.

"We're going anyway. If the general doesn't believe us, then we make a deal with Reid," she said, trying to hide her disappointment over the papers.

They drove south again down through the mountains, through Breckenridge heading for Spradley and Ft. Powell.

CHAPTER 21

17 December 2002

JOEL pulled up to the gated entrance of Ft. Powell at five o'clock in the afternoon. He wore Sheldon's uniform once again, and he was clean-shaven. They had stopped at a convenience store on the way where he had changed and shaved in the bathroom. He slicked back his hair, pulling his coat collar around the long pieces at the bottom. He looked very much like the picture Elaina had first seen in the file. Elaina was lying in the back of the Blazer, hiding under a canvas tarp. Joel slowed the SUV as the guard waved him to a stop. Stopping the car, he rolled down the window and saluted the guard. The guard saluted back, but walked over to the open window and leaned forward.

"Good afternoon, Sir. May I see your identification, please?" the guard asked pleasantly but professionally.

Joel reached into his pocket and pulled out Sheldon's ID, which didn't resemble him very much, but in the picture Sheldon's head had been shaved, and no one could tell that he had blond hair rather than black. Still, Joel hoped he would merely read the rank and name and not bother too much with the picture. He also hoped that word of his escape and the use of Sheldon's identity would not have traveled here. He thought it probably hadn't because the business of the Department of Scientific Research was usually kept quiet, even from other military installations.

"Here you are," Joel said, handing him the ID card. "I'm here to see General Sorenson."

The guard briefly glanced at the ID and handed it back to Joel. He stepped back and saluted him once again.

"Very good, Sir. I won't keep you."

Joel returned the salute and passed through the gate with a sigh of relief.

Elaina lay under the tarp, also breathing a sigh of relief. She hoped the guard wouldn't check to see if the general was expecting anyone. Of course, Joel hadn't said that he was expected.

Joel parked in the rear lot of the executive office building, and Elaina kicked off the tarp. They exited the vehicle, walking hurriedly toward the building.

"Sorenson was always a workaholic, so let's hope he's in there," Joel said, as they walked around the outside of the building toward the front. He opened the front door and held it for her.

"What about your uniform? What's he going to think when he sees your name? Won't he be suspicious?" she asked as they made their way to the elevator, not avoiding the gaze of the receptionist at the information desk.

"It doesn't matter; he'll hear me out, and if he doesn't believe us then, it won't matter anyway. I'll be going to the brig, and they'll probably take you into custody, too. If something happens, and it looks like things aren't going well, I'll distract them, and you make a run for it. Out past the field there's a forest; it'll be hard to find you there."

"You've been here before?" she asked.

"Not physically."

"I won't leave you here," she said, suddenly terrified that there was no way their plan had a chance of working. Why would this general believe anything they said? Reid would just convince him that Joel was psychotic.

"Hopefully you won't need to, but if something does happen, it's better for me, you, and Luke if you get out and get some help," he said logically, and she couldn't argue with his reasoning.

They walked down a dimly lit corridor with very few windows. Joel passed several offices and stopped when he saw the one he was looking for. The sign on the door read GENERAL MARK L. SORENSON. There was a soft stream of light coming through the crack under the door.

Taking a deep breath, Joel listened at the door a moment, hearing nothing, then knocked softly.

"Who is it?" the general called gruffly through the door.

"It's Carpenter, Sir. Sergeant Joel Carpenter," he said, his voice taut and quiet.

The door swung open and a tall gray haired man with a big smile greeted them heartily.

"Carpenter! How the hell are you?" He shook Joel's hand. "It's great to see you. And who is this?" he asked, smiling at Elaina. "What the hell are you doing here? Shit, I never expected to see you here," he said turning back to Joel. He stepped back and gestured for them to come in.

Elaina went in first, and Joel shut the office door behind

him as he followed her in. It was a plush office with thick carpet, richly stained wainscoting, walnut bookshelves filled with leather bound volumes, and an Italian leather sofa and chairs that sat in front of his enormous walnut desk. Sorenson motioned for them to sit down, and they sat in the large armchairs facing the desk.

"Sir, I'm sorry to bother you, but I have some information that I don't know who else to go to with," he began. He motioned toward Elaina and continued, "This is Elaina Tessier. She's the wife of Colonel Reid Tessier of Ft. Clairemont. I don't know if you've ever met him, but he was in the Gulf as well."

"Hmm. The name's familiar, but I can't quite place him. What's the problem?" he asked, taking a seat behind his desk, facing them.

Joel reached into his coat and pulled out the papers from Elaina's house.

"Take a look at these, Sir," Joel said, handing the papers across the desk to the general. "I've been held in a research facility for two years by this man. I have reason to believe that he's behind some unauthorized research—including the use of an untested drug on veterans of Desert Storm."

Sorenson read through the papers, and then looked up gravely at Joel, reading the name on his uniform for the first time.

"Am I to understand that you just recently took it upon yourself to leave this hospital with stolen and classified documents?" the general asked somberly, and Joel stiffened.

Elaina's heart began to pound again, and her throat went dry. He was going to turn them in. Why had they thought a general would ever approve of a lowly sergeant escaping and trying to fight his superior officers? She glanced at Joel nervously, and his eyes met hers briefly, reassuring her.

"Yes, Sir," Joel said, his voice unwavering and strong. "I also had reason to believe that Mrs. Tessier, here, was in danger because of Colonel Tessier," he stated, meeting the general's gaze, unintimidated.

Elaina disliked hearing Joel refer to her as "Mrs. Tessier." She never wanted to hear that name again, but right now it was the unfortunate truth. She swallowed hard and broke into the conversation.

"Sir, my husband, Colonel Tessier, is a dangerous man. I saw him kill someone—a fellow officer he worked with at Ft. Clairemont."

"This is quite a story you're spinning. If you have any proof of these allegations, I'll be glad to have him arrested immediately," Sorenson said soberly.

Elaina and Joel looked at each other again.

"Sir, he has my son," Elaina explained. "I'm sure he's in danger. Please. All we have are those papers—and I took them from our home where Reid left them. Joel didn't steal them," she added. "But Joel can take you to the facility, and you can see for yourself what's going on."

"General, I know it's hard to believe, but you know me," Joel implored him, "and I can prove it if you send someone there. But we need to stop Tessier now. He's on his way here. Is there any way you can hold him for questioning?"

The general pushed himself back from his desk and stood up.

"I'll see what I can do. These are serious allegations, and if they are true, you can bet that I'll do something about it. You two wait here, and I'll make some phone calls." Sorenson left the office, and Elaina smiled at Joel, but Joel didn't smile back.

"That was too easy, and I don't have a good feeling about this. Come on," he said. He took Elaina by the hand and opened the door to the office, looking both ways up and down the hall.

"When I shook his hand," Joel continued, "I felt something—not a vision. It was like he was trying to block me from his mind. He knew I could see, and he didn't want me to."

"Are you sure? But what if he can help?" she asked, reluctant to leave after what Sorenson had said.

"He won't. Trust me." Joel led her down the hall and out a back exit into the parking lot. They got in the Blazer and drove calmly toward the gate.

* * *

Inside the building, in another office, Sorenson argued with Colonel Reid Tessier while Luke rested on the couch in the corner.

"They're here, you idiot!" Sorenson began, red faced with anger. "How did they know you would come here?"

Reid stood up, surprised.

"Elaina—and Carpenter?" Reid asked hesitantly.

"Yes, they're in my office, waiting to find out how I can help them put you away and shut down The Ezekiel Project. They brought this," he said furiously.

Sorenson shoved the papers from Reid's file into his hands. Reid glanced at them and then looked up at Sorenson, embarrassed.

"How could you let her get a hold of these?" Sorenson demanded.

"I don't know—I told you, she took them out of my briefcase one day, and when I caught her looking at them, she dropped them. I guess I missed some of them when I picked them up," Reid said lamely.

"You're lucky this is all she got. How could you be so careless? And they knew you were coming here."

"Well, he is psychic," Reid defended himself.

"He doesn't need to be psychic with you around."

Luke stood up and inched toward the door, hoping they wouldn't notice him.

"Where are you going?" Sorenson turned toward him quickly.

"I have to go to the bathroom," Luke lied.

"Just wait a minute, Son. I'll go with you," Reid told him, looking at Sorenson.

"I can't believe you brought him here," Sorenson said again.

"I want to see my mom," Luke said, and Sorenson's fist clenched, and his jaw tightened with fury.

"You're not going to see anybody," Sorenson told Luke.

Luke backed away from him, frightened.

Sorenson turned to Reid, "I want her taken care of now, and I want Carpenter back in the research facility by the end of the day."

"How? I can't—" Reid began, glancing at Luke, then lowering his voice, "take care of her on post."

"I'll tell them that I'm sending someone to Ft. Clairemont to check out the story, and that I'll be in touch.

Then follow them out of here. I'll send someone behind you to pick up Carpenter."

Outside, Joel and Elaina reached the gate. Joel saluted the guard, slowing down slightly. Elaina, this time in the passenger seat, gripped his elbow and whispered to him.

"Is he going to stop us?" she asked.

"I don't know," he started, "not unless he knows."

The guard saluted and waved them through the gate. Joel started to speed up, but before he could get past the gate, the second guard in the booth shouted.

"Hey, stop them. Stop that car!" he shouted to the first guard. The guard that waved them through, shouted, hitting the side of the Blazer with his hands to tell them to stop. Joel ignored them and hit the accelerator just as he saw the guard in the side mirror pull his weapon.

"Get the MP's after them!" shouted the first guard to the one inside the booth. "Get the MP's after them!" he shouted again.

Elaina and Joel sped through the gate and onto the highway. Joel watched the rearview mirror for anyone following them while Elaina sat, turned all the way around in the seat, checking for MP's. They heard sirens in the distance.

"We need to get off this road and dump this car," Joel said, looking for an exit. "They're going to set up a road block."

"Where? Where do we go now?" Elaina asked, close to tears. The only thing stopping her from crying was her extreme anger over the situation. "Is Luke back there? You said he would be there with Reid!" she shouted at him.

"I don't know. But even if he is, it won't do him any good for us to get caught."

"We can't even make a deal with Reid now! We don't even have the papers anymore. We have nothing." She was dangerously close to tears now.

"Then we'll get something," Joel said quietly staring at the road ahead. Seeing a turnoff, he went up the exit ramp, squealing the tires of the Blazer as he took the turn at the end of the ramp.

CHAPTER 22

17 December 2002

GENERAL Sorenson could scarcely contain his anger when he discovered that Elaina and Joel had escaped. He dragged Reid and Luke into his office and slammed the door.

"That's it! You are not involved in this recovery anymore!" he shouted. Luke cowered in the background.

"You can't blame me for this, Sir," Reid said calmly. "Carpenter is the best precog we've got. He must have seen that he couldn't trust you, and they split."

"I've already assigned Harris to eliminate your wife and bring back Carpenter. I want you to give him whatever you've got. Any information that would help him. Friends, family, besides her parents, where she would go for help."

"Harris?" Reid was shocked. "When did you assign him? Why didn't you say anything?"

"It was just as a back-up. He obviously hasn't done any better than you so far, but I wanted some insurance."

"How long has he been on the case?" Reid asked, looking at Luke. "I mean—"

"I know what you mean," Sorenson said, smiling. "He was on it from the beginning."

Reid couldn't believe what he was hearing. Did that mean that Luke was on the list, too?

"You can't keep him quiet," Sorenson said gently as if he were trying to console Reid. "It's clear whose side he's on here." Sorenson nodded to the boy. "And even if he weren't, he's a kid; he's got no loyalty to us, and he knows too much." He continued to smile as if he weren't suggesting the death of a small boy right in front of him and his father.

"I won't let you do this," Reid said, backing away and placing his hands protectively on Luke's shoulders. "I can control him. You've got to believe me," Reid said.

Sorenson took a step forward, and Reid shoved Luke aside. Luke fell to the floor. Reid overturned one of the large chairs to block Sorenson's path and shouted for Luke to run.

"Run, Luke," he said. "I'll be right behind you." Luke scrambled to his feet and ran for the door.

Reid saw the general's golf club, a nine iron, resting against the wall in the corner and snatched it up. Sorenson turned to grab the boy, but Reid was on him too quickly, knocking him out with one blow to the back of his head. The general fell to the floor in front of the door with a thud. Luke stopped with his hand on the door, turning to see Sorenson lying face down on the carpet. Luckily, there was no blood. Reid thought he would live. But that was probably not a good thing. He could identify his assailant, and he would have a hit out on him and the boy within the hour. If he woke up sooner, they would never get off the post.

"Don't open the door," he told Luke. Luke let go of the handle.

"Is he dead?" Luke asked.

Reid knelt next to the body and checked the pulse.

"No, lock the door."

Luke turned the lock above the door handle until it clicked. No one had come running. Sorenson had sent his secretary and the other sergeant home for the day because he hadn't wanted to be seen meeting with Colonel Tessier. Apparently no one else had been close enough to hear the scuffle. They were all out looking for Sergeant Carpenter and his wife, most likely.

The thought of Elaina helping Carpenter or Carpenter helping Elaina, whichever was the case, infuriated him. He was sure they must be sleeping together. Maybe they had known each other while Carpenter was still in the research facility. Maybe they had planned this whole thing just to be together. But Reid couldn't see how. She had only been to his office at the facility once or twice. She wouldn't have talked to any of the subjects. The first she could have known about Joel Carpenter was when she saw his file. Then she must have contacted him somehow to conspire against him. Or maybe he psychically saw that she had discovered his file and decided to enlist her help and contact her. Yes, that made more sense. *The bitch.* She conspired with a total stranger to bring him down. What had Sorenson said? He had asked the general if he would help them bring Reid down. *That unfaithful, disloyal bitch.* And she had tried to take his son with them. Now, because of her, they wanted his son dead, too. It was all going to hell. But if he was lucky, maybe they would think that Carpenter was somehow responsible for the general's death, either by coming back here unseen, or by tele-kinesis—they would believe that with Carpenter's record. Especially, after what he'd just done to Dr. Andrzejczak. He just had to think fast.

He scanned the office for something to kill the general quickly and quietly that would not point to him as the killer. He could shoot him with his pistol. The silencer would muffle the shot, but that could be traced back to him. The general probably had a weapon in his office somewhere, but it would be harder to believe that Carpenter had first hit him with a club, and then shot him with the pistol. No. It was the only way. As messy and unpleasant as it would be, especially in front of Luke, he would have to finish him off with the nine iron.

He picked up the club. It was a good one, custom made, titanium. Of course, the general would have no less, he thought as he raised it over his head and swung a long drive into the general's skull. He got a bit of a kick out of using the general's head for a golf ball, remembering how many times Sorenson had beat him at the game. True, his handicap was a little high, but that was okay. At least he'd won the game. Nobody threatened his son, he thought with satisfaction. As the club smashed into the general's head, exploding tissue, hair, and blood spattered the room. Blood spattered across Reid's face, and he laughed until he heard Luke whimpering in front of the door. Luke hadn't screamed. He'd been too frightened. But now he stood there weak-kneed, ready to collapse at any moment, small, terrified sounds coming from his throat. Reid looked at him and saw that the boy's face had been splattered with the general's blood as well. Luke stood, holding his hands out in front of him, looking at the splashes of blood on the backs of his hands. His jeans were slightly spattered as well, but the majority of the blood had spurted upward.

Damn, Reid thought. Why hadn't he made the boy stand out of the way? Not only was it going to be a bear to clean all that blood off him before they could stroll nonchalantly out of here, but he hadn't anticipated what the blood pattern would look like to the police until he saw the blood on Luke. When Luke moved, it would be obvious that there had been someone his size standing there because the blood pattern on the wall would be an outline of the boy's figure. There was, indeed, blood all around the boy on the door and wall behind him.

"Shit," Reid said, staring at Luke. "Come over here, Squirt," he said.

Luke slowly took his eyes from the body and looked at his father, still making that whimpering noise.

"Come on, Son. It's okay. Nothing to be afraid of. He can't hurt you now." Luke didn't move.

Reid stepped carefully around the body and pulled Luke gently by the arm, sideways away from the door. Luke moved willingly but never stopped making that damn annoying noise. Reid backed up and examined the wall and door behind where Luke had been standing. There was a clearly a clean area of wall surrounded by the outline of Luke's figure in blood. He pulled Luke farther out of the way.

"Okay. Stand there for a minute," he said. "If I hit him one more time, I ought to get enough blood on the wall to cover up that spot." The body was still covered in wet blood and only seconds had passed since Sorenson had died. The blood would not have coagulated, yet.

Reid raised the club once more and aimed for the imaginary ball in place of Sorenson's head. He took the classic golfer's pose, his hands stacked on the grip of the club, thumb over thumb—coincidently, just as Sorenson had taught him, and he threw his arms back, twisting at the hip. His feet were straddled but straight, one heel coming up as he followed through with the swing, eyes never leaving the ball. This time the club embedded into Sorenson's head and almost turned the body over. Reid wiggled and pulled the club until it came out of the gaping wound in the back of Sorenson's head and lifted the end of the club to his eyes. The general's silver hair was mixed with blood, and there were hunks of scalp on the head of the iron. *Hole in one*, he thought, although he had technically hit the general's head three times. *This was kind of fun*, he thought. It beat the hell out of strangling Tom in his kitchen.

He looked up at the wall, and to his satisfaction, the previously clean area was now covered in, not only blood spatter, but bits of hair and scalp. He smiled over at Luke who was now sobbing quietly in the corner, covering his eyes with one hand, and his other arm wrapped around his head, covering one ear with the upper arm and the other ear with his hand.

Reid took a tissue from the general's desk and wiped down the club for fingerprints. He wiped the desk and the telephone that he had touched earlier. Still holding the club in the tissue, he picked up the general's hand and placed it over the grip, closing Sorenson's hand over it. Then he took the club and placed it Sorenson's other hand, slightly below where his first had been. When the investigators checked for prints and found only the general's, it would support the theory that Joel Carpenter had committed the murder telepathically. He dropped the club next to the body and scanned the office for any incriminating personal items he might inadvertently leave. He grabbed Luke's jacket, backpack, and the papers from his file, then took Luke by the arm and led him out of the office, wiping the prints from the door handle as they left.

CHAPTER 23

Night
17 December 2002

JOEL drove the 1980-ish, yellow Toyota pickup truck he had boosted down the beautiful snow-covered Victorian streets of Breckenridge, Colorado, about fifty miles south of Spring Forest. A busy ski town, Breckenridge also boasted a Victorian village filled with excellent cuisine and bed and breakfasts that were a little more removed from the ski slopes than the condos and lodges were.

"Let's get something to eat and a little rest," Joel said.

"I want to get back to Spring Forest before Reid does," Elaina said anxiously.

"We will. He left hours after we did, and he's stopped along the way as well," Joel told her reassuringly.

"Are you sure? You said you were getting weaker," she asked.

"I'm positive," he told her. He had seen Reid kill the general in a vision and had told Elaina about it, but he hadn't mentioned the part about Luke witnessing it. He did tell her that Reid had done it to protect Luke, which put her slightly more at ease that Luke was safe; however, she could never feel good about leaving her son with someone capable of such brutal murders. And if the general had wanted Luke dead, then that meant there would be others from the Department of Scientific Research that would want him dead as well.

Snow continued to fall steadily, and it was getting late—almost nine already. They had still found no vacancies in any of the places they had stopped. Joel turned into the lot of a large Victorian bed and breakfast on the edge of town, lit decoratively for Christmas. After parking in the back, they entered with only the gym bag. They had gotten rid of the paper sack and had combined their things into Elaina's bag.

Inside, Joel approached the front desk while Elaina wandered around looking at the paintings on the highly festooned walls. There was a large Blue Spruce in the middle of the room with mauve and blue Victorian Christmas ornaments and pearls adorning it. Elaina stopped to admire a nativity scene that sat on the coffee table in front of a Queen Anne sofa. Joel rang the bell on the front desk, and a kindly looking older man with gray hair, pale blue eyes, and a warm smile came out to greet him.

"What can I do for you this evening?" the man inquired.

"Hello. My wife and I were just passing through town and noticed your place. She loves bed and breakfasts." Joel smiled warmly. "Is it possible to get a room without a reservation?" he asked.

"Name's Walt." The man put out his hand for Joel to shake.

"Daniel—Daniel Martin," Joel introduced himself, and then pointed to Elaina. "That's my wife, Marie."

Walt looked toward Elaina and waved. Elaina waved back.

"We'll be glad to put you up. How long you going to be in town?" Walt asked reaching for his registry.

"Just one night. Heading up the mountain for a little skiing," Joel said, relieved to see that the bed and breakfast wasn't computerized.

"Well, that'll put you in the Christmas spirit. I have number seven open. She's a real nice room overlooking the town. Not too fancy, but she's cozy," Walt said, turning the book around for Joel to sign.

"That'll be fine," Joel said, picking up the pen to write Daniel Martin next to the date and room seven.

"That'll be ninety-five dollars for the night, and that includes breakfast," Walt said, taking the book back from Joel with a smile.

"That's very reasonable." Joel counted out the money from Sheldon's wallet. They hadn't needed to dip into Elaina's emergency cash, yet. "I thought these ski towns charged a lot more during the season."

"Well, we're off the beaten path a ways, and we don't shuttle to the lifts. We do have a nice restaurant open till ten, if you haven't eaten, yet. We can even have something sent up to your room. It's pretty good," said Walt handing back his change. "Normally, I run a credit card as security against any damage, but you folks seem like nice people—not the party type."

"Thanks," Joel said, trying not to show his relief. They shook hands again, and Elaina walked over and smiled. Walt reached behind him on an old fashioned pegboard, taking down the key marked seven and handed it to Joel.

Elaina tried to stop the image of Bates' Motel that entered her mind when she saw him take down the key. At least it wasn't number one, she thought. It was ridiculous that she felt like this. This was a wonderful place, and Walt didn't resemble Norman Bates in the slightest.

Walt pointed toward the stairs with a smile.

"The room's just up the stairs to the right, down at the end of the hall. Sorry, my bellboy went home early tonight. Would you like some help up with your bags?" Walt said, looking around for their luggage and not seeing any.

Elaina lifted the gym bag for Walt to see.

"I think this is all we need for tonight. If we need anything else, we can run out and get it from the truck. Thanks, though," she said smiling. She couldn't believe that she had been looking for similarities between him and Norman Bates a few minutes ago. Walt was great.

"All right then. Goodnight," said Walt.

"Goodnight," said Joel, taking the bag from Elaina.

"See you in the morning," Elaina said.

Elaina and Joel walked up the stairs and down the hall of the beautiful old house, admiring the paintings, decorations, and the well-oiled woodwork. The house was kept up very nicely. Elaina wondered if Walt owned the place. When they reached room seven, Joel unlocked the door, and they were even more impressed with the room than the rest of the house. The room was elegantly fur- nished with antiques and tastefully decorated. There was a beautiful converted gas fireplace with an oak mantle and a marble inlaid hearth across from the queen-sized iron bed.

The snow fell silently, deepening as Elaina and Joel ate their Chicken Cordon Bleu dinner that had been brought up to their room. Walt had brought the dinner up himself, and with it he brought two long dinner candles in white porcelain candlesticks and a single, long stemmed rose in a crystal vase that he sat on the oak coffee table in front of the fire. After he left, Joel put the two wing-backed chairs on either side of the table and lit the fire. Elaina dimmed the lights and lit the candles. Joel pulled out one winged-back chair, motioning for Elaina to sit. Joel sat across from her, and Elaina felt somewhat awkward as if this were a first date. Joel laughed, and she blushed.

"What are you laughing at?" she asked shyly.

"This is nice," he said. "I guess I'm just nervous. I haven't been on a date in a long time." He smiled.

"Well, it's not exactly a date." She smiled.

"It could be one if we wanted it to be." Joel looked at her seriously.

Elaina couldn't believe his eyes were so bright even by candlelight. She looked at him and wished she could read his thoughts. Then something occurred to her.

"Can you read minds?" she asked, remembering that when he first told her about the project, he had mentioned mind reading.

"No. Not usually. I mean, I can't really control what comes into my mind, but it usually has something to do with the future or something traumatic in the past. A strong image, something emotional," he finished. "I used to have dreams when I was younger that came true, but not exactly as I dreamed them."

"Not exactly?"

"Like if I dreamed someone died in a car crash, then maybe they died, but in a different way, soon after. Once I dreamed that a guy that I worked with at my dad's lumber mill was going to be killed in a truck accident, driving off the road over a steep embankment, but the next day he was hit by a log and knocked off a high stack of lumber. He fell fifteen feet, hit his head, and died. Stuff like that. Back then it wasn't very clear, but I would get—" Joel hesitated, looking at her to see if she was laughing at him. She was listening intently. He continued, "Feelings about people, like if they were good or bad people, you know. I believe people can be evil, truly evil; do you?" he asked, looking at her seriously.

"I don't know. I guess I always thought that things just made people bad. You know, their environment or childhood or whatever, but now I think maybe there are people who are evil. I don't know. So many bad things happen in the world," she said. "So you always had these powers?"

"Not like now. Tessier had us tested before we went to the Gulf. They told us that it was standard emotional and mental health testing before combat duty, but I knew what he was doing. I guess that's why only certain people were selected to be in the strike force I was in. We all had a propensity toward psychic abilities."

"You said you worked at your father's lumber mill? Tell me about it," she said, trying to lighten the mood a little and because she was genuinely interested in his life. Besides, that's what a date was for, right? Getting to know each other better, and that included his past, she thought.

Joel told her that he'd grown up in a small logging community in Washington. His father owned a lumber mill, and his mother had died when he was still in elementary school. His father never remarried. His father, Bill, had been very much in love with his mother, Kathleen. Bill had spent a lot of time talking about her until Joel felt like he really knew her, more than he could have at the age he had been when she died. Joel, himself, had been somewhat of an outcast all throughout school because he was introverted and sometimes scared people with his prophetic dreams. He was different, and people tended to stay away from different. Joel was close to his father, though, and loved to work with him outside in the trees. He was good with his hands, and woodworking came easy to him. But when he graduated from high school, he'd wanted to see the world, so he joined the army. He became a truck mechanic serving overseas for most of his time until the conflict in the Gulf. He was shipped out, and by that time, he had made sergeant in the infantry and was attending college part-time. He was trying to decide whether to go to officer training school or to get out and start a different career. Or maybe even go home and work in his father's lumber mill again. He had even thought about carpentry.

Joel kept Elaina laughing, telling her stories of growing up with his widowed father. She felt very comfortable with him now, just as she had earlier. The first date awkwardness had gone, and she couldn't believe that she had actually ever felt uncomfortable with him. Especially, after what they'd already been through together. She felt like she'd known Joel her entire life.

"You really did that?" Elaina laughed in response to a story about how he'd accidentally set the kitchen on fire, trying to cook a fancy dinner for his father. "What'd your father do?"

"Well, ever since my mom died, my dad tried to cook these "home-style" dinners—he wanted to have a nice "family dinner" together, so there wasn't a lot he could say. He just put a fire extinguisher right next to the stove after that." He laughed.

Joel looked at her appreciatively. She was beautiful with her thick wavy hair and her pretty brown eyes. She had the most beautiful smile he'd ever seen. Her teeth were white and perfectly even, and she had the slightest little dimple on one side of her mouth that got bigger when she laughed out loud.

"It's good to see you laugh — it's good to be laughing myself. It's been a long time since I felt like it," he said, suddenly quiet but still smiling. "You're very beautiful when you laugh. I mean, you're always beautiful, but especially when you laugh." He looked down at his plate and said, "I hope you don't mind me saying that."

Elaina felt tears stinging her eyes, and she fought them back. *See what just a few nice words do to me?* she thought. How pathetic. Reid had really done a number on her if she couldn't even hear an admiring comment without getting all choked up. But it wasn't just that. It was Joel. He was so genuine that she couldn't help being touched by his compliment. Coming from him, it meant even more because of who he was. He was kind and good and gorgeous, she thought.

"I don't mind. I don't mind at all." She smiled again. "You and your father must have a great relationship — I mean it sounds like he really tried."

"Yeah, he did. And we did, have a great relationship. He died when I was in the Gulf. Heart attack — working in his lumber mill. He loved working outside in the trees. Our land was very important to him."

"I'm sorry. He sounds like a great man," she said, worrying that she'd upset him. "Do you still have the land?"

"No," Joel said, angry all of a sudden. "He owed a little on the mortgage and some taxes, and by the time I found out about it, they had already foreclosed. Not that it would have mattered — I never would've been able to go back," he said bitterly.

Joel looked away, trying to hide his feelings of anger and disappointment. Elaina reached out and touched his hand. He looked back at her and gave her a small smile. She wished she had never brought up the land, or his father for that matter, yet it seemed like he needed to talk about it. Elaina found herself stroking his hand gently, and realizing what she was doing, she pulled her hand away self-consciously, running her fingers nervously through her hair, smoothing the waves. She pushed away her cheesecake and stood up.

"I'm too full for dessert," she said, walking away from the table towards the bed. She was uncomfortable again and even slightly embarrassed. *Why? Just because you were rubbing his hand? You were just being comforting*, she thought. But she knew she was attracted to him, and she was both afraid and embarrassed about her feelings. She decided to change the subject.

"How do you want to do this thing with Reid? Just call him up on his cell phone?"

Joel followed her with his eyes.

"Let's wait till morning, and see if we can think of any other way," he said, looking at her curiously.

"What about his office? If he really keeps everything in his safe and on his computer—maybe we should go there?"

Joel shook his head adamantly.

"There's no way. That place is heavily guarded. Besides, do you know the combination to his safe—or the password to his computer?"

"Maybe. I mean, Reid has a terrible memory—I bet he uses the same combination at work as we have at home. Our alarm number is the same as our safe because he can't remember which is which if they're not. He uses his birthday numbers, for Christ's sake! I bet I could figure out the password, too."

"Elaina, it's too dangerous." Joel paused for a moment,

thinking it over. "But if you think that's the only way, I'll go. If they catch me, I'm just back where I started—and if I'm back in, I might be able to get into his office and get you the information somehow. But you can't risk it—they want you dead."

"No," Elaina shook her head, "I won't let you go back in there to help us. You've done too much already." Elaina stopped to think for a second. "I've been there a few times, but not very often. Reid never has people over, so most of them wouldn't recognize me. Why don't you draw me a map of the place, just in case. A back up plan if we can't think of anything else. I'm sure I could get on the post as a delivery person or something."

Joel stood and went to the desk, rummaging through it till he found some writing paper and a pencil.

"I don't like it, but I'll show you—just in case." He began drawing a diagram of the research facility. Elaina walked over to Joel and took the pencil from his hand. He turned to her, surprised, and she embraced him. Joel put his arms around her and held her back. It felt so right to Elaina, to be here with him, holding him. She tried not to think of Luke, alone somewhere in the night with her husband. Her husband, the words didn't even sound right to her anymore. She had never really been married to Reid; she couldn't have because she had never really known him, and he wasn't the person she had thought she'd fallen in love with.

Joel's arms tightened around Elaina, and she melted in to him. He buried his face in her long hair draped across her shoulder, and she could hear his breathing. It was getting faster, and she was afraid he would feel her heart hammering in her chest. She didn't know why she cared, but she didn't want to seem desperate—but that's exactly how she felt. Her arms slid up his back across his taut muscles and a wave of gratitude washed over her, temporarily overcoming her, even making her forget her desire momentarily.

"Thank you, Joel. For everything you've done. I don't know what to say to you," she said. She could hear the emotion in her own voice and hoped he didn't think she'd started crying again. He might let go of her, thinking she needed space or time or something, when all she needed was for him to keep on holding her like this.

He released his hold slightly, as she'd feared, but he didn't let go. He just backed up enough to look down into her eyes.

"You're so different from anyone I've ever known," she said, getting pulled into the radiance of his blue eyes.

Joel gazed at her — lovingly and longingly. He tipped his head slowly toward hers, and their lips met softly at first, then more passionately as their kiss deepened. Their kiss lingered as they caressed each other slowly. Elaina buried her fingers in his hair, and with the other hand unbuttoned his shirt, running her hand inside and over his powerfully built chest. She couldn't believe she was doing this. This was so not her. As unhappy as she had been for so long, she'd never been unfaithful to Reid. But she wasn't being unfaithful; she was being completely faithful to herself and to Joel. This was the person with whom she was meant to be. She had been unfaithful all these years when she'd been with Reid. Reid, who could never be her real husband.

Joel lowered his head and kissed her neck. She lifted her head to expose more of her tender flesh to him. He ran his hands over her breasts, groaning with desire, and pulled up her sweater, exposing her breasts, then up higher, pulling it off over her head.

"Elaina," he said, murmuring into her hair, "you're so beautiful."

"Joel," she whispered.

Elaina pulled his shirt off over his shoulders, and Joel shook his arms out of it, dropping it to the floor. His arms were powerful and strong, though scarred with a hundred needle marks. She even thought the marks were beautiful. Everything about him was beautiful. Joel bent down and picked her up, effortlessly, in his arms and carried her to the bed, lowering her onto it. He climbed gently, but passionately on top of her, covering her breasts with his chest. Holding up his weight by his elbows on the bed, Joel looked into Elaina's eyes.

"I love you, Elaina. I've loved you ever since I first met you in my dreams."

She reached up to stroke his head, and he leaned down to kiss her again. They made love until they fell asleep in each other's arms. Joel slept more soundly than ever before, Elaina's head resting on his chest.

Downstairs, Walt was sitting in the office, just past the front desk on the sofa with his feet up on the coffee table. He was watching an old episode of *The Andy Griffith Show* when he heard a noise outside the house. He got up and went to the window, pulling the curtain back for a look.

He did not see the white Oldsmobile pull up in the shadowy dirt lot of the bed and breakfast on the side that was not visible from the office. Harris stepped out, screwing a silencer on the end of his gun, then holstered it in a shoulder strap under his coat before walking toward the house.

CHAPTER 24

Early Morning Hours
18 December 2002

ELAINA woke suddenly in the dark room, the only illumination a dim glow from the street below streaming onto one corner of the bed. Joel's sound sleep had turned restless again. It seemed he was having a premonition. He moaned, rolling back and forth, mumbling something inaudible. Elaina moved over to him, laying her head on his chest as she did earlier when he had slept undisturbed, hoping to comfort him. As soon as her head touched his chest, the room faded away, and she entered his dream.

They are in a room, but she can't make out the details. She just knows it's not this room, and Joel is hurt. He's lying on the floor. He's unconscious or – or – God, no! Don't let him die, she's thinking as she rocks his head back and forth in her arms, sobbing.

Elaina sat up startled, waking Joel from the dream.

He was sweating and shivering. Elaina looked down at him, upset.

"You had a dream. I saw it—you—you were dying or dead—I was trying to wake you, but you wouldn't wake up." The dream had been so real that her emotions were real as well. Tears were now streaming down her face as she looked at him.

Joel sat up and took hold of her, pulling her close, trying to calm her, but he began convulsing. She pushed him back down.

"I know," he said, trying to speak clearly. "It's okay, Elaina. It's okay." He touched her shoulder, but she pushed him away.

"No," she raised her voice, "it's not okay. You're not going to die—I won't let you. When we stop Reid, they'll have to help you, you and all the rest."

She fell onto his shuddering chest and began to cry silently, letting her tears flow freely down his body. "I can't lose you now, Joel. I can't," she sobbed.

Joel held her in his arms. He began to seize more violently, and she sat up.

"You need your medication," she said. He tried to nod.

She ran for the gym bag, but as she set it down next to him, a shadow fell across the window and onto the bed. Catching her breath, she looked towards the window and heard voices below. Joel struggled out of bed and went to the window. Elaina stood frozen behind him.

"What is it?" she asked, terrified.

"Let's go," he answered anxiously.

"But your medi—"

"There's no time," Joel said, pulling on his clothes shakily. "Get dressed."

Elaina dressed and grabbed the gym bag. Turning to the door, she saw Joel drop to his knees. She ran to help him up.

"Come on. You can make it," she told him, pulling him to his feet.

Joel managed to stand, leaning on Elaina for support. They hurried down the hall quietly. As they reached the edge of the staircase and started to descend, a shadow fell across the bottom step.

"Somebody's coming," she said. They stopped and listened. The shadow moved closer. Turning the other direction, they went back the way they had come.

"There should be a fire escape in the back of the house," Joel whispered. "There always is in these old houses."

Elaina helped him to the end of the hall, his arm around her small shoulders. He leaned on her a little, but tried to support his own weight. His convulsions were not constant. He shuddered regularly, but didn't seize violently as much as he had before. When they reached the end of the hall, they turned right, and the hallway dead-ended into a row of bookshelves on one wall. On the other wall, there were French doors leading to a small balcony.

"Come on, maybe there are stairs," Elaina said, pulling him faster than he was able to go. He stumbled, and she had to help him to his feet. She heard footfalls on the stairs. "They're coming."

The doors to the balcony were locked at the top with a sliding bolt. She couldn't move the bolt, which was almost too high for her to reach with Joel leaning on her. Joel leaned against the wall, and Elaina jumped up hitting the bolt, knocking it somewhat loose but not open.

"I can't reach," she whispered frantically.

Joel reached over her and slid the bolt open. Elaina opened the door. She rushed out onto the balcony and Joel followed, shaking badly again, sweat beading on his forehead.

But the balcony was enclosed and led nowhere. Elaina leaned over the side and looked down. It was way too high to jump safely, and directly below them was nothing but rocks and thorned bushes. Next to the balcony, however, she saw the fire stairs along the side of the house. She followed the stairs up with her eyes and saw that they came from above them on the third floor.

"Come on," she said to Joel. "We have to go up."

They went back in, turning the other way down the hall, searching for a staircase leading to the third floor. Elaina ran, pulling Joel along the hallway, but he was beginning to lean more heavily upon her, slowing them down, when she saw a staircase ahead, smaller than the one leading from the first level to the second.

"Please, Joel—try. You can make it."

Running up the stairs, Joel stumbled and fell to his knees.

"Go without me," he said, struggling to breathe. "I need the drug. Just get out."

"No," she said angrily, pulling him to his feet, "you can make it a little farther. We'll get you your medication when we get out."

He managed to get to his feet, and they struggled up the stairs. Elaina noticed a light come on in the hallway behind them. At the top of the stairs, Elaina pulled Joel in the direction where she assumed the door to the fire stairs had to be. She just hoped they weren't located inside someone's private room. She rounded the corner with Joel following and spotted a plain brown door locked with a dead bolt. She ran forward, turned the knob on the bolt, and pulled the door open. A small wind blew in snow, and she saw the fire stairs leading down into the parking lot near the yellow Toyota pickup.

"Let's go," she told Joel. They headed down the stairs holding onto the freezing metal railing, trying not to slip on the wet and icy metal stairs. She couldn't hear anybody following them, but the wind was blowing. All she could hear was the wind, the beating of her own heart, and Joel's labored breathing.

Inside the bed and breakfast, Harris descended the stairs leading to the lobby and stopped at the front desk. Lifting the hinged oak counter top, he slipped behind the desk. Harris stepped over Walt, lying dead on the floor in a pool of blood with *The Andy Griffith Show* still playing in the room behind him. Harris pulled out his cell phone.

"They got away," Harris said into the phone and paused waiting for a reply. "I don't know; they were just here." He paused again listening. "Well, what do you expect? The guy's a psychic." He waited again. "You tracking him?" Harris was annoyed. "The link is down? When will it be up?" He nodded his head. "Yeah, all right." Harris flipped the phone shut, put it back in his coat pocket, and left the house.

Elaina drove while Joel sat unconscious in the seat next to her. When she was sure no one was following them, she pulled onto a side road and stopped. She leaned over to him, nudging him gently. He lay there twitching unconsciously, every once in awhile convulsing more violently, not responding to her gentle shakes. She pulled out the half empty bottle of Anasymine and the last syringe and prepared his injection. Nervously she rolled up his sleeve, looking for a vein that wasn't collapsed and without too many puncture wounds. She hesitated, then turned on the dome light.

"Joel?" she asked, quietly at first and then louder, "Joel? Please wake up."

He stirred slightly and mumbled something inaudible. Elaina worriedly tapped the syringe as she'd seen him do so many times before, then released a small amount of the medication. She tapped his arm as well, hoping for a vein to become apparent. A couple of his veins had collapsed in his left arm, so she tried his right. The only vein she could see clearly was in his forearm close to his wrist, so she took a deep breath and poked the needle in. Joel never moved as she released the drug into his vein. She shook him gently again.

"Joel, are you okay? Please, say something," she pleaded.

Joel stirred again, this time his shaking subsided a little. He opened his eyes and smiled feebly.

"Couldn't be—better," he said, his words barely perceptible.

Elaina grabbed him up in a big hug and squeezed him, relieved.

"Thank you, God. Thank you," she said.

She released him, shut off the dome light, and put the truck in gear. Pulling back onto the road, she glanced back at Joel, who looked somewhat back to normal, but still weak.

"Elaina, I've been thinking. I have to go back—it's the only way to get the informa—"

"No way!" she said sternly, staring straight ahead. "We're going back to Spring Forest, and we'll check into that little motel on the edge of town. We'll just rest for awhile, until you're better, and then we'll try to get into Ft. Clairemont together. Like we got into my house," she said, remembering how Joel had made the men watching her house see an image of an empty street as she crossed right in front of them. He would have to rest and probably have more medication before he could pull that off again, she thought, and they were almost out of the Anasymine.

Joel didn't argue, but looked at her sadly, knowing that it wasn't possible. He should just turn himself back in to the facility, he thought. He could get all the medication he needed, and try to get some information to Elaina on the outside. But whom was he fooling? If they got him back, they would never let him out of their sight again, not for five minutes. Besides, he didn't have much time left, he felt, and he wanted to spend it with Elaina. He leaned back and closed his eyes and dreamed of making love to her again.

CHAPTER 25

Spring Forest, Colorado
18 December 2002

ELAINA stopped the truck in front of the small motel on the outskirts of Spring Forest. It was late morning, and they hadn't even stopped for breakfast, yet. She leaned over and woke Joel.

"Joel. Joel, we're here," she said nudging him.

He sat up slowly and pushed the hair out of his face. His beard was growing back again, and he had that dangerous unshaven look about him. Elaina liked him like that, although he would never seem dangerous to her, she could imagine him in Desert Storm during combat, a formidable foe. Now, he was reduced to taking drugs to keep up his strength, which seemed less and less useful and never lasted as long as the time before. He felt much better than he had the night before, however, and he flashed her his winning smile. His teeth looked even whiter in contrast to his olive complexion and against the dark colored beard growing in again around his smile, just as his bright blue eyes stood out against his darkness. Somehow, she thought, those eyes would stand out even if he was pale skinned and blond.

She smiled back, showing her own brilliant smile with a hint of a dimple in her cheek.

"Wait here," she said, looking toward the office of the motel. "I'll go in alone. It's best if we're not seen together." The motel was a one-level flat building that looked in desperate need of renovation. Each door had a large brass number with a covered walkway in front of it, room number one right next to the office. Again, she was reminded of the Bates' Motel, and this time the place looked a lot more like it than the cozy bed and breakfast had.

Remembering the bed and breakfast brought a smile to her face, and she thought of making love to Joel. It had been the sweetest thing she'd ever experienced, nothing like being with Reid. No matter what happened, she would treasure the memory forever. She smiled when she thought of Walt. Her smile faded as she remembered the intruder. She hoped Walt was okay, but then no one would have had any reason to hurt the old man. Walt was probably safely sleeping when the intruder came in, Elaina thought. She wondered if it had been Reid at the house, which meant Luke had been close by. But she didn't think so. It hadn't felt like Reid.

Now she thought she was psychic or something, she decided. But Elaina had been a lot more aware of her intuition now that she knew precognition existed. Reid had always said that everyone was capable of psychic abilities if they only knew how to tap into them. She wondered if she would ever get Reid's voice out of her head. It came back to her just like her mother's voice came back in times of trouble, only Reid's was a lot more frequent and a lot more upsetting.

She got out of the truck, and Joel leaned over to watch her. He quickly scanned the parking lot for anyone who might be watching. Only empty cars in the lot and mostly empty spaces.

The motel clerk was young, about twenty, and smelled like he hadn't had a bath in a few weeks. He looked Elaina up and down appraisingly and smiled with a mouth that was in serious need of dental work. He identified himself as Sean, the son of the owner. Sean was tall and thin, but other than that, he didn't look too much like Norman Bates. Norman was better looking.

Elaina checked in under the name of Sherry Mason, which just popped into her mind when she signed the register, and she had to tip Sean an extra fifty bucks when he told her the owners required a credit card number as security. She made up a lie about having spending problems, and her husband making her cut up all her cards, so now she only used cash. Sean didn't seem to care until she offered him the extra fifty bucks, which was ten dollars more than the room was. He was then very sympathetic and took the money eagerly, dropping the subject of the credit card. She held her breath as he reached up to the pegboard and hovered near number one. She relaxed as he settled on number three and took it down. She watched way too many movies, she decided. At least there wasn't a big scary looking house on the hill behind the motel, only an empty field. She took the key and went back out to the truck to get Joel. Halfway to the truck, she realized that the name she gave, Sherry Mason, sounded suspiciously like Perry Mason. She really did watch too much television.

* * *

At Ft. Powell, Reid drove down a dirt road. Luke stared out the window beside him.

"You hungry?" Reid asked, looking at Luke. "After I drop you off, I could grab some lunch and bring it back for us?" he said in his most cheerful, trying-to-sound-normal tone.

Luke continued to stare out the window and said nothing. Reid was getting annoyed by Luke's behavior. He didn't like to be ignored.

"Are you hungry or not?" he demanded angrily.

Luke moved then, shifting fearfully back in his seat, putting as much distance between Reid and himself as possible.

"I guess," he said quietly, his voice quivering.

Oh God, don't let him start bawling again, Reid thought.

"What the hell is wrong with you?" Reid asked, but didn't wait for an answer. "I should've left you with your mother—I was only trying to protect you."

Luke looked at his father and foolishly spoke in a moment of courage. "Joel Carpenter was right about you."

"Shut up—you're just like your mother," he shouted, his face red with fury. But he only clenched his fists tighter on the steering wheel and stared straight ahead. Luke slunk back into the edge of the seat and leaned into the door again, realizing his foolishness and thankful that his father managed to hold his temper.

Shadows fell across the Explorer as they entered a wooded area of the post. Luke saw an old warehouse or garage of some kind up ahead in a clearing, near the trees. It looked abandoned.

"Where are you taking me?" he asked, suddenly terrified at why they were going to this secluded place.

"It's just the old motor pool building. It's not used anymore. I want you to stay here for awhile, while I take care of some business," he told Luke, his voice returning to normal. "I want you to be completely quiet, so the bad men don't find you," he said, giving Luke an earnest look.

Luke couldn't imagine anyone coming that would be worse than his father, but his father had protected him from the general. The general had wanted him dead, and his dad said there were others who worked for the general that did, too. He fought back the tears that stung his eyes. He just wanted to be with his mom again. Everything she said had been true, and maybe the man she was with, Joel, could help them.

* * *

The sun was going down on the motel where Joel and Elaina rested in each other's arms on top of the double bed.

"Joel, let me take you to the hospital," Elaina said, knowing that he wouldn't agree. She had to make him see that it was the best thing to do.

"No, I don't want to go. It's okay, Elaina," he said, smiling at her.

Elaina sat up and leaned over him. She raised one hand and touched his face. He had grown pale again and still seemed weak, even though he'd had no visions since his last dose of medication. That had only been two hours ago, and now there was only about one dose left and one used syringe.

"Listen to me, Joel. You need a doctor. We don't have to give your real name," she rationalized.

Joel reached up and touched her face gently, lovingly.

"There's nothing they could do," he explained, hoping

she would realize that he was better off staying with her. If he could do anything at all to help her find her son and get him back, he wanted to do that, even if it meant dying in a cheap motel room. "They don't understand my brain chemistry or the medication I've been taking," he said logically. It was true. What would they be able to do for him, anyway? He jerked violently with a sudden seizure. The convulsions were coming on more suddenly and strongly than they were before.

Joel sat up and reached unsteadily for the last of his medication, but his arm was shaking too badly to reach it, and he fell weakly back to the bed. Elaina picked up the bottle and the used syringe wrapped in cloth. She held the bottle up to the light and saw that it was almost empty, not even a full dose.

"Here, let me do it," she said, preparing the injection.

He didn't try to resist as she rolled up his sleeve and tapped on his arm, finding a vein, this time in the upper arm close to the muscle.

"This might hurt," she said apologetically.

"That's okay," he said, not really caring.

She injected the Anasymine into his bloodstream, and his convulsions subsided. He rested back against the pillow.

"I'm going alone."

At this declaration, he opened his eyes wide, surprised.

"To Ft. Clairemont—I'm getting the file on the Ezekiel Project," she clarified. "And I'm going to find some more medicine for you," she said, determined he wasn't going to talk her out of it.

He shook his head and tried to sit up, but she pushed him back against the pillow.

"Then it will be too late for them to do anything. I'll get Luke back, and we'll take you to a doctor—one who knows about Gulf War Syndrome, and they can give you that drug—Myo—whatever, that they gave the others who got better, and they can help you. I know it," she finished.

Joel smiled at her and took her hand. "I've seen my death, Elaina—and you're with me, holding me—and it's okay; it's really okay," he said.

Elaina pulled her hand free angrily. How could he just give up like that?

"No," she cried. She didn't try holding back her tears anymore. She remembered the dream; she'd seen it too, but she didn't believe that it was set in stone.

"It doesn't have to come true—we can change it, can't we? Otherwise, what's the point of seeing the future?"

Joel pulled her down on top of him and held her against his chest, stroking her hair.

"Who said there had to be a point to it?" he said bitterly, thinking of all he'd been through, so men like Reid could prove their theories.

"You did," she cried. "You came to find me, to change what was going to happen to me. If we can't change what's happening to you, then we can't stop Reid from killing me, either," she said, turning his own words against him. She raised her head and looked down at him. He rolled over on top of her and kissed her forehead, her cheeks, and her lips. She kissed him back; their kisses became more passionate. He lifted his head, looking into her soft brown eyes.

"All right. But I need to go with you, to get you inside. I can wait in the truck like before, but I can't let you go alone," he said.

Elaina's face brightened as she said, "Aren't you the one who told me I have everything I need inside me to do whatever I need to do, if I just have faith?" she asked, smiling. "Well, I do." She was getting good at using his words against him. "Draw me a map of the facility, including Reid's office, and where I can find medicine for you," she told him confidently.

Joel stared at her, amazed at her new confidence. He felt a burst of pride and admiration for her.

"Okay," he said, pushing himself to the edge of the bed and slowly getting up. "Let's see if there's some paper in the desk. And this time don't distract me," he joked, remembering the last time he had begun to draw the map, and instead ended up in bed.

She laughed and jumped off the bed to follow him to the desk. He rummaged through the desk, found a pad of paper with the motel logo on it and a pen with an advertisement for some prescription medication printed on it, and he began to draw the outlay of Ft. Clairemont, explaining as he drew.

"I think the best way to get in is just to drive in the front gate, dressed in Sheldon's uniform. We can alter Sheldon's ID for you, using your driver's license picture and changing the name." He pointed to an area on his map. "Then, once you're in, tell the nursing staff that you're there to get some records for Dr. Andrzejczak. That should be safe because I doubt he's back to work, yet. The unclassified, ordinary medical records are in the nurse's station cabinet, right next to the cabinet of Anasymine. They'll have to unlock the cabinet to get to the records, and it's the same key for the drugs." Joel leaned down on the desk, holding himself up and took a deep breath. This little bit of exertion was already getting to him. He pointed to the drawing again.

"Then go down this hall. There is another exit that direction, so hopefully they'll think you're leaving that way. Tessier's office is at the end of this hall," he said, pointing it out on the drawing and putting an X where Reid's office should be.

Elaina nodded her head as she leaned over, examining the drawing.

"I've been there, just a couple of times—and that was a long time ago. Will his office be locked?" she asked.

Joel shook his head.

"I don't think so. He keeps everything important locked in his safe, so there's no reason to lock the door, and the staff doctors use his office for writing reports on his computer because only Simms and Andrzejczak have offices in the building, and they're usually using them."

"Good. Then I go in and try to open the safe and see if I can get into his computer files. I don't need much— just something with Sorenson's name on it, and if I'm lucky, something about the order to bomb the biological weapons plant in Iraq, and the order for your platoon to go in there at the same time."

"Yeah, nothing much." He laughed. Then he became serious. "Anything goes wrong, you get out of there. Use the back exit to leave after you go through Reid's office, so you don't have to go back and pass anybody else. I'll have the truck parked back there, waiting. I know you can do this. Remember when I asked if you believed in destiny?" he asked, letting go of the desk and standing up straight, looking into her eyes, his eyes brighter than ever. "I thought I was supposed to save you, but now I think you were meant to help us—me and the other vets, and to stop Reid and Sorenson.

Elaina's smile faded, and Joel brushed the back of his hand against her face.

"I hope I don't let you down," she said quietly.

"You could never do that." He smiled.

Joel swayed slightly and reached out to steady himself.

"I think I need to sit down."

He sat on the bed, and Elaina pushed him into a lying down position.

"You need to get some sleep first. That's why we came here."

"I've slept more in the last couple of days than I have in a whole month. I usually can't sleep, but with you I sleep like a baby." Joel smiled sleepily at her and shut his eyes, a faint smile still on his lips.

While he slept, Elaina called the clerk at the front desk and asked Sean if he had a portable typewriter that she could use. When he said maybe and left it at that, she told him there would be an extra twenty in it for him if he brought it to her room immediately along with some clear tape.

Sean brought an old Underwood that looked like an antique, but he assured her it had a fresh ribbon and handed her a small dispenser of tape.

"What are you doing in here with this stuff?" he asked, glancing around the room.

"Just fixing something," she replied, handing him his twenty-dollar bill and waiting for him to leave. He looked suspiciously at Joel sleeping in the bed.

"There's an additional charge for double occupancy," he said.

She slipped him another twenty, and he went away happy.

Joel slept as Elaina finished sliding her driver's license photo into Sheldon's military ID slot, covering his picture. She had split open the worn out laminating plastic and rubbed off part of Sheldon's name with an eraser. She typed over the missing letters and replaced the plastic, fastening it back together with clear tape. The ID that had once read Michael Clarence Sheldon, now read Michelle Clarice Schneider. It wouldn't withstand close examination, but from a distance, it would pass. Elaina dressed in Sheldon's desert camouflage uniform and military t-shirt. She pocketed the ID and bent down to roll under the cuffs of the overly long pants. She looked down at her Nike hikers and frowned. Picking up Joel's army boots, Elaina shook her head. They were about four sizes too big.

"There's no way," she said. She put them down, looking at her own hikers again. At least they were black. Elaina scanned the room for anything else she might need. She grabbed her gym bag and Sheldon's army coat and tried it on. It was way too big, not to mention the fact that Sheldon's name was printed over the pocket. She decided that she would take it just in case, but not wear it unless it seemed necessary. Walking over to the mirror, Elaina evaluated herself.

"Shit. I'm never going to get away with this," she said to herself.

Taking one last glance around the room, her eyes came to rest on Joel, sleeping. She had purposefully waited until he went to sleep, so that he would not try and stop her from going to Ft. Clairemont alone. Now she wondered if that was wise. She needed Joel. What if something went wrong? And he could just wait in the truck, be there, just in case. But if they were found, he would be locked up again, used as a lab experiment. She went over to Joel's side and leaned close to him and whispered in his ear.

"Wish me luck." She kissed him lightly on the forehead, but he didn't stir. She smiled, admiring him a moment longer, then opened the door silently and left. She went out to the pickup truck and brushed the snow from the window. Throwing her things in the passenger seat, she reached under the steering wheel, touching the wires together and starting the engine. She was getting good at hotwiring now; she had watched Joel enough times. Pulling the truck out into the lightly falling snow, she drove toward Ft. Clairemont.

CHAPTER 26

Ft. Clairemont, Colorado
18 December 2002
2100 Hours

OUTSIDE the Ft. Clairemont Research Facility, it was cold, but it had stopped snowing. Elaina drove up to the heavily guarded, gated entrance and the guard on duty motioned for her to stop. Corporal Bill Fishe stepped out of his booth and approached Elaina, still in the yellow Toyota pickup. Despite the cold, she had taken off the oversized uniform coat, and it was lying on the seat beside her.

"What business do you have here, Ma'am?" Fishe asked.

Running her fingers through her hair nervously, Elaina forced a smile to her shaking lips.

"I'm here to pick up some records for Dr. Andrzejczak. He's working at home since his little accident," she said, hoping that Andrzejczak wasn't inside the facility at that very moment.

"And you are?" Fishe asked, raising one eyebrow. He didn't recognize her. He was sure he would've remembered someone that beautiful if he'd seen her before.

Elaina reached unsteadily into her pocket and pulled out the doctored ID card.

"I'm Lt. Michelle Schneider—" she said, holding the ID card up in front of the guard's face just long enough for him to glance at it and then dropped it. It landed on the floorboards at her feet, and she quickly covered it with one foot. "Oh, I'm sorry," she said, bending over under the steering wheel, pretending to reach for it. "I'm Dr. Andrzejczak's new administrative assistant—just a minute; I think I feel it," she said, still fumbling under the seat.

Fishe looked bored and annoyed as he saluted her and waved his hand, motioning towards the gate.

"Go ahead, Ma'am. You're clear. I'm sorry to have kept you. Have a nice evening," Fishe said politely, backing up to let her pass.

She returned the salute, hoping she was doing it right as the gate swung open. She let out a deep shaky breath as she drove through the gate. She turned left, the way Joel had shown her. Looking behind her through the side window, she saw that the exit stood open on the opposite side of the guard's booth. Elaina drove around to the second building and parked in a utility vehicle space behind the main medical building. No one seemed to be anywhere around the area, thankfully.

She stepped out of the truck and the freezing wind sliced through her thin t-shirt. She looked on the passenger seat at the oversized coat, but decided again to leave it. No one would believe it belonged to her, and she couldn't risk them noticing Sheldon's name, so she would just have to be cold. Elaina walked to the front of the building, her knees shaking from fear more than the December air.

* * *

Luke sat shivering in the corner under an old army blanket his father had given him. It was uncomfortable, and he was getting sleepy and hungry. It had been hours since his father had brought him lunch. He didn't know what time it was, but it was dark outside and a light snow had begun to fall. He'd rubbed the dirt off in a small circle on one of the windows, even though his father had told him to stay away from them, and he'd seen the snow. It would have been pretty if he'd been back home in his room, watching it fall outside his bedroom window. He thought he'd heard a car, and he wanted to check in case it was one of the bad men. Then he would know whether to run or hide, or something, but he hadn't seen anything except the snow.

Shivering from the cold, he got up from the corner and climbed into one of the old broken Jeeps. It wasn't very padded, but at least it was warmer than the cement floor. He crawled into the back seat, curling up in the wool army blanket and went to sleep hungry.

Reid was busy answering questions about Sergeant Joel Carpenter and why Reid had been in to see the general. He couldn't believe their nerve. Someday he'd be beyond this type of interrogation; if he needed someone dead, no one would question it. They couldn't expect geniuses to live under the same rules as other people. But for now, he had to go along with the authorities in power.

He told them that Carpenter was a Gulf War veteran that suffered from an extreme case of psychosis, as a result of his exposure to toxins during the war, and that he had recently escaped from Ft. Clairemont where he was being treated and held because he was dangerous. He had to tell them that Carpenter was involved in a project, and that project had to do with telekinesis, so they would believe what he wanted them to believe — the way he'd set up the crime scene to look as if Carpenter had used telekinesis to kill the general. Reid told them that Carpenter had the ability for telekinetics, and that he could be very dangerous in his current condition. He also told them that Carpenter may have believed that the general had something to do with the project and resented being held against his will. Those with high enough clearance would find out that General Sorenson was directly responsible for Carpenter's presence in the facility, and that would secure Carpenter as a suspect in the murder.

Because Reid had been seen meeting with the general earlier that day, he was told to remain on the post for a day or two, in case they needed him for further questioning. Luckily, no one had seen Luke; he couldn't take the chance of anyone talking to him just yet. He had been pretty lucky all around. No one knew the exact time he was with the general, thanks to Sorenson having cleared out his office personnel for the day.

Reid was in charge of Harris now. He would depend on him to take care of Elaina and take Joel Carpenter back to the facility. Then Reid would personally supervise Carpenter's case and make sure he was under control. At least long enough to figure out why Carpenter was able to do so much more than the others. And after that, if he couldn't keep him under control, he would do away with him. But for now he needed him. Since Thompson and Montoya had died, Carpenter was the only one who showed any real promise. Sure, all of them could do little mind reading tricks or had precognitions, but none of them had the power of telekinesis or mind control—and Carpenter had both. He suspected that he might even be able to remote view, but he had not found a way to test that theory, yet. Soon, everyone would know that Reid Tessier had been right about all his theories. No one would be laughing at him anymore.

He was sure that if he found the key to Carpenter's success and could prove it with other subjects as well, he would not only get funding for the project, but would go down in history as one of the greatest scientists of all time. They would all believe him then. He would be assured a high dollar civilian position upon retiring from the military. Maybe he would even run for office. Everyone who had ever scoffed at him would be eating their words. Of course, the general's death wouldn't be good for public opinion of the project, but that would eventually blow over.

The interview had gone well, and he thought he would pick up something for dinner and go see Luke. Maybe he would even sneak Luke into the temporary quarters he would be occupying that night. It was just a matter of time before the boy came to his way of thinking. After all, they were from the same blood, and although Luke didn't seem to have the genius that Reid had, and he had inherited a few annoying character traits from his mother, he was still his father's son. Soon he would come to know that his father was right; his father was always right.

* * *

Elaina pushed the door buzzer and waited. A large female guard of about fifty, named Hackett, came to the window and looked out. Elaina held up her fake ID, several inches from the window just to make sure, and the woman buzzed her through. She pushed open the door and was surprised when the female guard began to pat her down for weapons. Finding nothing, Hackett stood and looked her up and down with a frown.

"You trying to catch your death out there?" Hackett asked in a condescending tone. "No jacket; it must be twenty-five degrees." She shook her head in disgust.

Elaina turned around and lowered her arms since the search appeared to be over.

"I forgot it in the car," Elaina said, shivering.

The guard gave her a look of disapproval and then saw her shoes. Elaina followed the guard's eyes down to her feet and saw the white Nike stripe shining on her black hikers.

"They're a lot more lax than they used to be—used to have to be in complete uniform wherever you went. Anymore—" she looked at Elaina with disdain, "they let you dress however you want."

"I was redoing the filing system for Dr. Andrzejczak today—in his home office. Moving a lot of boxes and stuff," she said, hoping that this woman didn't know Andrzejczak very well.

Hackett, apparently losing interest, motioned for her to continue into the building and buzzed her through the second set of doors. It appeared that Elaina's ability to sufficiently bore the guards was the best strategy, yet. Elaina followed the sounds of chaos into the day lounge where Marshall was going off again, and two vets in the corner argued loudly over their card game. One accused the other of using his psychic powers to cheat. Another rocked himself in the corner in the exact same position he was in when Joel was there.

"Jared, you're cheating!" the angry vet yelled at his card partner. "I can tell by the look on your face."

"What? What's the matter with my face?" shouted Jared in return. "You're fulla shit, Charlie!"

"You were staring right through me, and your eyes were all glazed over," Charlie accused.

"Oh man, that's pretty desperate—just 'cause you can't play poker doesn't mean ya gotta accuse somebody of cheating," Jared shot back.

Marshall drowned them out with a loud scream. He ran across the room, throwing chairs between him and the nurses. Elaina watched, horrified that Joel had been made to live here in all this pandemonium. Her attention was drawn to the nurses' station. She walked calmly over to it. With no one paying any attention to her, she moved behind the counter and took a look around. There were several cabinets underneath the counter, and she tried them all. They were all locked. She stood up to ask some-one for help and to try out her story when she noticed a set of keys on top of one of the charts. Glancing around, she picked up the keys and bent to unlock the cabinet to her left. Just as she opened it, Nurse Blancett came around the corner.

"Can I help you?" he asked from behind.

She jumped up, startled, and looked at him. Her hand was still on the key in the lock when she jumped, and she accidentally turned the key into the locked position, but the door was still open about an inch. The lever that held the cabinet closed now prevented it from shutting.

"Oh, you startled me," she said, facing him. "I was try-ing to find what I needed on my own because you looked like you had your hands full." She smiled at him. He smiled back. "I'm Lt. Schneider, Dr. Andrzejczak's assist-ant. He sent me to pick up some records. He's still work-ing at home."

Blancett looked her up and down admiringly and smiled lustfully.

"Lieutenant? Why haven't I ever seen you before?" he asked, but there wasn't disbelief in his voice, only interest.

"Oh," she laughed flirtatiously, "you're hurting my feelings. You don't remember? We met a couple of months ago when I came to help Dr. Andrzejczak sort out some charts.

His face changed slightly, and she thought she saw suspicion. She must have said something wrong.

"Oh, yeah," he said slowly, "it's been a long time." He was smiling again, but she thought he still looked different.

"Yeah, too long," she said, resting her arms behind her on the countertop. She set the keys down quietly on the counter behind her without turning around, and he didn't seem to notice. "If you could just help me find some records, I'll let you get back to your patient," she said sweetly, nodding to Marshall who was now rolling around on the ground. At least he wasn't screaming for the moment.

Blancett stepped forward till he was right in front of her, and she thought this was it; she was caught. He would grab and her haul her off to the guards now, but instead he leaned over her, picking up the keys behind her, brushing against her breasts with his arm and coming within inches of her face with his face. Elaina remained still and somehow kept her smile. Blancett took a half step back and bent down to open the cabinet on the right, opposite the one that was still partially open. He pocketed the keys and stood up, again putting his face within inches of hers.

"There you go," he said, breathing in her face.

At that moment Marshall let out another scream and someone yelled for Blancett.

"Blancett! Get over here and help me," the other nurse shouted, trying to restrain Marshall.

Blancett smiled at Elaina and reluctantly went over to help. Elaina dropped to the ground and opened the partially ajar cabinet. It was filled with different medications. She looked through them until she found several bottles marked Anasymine and stuffed them in the large pockets of her fatigues. She saw a box of disposable syringes, grabbed a handful, and put those in another pocket. She tried to close the cabinet but the lever was in the way. Forcing the lever down with her hand, she managed to get the door shut.

Elaina was going through the files of medical records when Blancett ran over to get some medication for Marshall. Blancett pulled out his keys and bent down to the cabinet she had just forced shut. He tried to unlock the cabinet, but when he turned the key, it locked instead. He pulled on the door, but it wouldn't budge.

"That's funny," he said as he tried the key again, this time unlocking it easily. Opening it, he reached in and moved his hand around on the shelf. "What the hell?" he asked, shoving his hand all the way to the back to reach the drug. He bent down lower and stuck his head in, looking around.

Elaina glanced at him anxiously but continued to flip through the files, looking for Joel Carpenter's name. She found his name and pulled the file folder. Standing up, she smiled down at Blancett, hiding the name on the folder with her hand.

"Thanks," she said, and he stood up to face her. She turned to leave.

"No problem," he called after her. "Hey, don't be a stranger!"

Elaina waved goodbye and walked quickly down the hall towards Reid's office. She entered the hall lined with the offices and passed several people in lab coats. She smiled briefly at them, avoiding their eyes, slowing her pace as to not arouse suspicion. Further down the hall, she found herself alone. Seeing Reid's office ahead, she glanced behind her and found no one around. Checking the door, she breathed a sigh of relief as she found it unlocked. She slipped in quietly without turning on the light. She shut the door behind her and locked it from the inside. The light from the computer monitor illuminated the room enough for her to see.

CHAPTER 27

Spring Forest
18 December 2002

A COLD wind blew a light flurry of snow into the motel office as Harris opened the door, stepped in, and wiped his feet politely on the tattered rug in front of the door. The cowbell on the door clanged, and the weasely looking clerk glanced up from the small black and white television on the counter and put his cigarette in the ashtray, still burning.

"Can I help you?" Sean asked.

Harris pulled out a couple of photos, one of Joel— from his file and one of Elaina and Luke, placing them in front of the clerk.

"By any chance have you seen these two people around here?" Harris asked. "The kid isn't with them," he added.

"You a cop?" Sean asked, grinning, revealing several rotten teeth.

"No." He laughed. "Definitely not. Just somebody looking for a couple of friends."

"Well, I can't remember every face that walks through that door." Sean smiled and rubbed his head.

Harris pulled a twenty out of his wallet and waved it in front of the clerk.

"I can see how that would be difficult in a nice place like this—I mean you must have a couple of people in here every week," Harris said sarcastically.

Sean smiled even wider at the joke, took the money from Harris, and stuffed it in the pocket of his filthy jeans.

"Well, I try to stay on top of things," he said as he checked out the pictures again. Pointing to Elaina, he said, "She checked in by herself, but she called down asking if I could bring her a portable typewriter, and when I brought it to her," he said pointing to Joel's photo, "there was a guy in there. It could've been him, but he was sleepin' and his hair was longer. Looked kinda like him, though. Didn't look too good."

"Are they still here?" Harris asked excitedly.

"Yeah, I just gave her a typewriter a couple of hours ago."

"What room?" Harris asked.

"Room three."

"You wouldn't have an extra key?" Harris asked, pulling another twenty from his wallet.

Sean smiled greedily. This was his lucky day. He'd never made so much side cash in one day before. He turned around and pulled a master key from the peg board and started to hand it to Harris, but pulled back abruptly as Harris reached for it.

"Not so fast," Sean said.

He pointed to the money, and Harris handed over the cash. Sean gave him the key with a smile.

"A pleasure doing business with you," Harris told him, heading for the door.

"Anytime, Man," Sean said, counting his money.

Harris noticed that there was no light coming from underneath the door of room number three as he listened with his ear pressed against it. Silence. He wondered if they could be out, but the clerk had seemed to think that they were just here, or maybe he was telling him what he thought would keep the money rolling in. Quietly using the key, Harris let himself inside room number three and shut the door. He looked around the room, adjusting his eyes to the darkness. He could just make out what looked like a person sleeping in the bed. Harris pulled out a silencer-equipped gun out of his coat and moved forward toward the sleeping person.

"Elaina, is that you?" Joel asked, sitting up in the bed suddenly.

Harris flipped on the wall switch, flooding the room with light. Joel shielded his eyes from the brightness and rolled out of the bed. His eyes darted around the room, looking for Elaina.

"Who're you looking for?" Harris said, scanning the room first with his eyes, then opening the closet and looking in. "Maybe I could help," he said as he walked over to the door leading to the small bathroom and swung it open. He pulled the shower curtain back and looked into the stall.

Joel got to his feet unsteadily and moved forward, afraid for Elaina. He saw the nine-millimeter, semi-automatic weapon with the abnormally long barrel and realized that this guy had a silencer screwed to the tip. That could mean only one thing—he meant to kill someone in cold blood, and it was probably Elaina. They needed him alive, but he knew Reid wanted Elaina dead. And this meant that the Department of Scientific Research also knew about Elaina and would want her dead as well. Of course, they knew about Elaina. He had taken her to them himself and let her tell what she knew. Joel became angry, angry with himself for putting Elaina in danger and angry with this man who intended to kill her.

"She's not here," Joel said. It was apparently true, but he didn't know where she'd gone. Maybe just to get some ice, or some dinner, and she would walk back in at any moment into an ambush. But he didn't think so. She had wanted to go to Ft. Clairemont alone. She thought he was too sick and weak, and she had probably gone to break into Reid's office alone. He looked around the room for her gym bag and saw it was missing, along with Sheldon's uniform. The old Underwood typewriter sat on the desk with little scraps of tape and paper strewn across it. Yes, she was gone. He was sure of it. This thought scared him more than if she had been here in the room with the man sent to kill her. At least he would be with her and could do something to protect her and know what was happening with her.

"Apparently not," said Harris, walking back towards Joel. He raised the gun to Joel's head and pressed it against his temple. "Where do you think she could have gone?" he asked with mock politeness.

"Where's Tessier? Doesn't want to clean up his own messes?" Joel asked, staring Harris directly in the eye, not even flinching with the gun at his head.

Harris smiled and looked at Joel for a moment, respect showing in his expression.

"You start talking or there *will* be a mess to clean up," Harris said, still smiling.

"You're not going to kill me. You're supposed to kill her and bring me back to the facility—isn't that right?" Joel asked coldly without a hint of intimidation.

Harris' smile faded as he became annoyed with Joel's impertinence.

"Don't overestimate your importance. There's plenty more where you came from. I was told to keep you alive if I could. But to tell you the truth, I don't think Tessier would care too much one way or the other. I've heard he doesn't think too kindly of you running around with his wife. He's got his kid with him; that's all he cares about. And the success of this project." Harris sneered.

Joel brightened at the mention of Reid's son. If this man knew Tessier had his son, then maybe he also knew where they were or would be going—something he could use to find him, to get him back for Elaina. Joel stared intently at Harris and his face grew very serious.

"You've seen Tessier and his son?" he asked.

"What do you care?" Harris looked at Joel quizzically, wondering what was going on in his mind.

"Where are they?" Joel demanded as if he were hold-ing the gun to Harris' head.

This annoyed Harris. He pressed the gun harder against Joel's head, turning his skin white where the silen-cer made a circular mark on his temple.

"Now you're asking the questions?" Harris pushed Joel backwards knocking him into the wall and followed him, standing in front of him with less than a foot between them, the gun now aimed at Joel's chest. He cocked the gun suddenly and clenched his teeth, apparently furious that Joel didn't seem afraid of him.

"I'm asking the questions here," Harris ground out the words between his clenched teeth. "Now, where's the little lady?"

Joel threw himself forward on Harris, knocking his arm sideways, making the gun point towards the window and grabbed him in a bear hug. They wrestled to the floor, and Joel landed on top of him. They rolled over, and then Harris was on top, trying to free himself from Joel's grasp. Joel held on, not fighting, just concentrating on seeing into Harris' mind, clutching him tightly.

Joel began to shake, and he cried out in pain as the overhead light faded away.

He is in a dark warehouse, the only illumination coming from an overhead lamp swinging slightly back and forth, casting weird, changing shadows all around the large area. It isn't night, Joel thinks, but the windows are covered with something, and they're not letting in any light. The warehouse is on an army post, he thinks, because he sees army Jeeps parked in rows, one with the engine pulled out and the hood open, and dusty filing cabinets next to a box of files. Luke is here, sitting on some kind of gasoline barrel, and Tessier is sitting in front of him. They're eating sandwiches. Reid's cell phone rings. It's Harris on the other end of the line.

"They were spotted heading into Spring Forest about two hours ago," Harris tells Reid.

"All right. You go. I can't be seen in the area when you do it. Who knows what she's told anyone about me being after her. I'll stay here at Ft. Powell. They want me here anyway in case Carpenter comes back. Ever since he killed the general, this place has been in a panic over him. I'm the only one who knows

exactly what's going on with the project around here, so they've put me in charge of the investigation," Reid lies.

"Yeah, okay. What about the kid?" Harris asks.

"What about him? He can stay here with me. I have him under control."

The motel room came into view again as Joel released his hold on Harris and fell back, lying on the floor with his head against the wall, exhausted.

"What the hell did you do?" Harris yelled at him as he retrieved the gun that had fallen to the floor during the struggle.

Joel stared at him, making no attempt to reply. Harris became furious all of a sudden, realizing what Joel had done.

"You're dead, you psycho. I don't care what Tessier says," Harris spat out, his anger out of control as he pointed the already cocked weapon at Joel.

Joel, breathing raggedly, concentrated all of his mental energy on Harris and the gun. Suddenly, Harris began to struggle to keep the gun steady. He shook as the gun began to turn away from Joel. His hand shuddered wildly, and he stared at his hand in confusion and horror as the gun slowly turned towards himself.

"What the — what the hell are you doing to me?" Harris screamed as he fought his own arm for control of the gun. "No!" he screamed. His hand tightened and his own finger squeezed the trigger. The gun went off and the bullet tore through Harris' chest, throwing him through the air and on to the floor, several feet away from Joel.

Joel's head collapsed backward on the floor as he was seized with convulsions, the most violent yet. When the seizure finally subsided, he curled into a ball on the floor, shivering with chills.

In the office, Sean heard what he thought sounded like shouting and a struggle with some loud thumping. Then all of the sudden it was quiet again; too quiet. *Oh man*, he thought, *I didn't give that guy a key so he could—* No, he wouldn't let his mind go there. It wasn't his fault. Didn't the guy say he was a friend? Yeah, well friends don't usually ask for a key when the people are home, either. He hoped nothing too bad happened, or he'd probably get shit for giving out a key. He could always pretend the guy stole it, but then he'd get it for leaving the front desk unattended. Besides, maybe nothing happened. Maybe they worked it out. He didn't think so, but he wasn't about to go to room three and knock on the door, in case the guy was still there and decided he didn't want any witnesses. What if the man decided to come back and get rid of him after his meeting with them went bad or something? Sean let his imagination run away with him. *Better safe than dead*, he thought, so he picked up the office phone and dialed 911.

CHAPTER 28

Ft. Clairemont Research Facility
18 December 2002

H ACKETT buzzed Dr. Rivers through the front entrance of the research facility at nine-thirty. She hadn't bothered searching Rivers because only lower ranking officers and people she didn't know were searched.

"Gettin' nasty out there, ain't it?" Hackett asked, smiling.

"Yes, it is," he nodded, stomping the snow from his feet.

"What are you doing here so late, Sir?" Hackett asked, helping him off with his coat.

"I just stopped by to get some files for Dr. Andrzejczak. He's still working at home. He wanted to check something out. He asked me to drop in and get them on my way home from dinner."

Hackett looked surprised. "Well, why didn't he tell his assistant to get them while she was here?" she asked.

"His assistant?"

"Yeah, she was just here. She said she was picking up some records for Dr. Andrzejczak because he was working at home. I don't know why he made you make the trip. Why don't you call him?"

"Maybe I'll do that," he said, thinking. "Well, the ones I'm here to get are classified. His assistant probably wouldn't be able to get them. I didn't know he had an assistant. What was her rank?" Rivers asked curiously.

"Lieutenant, Sir. Is anything wrong?" she asked.

"No," he said, his smile returning. "I'm sure everything is fine. I'm sure it's as I thought; she wouldn't have the clearance to get these files." He went through the second security door and entered the hospital.

Elaina tried Reid's birthday numbers to open the safe, the same as their safe at home, and the same as their alarm code for their house. She finished the last turn and the safe clicked open.

"Unbelievable. You really do need to work on that memory problem, Reid," she said, laughing quietly.

She opened the safe and reached in, feeling around in the dark. Nothing. Completely empty. Disappointed, Elaina closed the safe and looked around the room. She went over to Reid's desk and sat down behind the computer. Using the mouse, she clicked on several different programs until she suddenly ran into a block asking for a password. She stopped and smiled.

"Let's try Ezekiel," she said and typed in the word. Password error, the computer informed her.

"That would be too easy, even for you," she said, undeterred. "How about — Prophecy," she said, typing the word. She looked at the computer screen. "No," she said, thinking for a moment. "Prophesy." Again, the computer refused it.

Elaina looked around the room. Her eyes fell on an old bible resting on a pile of books. She grabbed the book and flipped through the pages, stopping when she got to the book of Ezekiel. She read the first verse:

> *In the thirtieth year, in the fourth month on the fifth day, while I was among the exiles by the Kebar River, the heavens were opened and I saw visions of God.*

"Okay," she said, typing again, "let's try 30-04-05." The computer rejected the password. She flipped the numbers around to modern dating, 04-05-30. Nothing. She thought that Reid would probably use the military style of writing a date, so she tried, 05-04-30, and when the computer refused that as well, she picked up the bible and flipped through the book of Ezekiel some more.

"Reid, you're not as obvious as I thought you were." She found a few highlighted verses and stopped to read. Just one portion of Ezekiel 12:23 was highlighted, and it seemed promising. It read:

> *The days are near when every vision will be fulfilled.*

A few verses down she read:

> *The vision he sees is for many years from now, and he prophesies about the distant future.*

Elaina typed in "vision"—nothing, then "visions"—again nothing. "Prophecies" didn't work, either.

"Geez, Reid you're better than I thought," she said, getting frustrated and nervous. This was taking longer than she had anticipated.

A shadow fell across Elaina's face, and she caught her breath as she saw a silhouette in the window of the door. The doorknob rattled. Elaina sat frozen, and the knob rattled again. The silhouette disappeared, and she heard footsteps walking away. Elaina let out a deep breath and frantically started flipping through the book.

"Okay, Reid, tell me what it is," she whispered.

She flipped open a page with one word underlined in red, instead of yellow highlighter: *Prophet.* Elaina smiled and let out a small laugh.

"I knew you would have it marked somewhere, so you could remember."

Elaina typed in the word and the computer began making its whirring noise and a different screen appeared. On the screen, there was a symbol of a beast on wheels and below it were the words she was looking for: *The Ezekiel Project.*

"Yeesss!"

Elaina flipped from screen to screen, amazed.

"It's all here. The orders, everything. Sorenson, Senator Phillips. Oh my God, Joel, we did it!" she told him, hoping he was telepathically listening.

Elaina threw open a couple of drawers until she found a box of disks. She put one into the floppy drive and clicked on save to disk. As it downloaded, the bar measuring how much had completed appeared and moved slowly forward.

As she watched the completion bar crawl imperceptibly toward complete, the footsteps returned, and this time they were accompanied by voices. Her breath caught in her throat, and her heart knocked against the wall of her chest. She stared at the frosted glass in the door and saw nothing. She looked back at the completion bar—sixty-two percent complete. Her eyes moved back and forth from the screen to the door, and she held her breath. She ran a hand through her hair nervously.

"Come oonn!" she whispered.

The voices and the footsteps grew closer, and again she stared toward the door.

"I don't know; maybe somebody's in there. It was unlocked earlier." She heard Blancett's voice behind the door.

"With the light off?" she heard Rivers ask skeptically.

The silhouette of the two men covered the white glass. Her eyes searched frantically around the room and stopped on a high vent on the wall above some book-shelves. Elaina looked down at the computer. The bar read eighty-eight percent, then suddenly jumped to the end of the bar, one hundred percent. She pushed the but-ton, popping out the disk and clicked on the close icon. The screen went back to its original start-up menu. Elaina jumped out of her chair as a key was inserted into the lock. She stuffed the disk into her side pocket in with the disposable syringes and grabbed Joel's medical file from the desk. She scrambled to her feet, the sound of the key being turned in the lock amplified. She could no longer hear the drumbeat of her heart that had filled her ears moments earlier.

Elaina dropped the file on top of the bookcase and grasped the shelf, stepping on the second shelf sideways because the books were large and left only about an inch of shelf room for her footing. She never noticed her altered ID slide out of her pocket, hit one shelf of the bookcase, and bounce, landing silently to the floor next to the desk's chair. Climbing the bookshelf like a ladder, she reached the top and pulled open the vent cover. It swung open like a door on hinges, and she silently thanked God that it hadn't been screwed shut. Standing, crouched on top of the bookcase, she shoved the file into the duct and dove in behind it, only her feet showing as the office door swung open.

Blancett entered the office first, Rivers following close behind.

"Nobody here," Blancett said, scanning the room.

"I guess someone locked it when they left," Rivers surmised.

Walking further into the room, Blancett's eye fell on something lying on the floor next to the chair in front of the desk.

"Hey, what's that?" He bent down to get a closer look and noticed it was an ID card. He picked it up, examining the card, easily spotting the tape holding in the photo and the alteration of the name. He turned quickly to Rivers.

"Check this out," he said, handing Rivers the ID.

Elaina inched her way through the ventilation duct on her stomach, holding Joel's medical file in her hand. She opened the file folder and removed the contents, discarding the empty folder behind her. She folded the papers, shoved them into the back waistband of her pants, and started crawling again. It was dark, except for one small stream of light coming through an opening several feet away. When she reached the light, she peered through the cracks of another vent cover. The vent cover led to the hallway outside Reid's office, but farther down. She could hear the voices of Rivers and Blancett coming closer again.

"She said she worked for Andrzejczak?" Rivers asked.

"Said he wouldn't be in for awhile because of the incident the other day," Blancett nodded.

"Have you seen her before?" Rivers asked.

"No," Blancett said, remembering how she had tried to convince him he had. "She acted like I did, but I would have remembered her—real good looking. She wanted some records, and I unlocked the cabi—hey! She took the Anasymine!" he realized, recalling how he had to reach far into the back to find it, and there seemed to be some missing.

"I knew she was acting funny," Blancett continued. "When I went to get some Anasymine out of the cabinet for Marshall, I noticed the cabinet had been unlocked, and then there was hardly any Anasymine left. And I had just restocked it this afternoon. And the keys, they were on the counter where she was standing when I came up to her," he finished.

"It's her. It's got to be," he said thoughtfully.

"Who?" Blancett asked.

"Colonel Tessier's wife. She's been helping Carpenter. The Anasymine's for him. Let's go," Rivers said, heading back toward the day lounge. "Alert security. Have them hold all cars at the gate. I'm going outside and see if I can see anything."

Elaina looked back and forth down the long length of the duct. She couldn't see any light up ahead. It might lead only to more offices. According to the drawing Joel had shown her, there was an emergency exit in this direction, but it might set off an alarm letting them know exactly where to find her.

"Shit!" Elaina decided she had no other choice. She couldn't try to find the other exit Joel told her about because then she'd have to pass a guard who would surely know by now to be looking for her.

She rolled onto her back and kicked off the cover. It swung open and clanged loudly against the wall. Back on her stomach and facing forward, she stuck her head out and saw no one coming. She turned around again, pushing herself through the opening feet first. Lowering her weight with her hands, then letting go, she fell the extra distance, landing on her feet in a crouching position. She ran down the hall in the opposite direction Rivers and Blancett had gone. She saw a glowing green exit sign ahead. Below it was the emergency door. Reaching the exit, she pushed the bar across the front of the door, opening it and setting off the emergency alarm. The alarm blared out its deafening sound. She ran outside, slipping and sliding, trying to get her footing as she raced toward the Toyota.

CHAPTER 29

REID stopped by the officer's club and picked up the takeout he'd ordered. He ordered a steak and a cheeseburger, a side of macaroni salad, a loaf of French bread, and a two-liter bottle of Coca-Cola. He didn't eat vegetables, and he didn't expect his kid to either. Vegetables were for wimps, except maybe potatoes— yeah, potatoes were okay. He drove his blue Ford Explorer down the dirt path toward the abandoned motor pool.

* * *

At Ft. Clairemont, Elaina slammed the door of the truck and fumbled for the wires under the dash. Her fingers were shaking from the adrenaline rush, and the cold didn't help as she tried to make them work with the tiny wires. Finally, she managed to touch them together, and they sparked. She pressed the gas pedal at the same time, and the truck's engine groaned to life. Fortunately, the engine was still pretty warm since she hadn't been in the building very long. Elaina put the truck in reverse and backed up fast, hitting a garbage can and knocking it over. She hit the brakes, threw the car into gear, and hit the gas going forward, squealing her tires on a couple of feet of dry pavement before again encountering ice and fishtailing. She struggled to keep the truck going straight. She got the truck under control and headed for the front exit. It was the only way out she knew, so she had no choice. As she neared the exit, she saw two armed guards standing next to the closed wooden gate that had been open when she first arrived. *They're expecting me*, she thought, and pressed the gas pedal harder. She heard a siren coming from a vehicle behind her. Flooring the accelerator, she headed directly for the guards, rather than the wooden gate.

The guards were taken by surprise by the yellow Toyota pickup heading straight at them at full speed. They began to shout and run, scattering in two different directions, instead of shooting at her. One jumped backwards, misstepping onto the curb behind him, spilling him to the ground. The other ran for cover behind the booth. Elaina turned the truck sharply, almost losing control, but she recovered and aimed the truck directly at the gated exit. She hit the wooden barrier at full speed, bursting through it and barely slowing down as she drove over the broken pieces of the gate.

She sped down the road and headed up the main highway into heavier traffic. Moving in and out of traffic at a high speed, she lost sight of the military police vehicle that had followed her through the broken gate. She didn't think they were even close enough to have seen her enter the highway, but even if they had, she lost them, maneuvering through traffic.

Elaina couldn't calm her shaking as she checked her

rearview mirror for anyone following her. Not seeing any-one, she finally slowed down to a safer speed. She didn't need to get into an accident on the icy roads or be stopped by a traffic cop right now. She took the next exit, and headed down a different road that led toward the middle of town.

Elaina parked in the back lot of a cyber café with a large sign that read: Java.Net—Open 24 Hours. Getting out of the truck, she took a quick look around and walked cautiously inside.

Paranoid, Elaina examined everyone in the café while still avoiding eye contact. She asked the clerk for a computer key, made her way to the back of the store, sat down at an open computer, and inserted her key. She typed FBI & Crime Reporting into the search engine, and a list of possible sites appeared. Choosing their official home site brought up a menu of pages from which to pick. She decided on one called Crime Hotline and clicked on it. Following the directions on the screen, she downloaded the disk as an attachment. As she waited for it to down-load, she glanced nervously around the room for anyone who might be watching her.

Seeing no one particularly suspicious, she turned her eyes back toward the computer monitor and began her search for the major news networks, beginning with CNN. Something caught her eye in the computer screen—a reflection in the glare of the monitor. She turned around abruptly, but no one was behind her. The glass window, however, caught her eye as she faced the dark parking lot, seeing only her reflection. She was going crazy. If any-one were watching her from out there, she wouldn't know it. It was too bright in here and too dark outside. There couldn't have been a reflection in her computer screen coming from out there. It had to be coming from someone who had been standing behind her for a moment and then walked on. After staring hard into the glass a moment longer, satisfied that she couldn't make out anything, she turned back to her search, found what she needed, and downloaded the disk again.

It's too late to turn back now. The popular oldie popped into her mind. *Who had sung that song?* She probably wouldn't be able to get it out of her head, now. Probably some kind of stress reaction, she thought, running her nervous fingers through her thick hair again.

Swiveling her chair toward the entrance, she checked the front door for new arrivals, then did another sweep with her eyes around the café. Nobody new, she decided. Just then the door opening caught her eye, and she looked toward the entrance with irrational fear, as if she knew exactly who would be coming through the door and knew they would be after her. But it was only a young couple, laughing with their arms around each other. Letting her breath out slowly, she turned back to her work and began to look up the web sites of the major newspapers, starting with the *Chicago Tribune.*

She downloaded the information for the *Tribune*, but then had trouble finding the site to submit to *The New York Times. The Cornelius Brothers and Sister Rose, that's it*, she remembered the name of the group that recorded "It's Too Late To Turn Back Now." At least she didn't have to worry about that anymore. It was strange how the mind worked. She laughed quietly and busied herself with finding the last site on her list. She was engrossed in her search when a man startled her from behind.

"Excuse me," he said, smiling.

Elaina jumped, clearly stunned, and gasped audibly. She looked up at the man, shaking.

"I'm sorry. I didn't mean to scare you. I was just going to offer to buy you a cup of coffee," he said, nervously offering his hand. "I'm Jerry Gallegos."

Elaina stared at him, frozen, not at first comprehending what he wanted from her.

"Hey," Jerry said, putting up his hands to call a truce, "I'm sorry I bothered you." He smiled again and began to walk away when Elaina snapped out of her shock.

"I'm sorry. I'm just a little preoccupied here. But thank you, anyway," she said.

Jerry turned around, disappointed, "Sure."

Elaina found the *New York Times* information reporting site and began downloading. The idea that she might be damaging national security in some way went briefly through her mind, and she dismissed it. The people had a right to know what was going on. This was illegal, unethical, and immoral stuff that was going on, not defense codes or anything. Then she wondered if anyone would believe what she sent them enough to investigate anyway, or would they think it was just a crank? If anyone reading it had any military training, they would be able to recognize the government procedures and documents as authentic. She was lost in these thoughts when a man in a dark suit sat down at the terminal next to her. She noticed him immediately and watched him with her peripheral vision. He was obviously looking at her as he sipped his coffee, only occasionally glancing toward his own computer.

Her heart flopped in her chest and a trickle of sweat began to tickle her forehead at the edge of her hairline. He looked very FBI, and she prayed the Bureau wasn't somehow in on this, too since she had already downloaded to them. The army had their own investigators who dressed like this, she remembered — the CID, Criminal Investigation Division. And she had briefly considered going to them, then decided against it, thinking it would be too risky. He could, of course, just be a businessman on a trip, needing to get online for a few minutes.

The disk finally finished downloading. Relieved, she reached down and popped it out of the floppy drive, slipped it into her pocket, and grabbed the key out of the machine. She avoided looking at the man at all as she headed for the cashier to pay.

She handed the key to the cashier and paid the total, checking over her shoulder. The man who had been sitting next to her in the dark suit was heading straight towards her. She swung around abruptly, heading for the front door. The cashier called out to her.

"Ma'am, you forgot your change." Elaina kept walking, and by the time she made it through the front door, she was running.

CHAPTER 30

Midnight
19 December 2002

A T the FBI headquarters in Quantico, Virginia, Mike Piganni, a young hotshot agent, burst into the office of AD Davis, the assistant director in charge of civilian complaints against government agencies.

"Take a look at this, Sir." Mike handed some printed papers to Davis. "This was just received from the central office via email. They said it came from Colorado."

"What is it?" Davis asked, flipping through the papers.

"If it's authentic, it's a copy of an order to change the coordinates of a bombing raid on Iraq during the Gulf War, and another order for a group of soldiers to paratroop into the area — a few minutes earlier than the bombing," Mike explained.

"Why in the hell would they make a mistake like that?

Who gave the orders? And why didn't they communicate with each other?" Davis demanded, appalled.

"It wasn't a mistake, Sir. A General Sorenson gave both orders."

"Why in the hell?"

"That's what the rest of the documents are about, Sir," Mike moved closer to Davis' desk and pointed to one of the pages. "Here. It tells all about a project run by the Department of Scientific Research—The Ezekiel Project, it's called. The first group of soldiers were unintentionally exposed to Sarin gas in the Gulf. They were quarantined in Egypt. The military noticed some strange things about them. Real science-fiction stuff. Abilities such as height-ened awareness—some could even read minds, sup-posedly. A couple reportedly had visions. This General Sorenson was stationed over there—he sent a team from the Department of Scientific Research to Egypt to study these soldiers." Mike took a breath and went on while AD Davis listened intently.

"Needless to say the soldiers were very sick. They were treated with several drugs, one that later became known as Myotrophin, used for treating Gulf War Syn-drome. Some of them got better, but their abilities grew less and less, until they had none of their previous psychic capabilities. The rest died. The director of the research facility where the second group is still being held in Colo-rado is Colonel Reid Tessier. He's a biochemist and physi-cist, and he works with a team of doctors, neurologists, psychologists, and experts in chemical and biological war-fare—which was also his specialty, by the way. Anyway, this Colonel Tessier went to Egypt. He'd developed this drug, Anasymine, that enabled the brain to supposedly grow new pathways in the brain, which could, according to their theory, make these infected Gulf War vets' abilities permanent. He tried some experiments with the soldiers, but it was too late."

"He needed a new test group," Davis finished for him.

Mike nodded and continued, "The second group. I guess Tessier and Sorenson were in real tight. Tessier asked and Sorenson delivered. The second group was vaccinated with Pyridostigmene prior to exposure to prevent death and ward off some of the ill effects. But they gave them less than the usual dose. I guess they wanted to make sure they absorbed enough of the Sarin to have an effect." Mike leaned over again and motioned to the pages. "If you turn a few pages, you'll see how he picked who would get exposed. He used a computer software program he developed that examined and sorted the soldiers stationed over there according to red flags that showed up in their psychological profiling when they joined the army. Then he narrowed the group down and gave them a battery of tests that supposedly showed a propensity toward psychic phenomenon or the belief in it. His theory was that most people believing in psychic phenomenon had first hand experience. Then he selected from that group, seventeen men to form a strike force, the 151st battalion. They were trained as paratroopers with the 101st Airborne division to be sent in to check bunkers and warehouses for biological and chemical weapons that were ordered destroyed, but had not been. If they found weapons, they were to contain the area and send for a crew to dispose of the weapons, safely. Of course, that's just what they were told. Tessier had no intention of really doing that. They were set up," Mike finished.

"Unbelievable. How far up the ladder does this go?" asked Davis.

"He mentions one senator. It doesn't say how far up the knowledge goes in the Department of Scientific Research.

General Speare is the head of the Department of Scientific Research for the whole country. It doesn't mention him, but it does imply that all this had to be kept quiet and that only those in the Colorado research facility were privy. First they moved the men here to Virginia where they lived solely on post and never left for any reason. They were kept in isolation but worked jobs on base and went in for weekly testing. But many were getting worse, having long term effects either from the exposure to Sarin — resembling the same symptoms of other vets in the general public who claim to have Gulf War Syndrome, except worse. Still others were having psychological breakdowns and psychosis. They were addicted to the Anasymine and that might have been causing the trouble. No one knew for sure, and Colonel Tessier was put in charge of finding out and stopping their deterioration as well as turning them into something the government could use. As it was they were just costing the government money, and Tessier's drug was seen as a failure. They moved the men to the Colorado research facility with Tessier in charge of salvaging the project. But last week two men died. That's not in the report. I just found that out, checking the facility's medical files."

"From the disease, the drugs or whatever, or something else?" Davis asked. Davis spread out the papers on his desk.

"I don't know. The file just states complications from an illness, but I'm assuming if any of this is true, that it was something to do with this project. Anyway, those documents," he continued, pointing at the papers in Davis' hand, "mention that since they almost lost their funding, the focus on proving that the abilities have merit in the military has become a top priority to them. That's why I think there's this medical file on this guy." Mike pointed to the last page and to Joel's photo. "According to these papers, this Carpenter has more power than any one of the subjects, and hasn't been as sick as the others, although his condition has worsened."

Davis' phone rang, and he picked it up. It was his secretary telling him that the phone was ringing off the hook in the FBI's main office. Newspaper reporters and even CNN newscasters were trying to see if anything was being done about The Ezekiel Project. When Davis hung up, he turned to Mike.

"Get these documents authenticated, check it out, and then get on the phone with the president. We need to know how far this goes up before we get involved. Unfortunately, if it's a matter of national security, and it's all been sanctioned by the president, we can't do anything about it. Find out."

"Yes, Sir." Mike turned and left the room excitedly. This could definitely be the case that got him the attention of his supervisors.

CHAPTER 31

ELAINA headed for the motel. She had to get Joel and arrange to meet Reid. Timing was crucial because if the story hit the news or if FBI investigators raided the research facility, she wouldn't have any leverage with Reid. If he thought she alone had the documents downloaded from his files, then she had bargaining power to get Luke back. She wondered if she should have sent the files so soon, but she couldn't take the chance that Reid might somehow get the disk away from her, and if it came down to trading the disk for Luke, she would have to do it, even if that meant sacrificing all the other veterans' safety including Joel's. This was the safest way. She wouldn't have to make a choice, and she could freely give up the disk, knowing the information was already in the hands of the public. But now she had to hurry and hope Reid wasn't watching the news. She had only sent it to reputable sources and most likely each would check out the story's authenticity before airing it. That would buy her a little time.

Her thoughts were cut short by the sound of sirens behind her, closing the distance, becoming louder, and the sudden appearance of swirling red and blue lights in the rearview mirror. She continued to drive straight down the road, checking her speedometer. It read sixty-five mph. If they were following her, she should speed up and try to outrun them, but she doubted her ability to do that in the old pickup. She accelerated a little and the speedometer reached sixty-nine mph. But if they weren't coming after her, and she started to run, they might pull her over thinking she must be some kind of fleeing felon. After checking the mirror again, she decelerated, finally pulling over to the shoulder. The squad car raced past her and disappeared into the distance ahead.

She dropped her head forward and rested it on the steering wheel and began to cry. She hadn't realized how taut her nerves had become and how in control she had to be the past twenty-four hours. She sobbed out loud for a few minutes and then sat up looking at the night sky. That had felt so good, just to cry and let it all out. The release seemed cleansing, and she sat thinking about what she'd just accomplished. She had just broken into a top-secret military installation and had stolen classified information! *She* had done that. Not Joel or Reid or her father or anybody else she saw as being much stronger and more capable than herself, but she had done it, and she had done it alone. Thinking about this seemed to give her renewed strength, and she took a deep breath and signaled to reenter the highway.

Elaina took the exit right before the highway took her out of town and followed the small road to the motel where she had left Joel. He would be so proud of her when she told him what she'd gotten. And she would give him his medication, which she was sure he must be desperate for by now. She had his medical records, and as soon as they got Luke back, she would take him to a hospital, and not a military hospital either.

Elaina parked in the back and entered room number three without passing the office. There was no light coming from the tiny window or from under the motel room door as she approached it uneasily. He could be still sleeping, she supposed, but what if he'd gotten tired of waiting and thought she had just ditched him, deciding to go on alone? She should have left him a note, but she thought he would sleep the whole time. It had taken her longer than she anticipated. Elaina put the key in the lock and opened the door.

"Joel," she called softly into the dark, "are you asleep?" She stepped through the door. "Joel, I did it. I got everything, but I think we should go now."

Reaching for the light switch, she couldn't make out anything in the dark room. She found the switch and flipped it on, illuminating the entire room, softly. The first thing she noticed was that the bed was empty. Her eyes moved downward, and she saw Joel lying unconscious on the floor in front of the bed and Harris dead, his eyes wide open staring at the ceiling a few feet in front of him.

"Oh my God—Joel, Joel." She gasped and ran over to him, falling on her knees beside him. "Joel." She shook him gently. "Wake up. Are you okay?" Elaina lifted his arm up and put her fingers on his wrist. Not feeling anything, she put her fingers to his throat and felt his weak pulse, and she saw the rise and fall of his shallow breathing. Relieved that he was still alive, but still fearful of his condition, she leaned over him and shook him gently again.

He began to stir and weakly opened his eyes. Elaina grabbed a pillow from the bed, gently picked up his head, and propped it up on the pillow.

"Joel, what happened? Are you hurt?" she asked, stroking his head.

Joel smiled and tried to sit up, but fell backwards and then tried to speak, but he had trouble catching his breath, so Elaina propped another pillow behind his head, so that he could breathe better.

"Luke and Reid are at Ft. Powell." Joel stopped to breathe. He could hardly speak and the words came out like a whisper. "They're at the old motor pool — it's an abandoned warehouse. I think it must be on the south side of — the post because of the trees. Take his gun," Joel pointed weakly at the gun lying next to Harris on the floor, "with you — Reid's going to try — to kill — take the gun," he said unable to finish his thought. The gun was on the floor next to Harris' hand where he'd dropped it after squeezing the trigger against his will.

"Joel, I got everything — I emailed the disk to the FBI and the New York Times and even CNN. It has everything on it — and I got your medicine," she said, reaching into her pocket for the Anasymine. "I'm going to give you some; then I'm going to take you to the hospital — now they can't take you back — it's too late. Then I'll go get Luke. I'll give Reid the disk in exchange for Luke."

Joel shook his head.

"Elaina, set up the meeting with Reid now — before he finds out that you already sent it to the FBI and new — " He struggled to catch his breath. "You need to go fast before he knows — hurry."

Elaina's eyes were brimming with tears as she shook her head.

"I can't leave you like this," she said, pulling out a syringe and tearing off the wrapper. "Let me give you your medicine."

Joel put his hand up to stop her. "No—I don't need it anymore," he said, trying to smile, but instead it came out like a grimace of pain. He reached up and touched her face and tried to wipe away her tears, but they were coming too fast. "You did it, Elaina—I knew you could." He shivered violently and his eyes glazed over for a moment, and she'd thought she'd lost him. She lay her head down on his chest, and he took a sharp and painful breath and put his hand on her head.

"Did I tell you how beautiful you are?" he asked, and she lifted her head and looked into his amazing ocean blue eyes. She completely broke down this time and began to sob. She felt a crushing weight in her chest, and she thought she couldn't stand the pain for one more moment. Elaina fell onto his chest and lay on top of him, holding him and weeping.

"Joel," she pleaded through her tears, "please don't go—don't give up. I need you—I love you," she said as he stroked her tear-dampened hair.

"You don't need me—you're going to be all right," he said gently.

She sat up and shook her head angrily. "I can't face Reid without you," she shouted at him, swiping at her tears with the back of her hand. "I don't want to do anything without you."

Joel lifted one arm weakly and touched her breast right over heart and said, "I will be with you." His hand dropped, and he began to convulse again, this time more violently than before, but he continued to speak. "Don't forget the gun—remember the vision," he said, and she knew he referred to the vision they shared, but she instead, remembered his dream she witnessed where she held him in her arms as he died.

Elaina picked up his head and cradled it in her arms, rocking him back and forth, sobbing.

"Please, Joel—let me take you—"

"It's okay, Elaina—I want to go now; it's okay."

She leaned over and kissed his lips.

"I love you, Joel. I love you so much," she said, and she thought she couldn't bear how bad it felt to lose him.

Joel smiled weakly at Elaina and moved his lips to speak, but she couldn't hear anything. She knew what he was trying to say. His lips formed the words, "Love you." His eyes became fixed and vacant, and his arms went limp.

"Joel—Joel," she said, still rocking his head, not believing he was really gone. She thought she would die if she knew he was really dead. Elaina let his head drop to the pillow, and she threw herself on top of him, crying for a few moments, and then Luke entered her mind. She forced herself to sit up. She stared down into his beautiful blue eyes, and then gently shut them with a brush of her hand. The tears dripped from her face and plopped softly onto his.

Slowly getting to her feet, she emptied her pockets and filled her gym bag. She stripped off her army t-shirt and baggy fatigue pants and pulled on her jeans and long sleeved top. She picked up her white jacket and looked at it, then looked over to where Joel's jacket with New Mexico printed on the back in the colors of the sunset sat draped over the back of the chair. Walking over to the chair, she picked up the jacket and buried her face in it, inhaling the scent of him. His mild and tangy aftershave clung to the fabric, and she remembered lying on his chest, her face up against his neck, smelling this scent after they had made love and falling asleep, this scent of him filling her senses. She began to cry again as she buried her face in the jacket;

then pulling herself together, she put the jacket on instead of her own, hoping that it wouldn't lose his aroma too quickly. She grabbed the disk from the bed and put it in her jacket pocket. Elaina went to the phone on the night table and dialed Reid's cell number.

She wiped the tears from her face and sniffled as she waited for an answer.

"It's me," she said without a trace of emotion. "How's Luke?" she demanded on the verge of sounding angry but in control.

"Elaina." Reid was clearly taken off guard. "I'm surprised to hear from you."

"Is Luke all right?" she asked impatiently.

"He couldn't be better," Reid answered defensively.

"I have all your files from your computer—I have proof of everything. I want to meet. I'll give it all to you in exchange for Luke," she said calmly and forcefully.

Reid was so shocked by her statement that he didn't answer at first, and when he did, he didn't try to hide the laughter in his voice. "You expect me to fall for that?"

"It's true," Elaina said, angry now. "I'm surprised you haven't heard about it, yet. They'll probably be calling you shortly to tell you I broke into your office," she said, hoping that wasn't true because they might also know that she'd leaked it to the press and tell him that too.

"You?" he asked sarcastically. "Break into an office in a top-secret military installation?" he said in a condescending tone, although his laughter was gone. "Give me a break."

"Does the word "prophet" ring a bell?" she asked flippantly. It was her turn to be condescending. "You really shouldn't underline your secret passwords in the very book your project is named for."

"How?" Reid's voice became weak, and she imagined how his face must have paled.

"It wasn't that difficult—you made it easy," she goaded him. "Where shall I meet you?"

"On Ft. Powell. I know you know where it is since you met with General Sorenson here. Drive in through the south side by the forest. There won't be any manned gates over there. I'll make sure it's open. Drive around to the south side of the barracks, and you'll see the motor pool. There's a warehouse there. We'll be inside. Come alone," he told her.

"Oh, I will," she said and hung up the phone.

Elaina looked back at Joel one last time and pulled the coverlet from the bed. She gently covered Joel with the blanket and hesitated, blinking back another set of tears. She turned and picked up her gym bag with Joel's medical records and her few belongings. Luke's backpack was still in the truck. She started to leave and then looked down at Harris. She still didn't know exactly what had happened here, but by the looks of it, Joel had used his telekinesis, knowing it would probably kill him in his weakened state, to overpower the man to get information about where Reid was hiding with Luke. Elaina bent down and picked up the gun. She removed the silencer and tucked it into her jacket and taking one last look at Joel, she left the motel. As she drove toward the highway, she saw a squad car coming toward her from the opposite direction. The car sped by without running lights and sirens, and she breathed a sigh of relief as it passed without seeming to notice her.

CHAPTER 32

19 December 2002

ELAINA drove slowly and quietly onto the post through the open gate by the edge of the forest. It was very dark, and the tall pine trees were thick. Elaina turned off her lights and killed the engine when she saw the old warehouse come into view. She didn't want Reid to know she had arrived. She didn't know how much advantage that would give her, if any. Getting out of the truck, she pulled the gun out of her jacket and tucked it into the back of her jeans, thinking it would be easier to get it out faster. She crept quietly toward the building.

When she reached the building, she tried to peek in the window, but it was so dirty that she couldn't see through it. She rubbed it with the sleeve of her jacket until she had a small opening she could see through. Inside, she saw Reid and Luke talking. Reid seemed calm, but Luke looked frightened and dirty, still wearing the same clothes as when she'd picked him up from school five days ago. A tear rolled down her face as she watched Luke and imagined what he'd been put through. She took a deep breath and opened the door as quietly as she could.

Elaina stepped inside the warehouse and felt a strong sense of dejá vu as she saw the overhead lamp swinging slightly and the army Jeeps parked in rows, one with the engine pulled out and the hood open, and dusty filing cabinets next to boxes of files, just as in Joel's vision.

Luke spotted her at the same time as Reid. Luke jumped up and attempted to run toward her, but Reid pushed him back down in the chair.

"Mom!" Luke cried. "Mom!"

Elaina stepped forward cautiously.

"It's okay, Luke. Everything's going to be okay, now," she said, her eyes going back and forth from Reid to Luke.

"Hello, Elaina," Reid said smoothly, trying to turn on the old charm again. "It really is too bad," he said, looking her up and down lustfully, "things had to turn out like this—I loved you, you know," and she thought he really believed that.

"You have no idea what love is," she said.

"Oh, I get it—you spend a few days with Loverboy, and now you understand what love really is; is that it?" he asked his jealousy showing.

"Something like that," Elaina said.

"Well, you have changed—you're sure getting ballsy, aren't you? Coming here and demanding Luke back. My son!" he shouted suddenly, shocking her into taking a step backward. "Threatening me with your little disk," he spat, stepping forward past Luke, putting himself between them.

"Here," she said taking the disk out of her pocket and holding it up. "Take it. I just want Luke back."

"He's my son." Reid seemed to be getting angrier with every word she said. "What makes you think I would give him up?"

Elaina's heart slipped into her stomach as she realized what she'd always known—Reid would never give up his son. She took a step forward and swallowed hard.

Suddenly Luke stepped forward and said, "Mom, I want to go with you."

"Stay back!" Reid shouted, looking at Luke.

Elaina took a deep breath and nodded at Luke.

"Luke, it's okay. Just let me talk to your dad for a minute."

"Give me the disk, Elaina," Reid said.

"Okay," she said but made no move to give it to him, "you can have it." She looked at Luke and smiled. "Come here, Luke."

"Don't you move," Reid said between clenched teeth, never taking his eyes off Elaina. "Give me the disk first."

Elaina threw the disk to Reid, and he caught it, glanced at it quickly, put it in his pocket, and looked up at her.

"How do I know this is the only one?" he asked.

"Look, Reid. It's the only one—I only did it to get Luke back."

Reid pulled a gun out of a holster inside his coat and pointed it at Elaina. Elaina stepped back in fear, and she looked fearfully at Luke who took a step closer.

"Dad, no. Don't hurt her," Luke said.

"What about your boyfriend? Aren't you doing this to help him?" he asked.

"Reid, listen to me. You—"

"Why did you have to do this? Huh? You couldn't leave it alone—and now it comes down to this," he said, waving the gun. "I never wanted this to happen, Elaina," he said quietly.

"Reid, it's too late. I already emailed the disk to the FBI and to the major networks and papers. You might as well let us go," she said, figuring it wouldn't matter if he knew. He wasn't planning on giving up Luke, and she wasn't leaving without him. Maybe if he thought the whole thing was hopeless, he could see that she would have to take Luke. But Reid was furious, and his face turned red with anger as he leveled the gun on her.

"You bitch!" he screamed. "You're lying! If you had minded your own god damned business—none of this would be happening. Everything would be fine."

"Everyone except Joel Carpenter!" she shouted back, so sick of his selfishness and loathing him for what he'd done to her and Joel and Luke and all the other vets suffering in the research facility. "He's dead; did you know that?"

Reid stared at her a moment as if what she said didn't register.

"They weren't supposed to kill him," he said quietly. "But I can't say I'm sorry after what he did—running off with you," he admitted.

"They didn't kill him," she shouted. "You did."

"He died—from the illness?" Reid lowered the gun slightly and seemed almost remorseful. "I didn't want this, Elaina. But now everybody knows," he looked down at his gun, cocked it, and lifted it, pointing it at her again, "how much you know, and I don't have a choice."

"Dad, no!" Luke shouted.

Reid, momentarily distracted by Luke, turned and

glanced back at him. Elaina pulled the gun from the waist-band of her jeans and aimed it at Reid. He turned back, see-ing the gun. He whirled around and grabbed Luke by the collar, pulling him close and put the gun to Luke's head.

"Put the gun down," Reid said, sounding like a stranger.

Elaina didn't hesitate. She bent down and placed the gun on the floor and raised her hands in front of her, shaking.

"Reid, please — just let him go," she said. "Can't you see it's too late?" Tears ran down her face. "You can just let us go. Run away before they come for you," she pleaded.

Reid motioned with his head toward the gun on the ground.

"Kick it over here."

Elaina kicked the gun to Reid, but kicked too hard, and it slid past him. He let go of Luke and took a couple of steps toward Elaina, furious. He raised the gun, aiming at Elaina with a look of steely determination and addressed Luke, who was now behind him.

"Luke, I want you to turn around and shut your eyes," he said calmly but with hate in his tone.

Luke shook his head, knowing what his father meant to do. Elaina's head reeled remembering all this as if it had happened before. Nothing — there was nothing any-one could do to change fate — it was destiny, she thought, and she saw Luke rush forward.

"No! Luke, run! Run!" she shouted as she saw Luke fall forward on the ground behind Reid. He was picking up something. It was the gun she'd kicked forward. Reid raised his other hand to steady the gun. Luke had the other gun now, and he raised it, pointing it at his father's back. Reid continued to walk toward Elaina slowly, aiming.

Luke pulled the trigger on the nine-millimeter semi-automatic, and Reid was thrown forward just as Luke was thrown backwards. One by the impact of the bullet tearing through his back, and the other from the kick of the powerful weapon. Reid lay face down on the concrete floor, blood spreading out beneath him. His face was turned to the side, and he looked up, blood beginning to ooze out of his mouth.

Elaina ran to Luke and hugged him and gently removed the gun from his hands. Luke pushed free of her and stepped closer to Reid and looked down into his face. Reid looked into Luke's eyes and tried to speak, but the words came out garbled because his mouth was full of blood.

"You shouldn'ta done that, Squirt," Reid said, bubbles of blood exploding on his lips. "What am I gonna do—with you?"

Elaina pulled Luke away from Reid.

"Hey, Squirt," Reid said in words even more difficult to understand. "I'da don-done the same thi—you—take aft—you—da—" his words tapered off, and he became silent and still, his eyes staring forward at Luke. Elaina turned Luke away from him and held him, rocking him back and forth. Luke seemed to be in shock as he kept repeating the same words over and over.

"He's not my dad—not my dad. That's not my dad."

Elaina lifted Luke to his feet and sat him in a chair. She went over to Reid's body and took the disk from his pocket. She might still need this, just in case nobody believed her before. She had a feeling they would start listening when they found all the bodies. She took Luke by the arm and pulled him with her.

"Come on. We have to get out of here. It's going to be

okay, but we have to move." She still didn't know if there were any others at Ft. Powell who were part of the project, and she didn't want to take any chances.

Luke clung to his mother as the sound of vehicles came closer. As an afterthought, Elaina let go of Luke and ran back to the gun she had taken from him. She picked up the weapon and wiped all the fingerprints from the gun, and then set it back down. Grabbing Luke by the arm, she ran out of the building, pulling him behind her.

She shoved Luke into the truck first, and then got in behind him. They took off in the truck, blowing up dirt behind them as a Jeep drove in from the other direction. The Jeep chased Elaina over potholes and hills on the ungraded dirt road, and Elaina drove off of the road and into the bushes, knocking the bumper loose on the battered truck. The Jeep followed until Elaina crashed through a low barbed wire fence and popped one of her tires. She struggled to keep control of the Toyota as she hit a rock on the opposite side of the flat. The truck went off balance and turned over, rolling sideways down the hill. The truck landed upside down at the bottom of the hill and stopped on a patch of ice and slowly began slipping forward, sliding into a deep ravine and finally coming to a halt.

CHAPTER 33

19 December 2002

THE squad car pulled into the lot of the seedy little motel at about 12:15 AM, and Sean Pinker met the officer in the parking lot. The fifty-something year old cop squeezed out of the driver's seat, extricating his belly out from under the steering wheel, his nightstick in hand. He holstered the nightstick and sauntered heavily over to the motel clerk.

"You got some trouble?" the cop asked, scanning the all but deserted lot.

"Yeah. Some strange noises coming from room three. It sounded like a fight, then nothing," Sean said, purposefully omitting the part where he gave a certain shady looking character the room key. "Can you check it out?"

"Who's staying there?" the cop asked, already walking towards the front of the motel.

"A woman—and some guy. He seemed a little sick or

drunk. Maybe he OD'd; I don't know. I usually don't ask too many questions, but I don't like the sound of what I heard."

"You got a key?" the cop asked. "Just in case they don't want to open up? Otherwise I gotta break it in. The city's not liable for the damage since you asked me to open it up," the cop clarified.

"W-well," Sean stuttered over his words, "that's the thing that's got me worried. See I- there-I couldn't find the key. It's missing. It's the master key, and it fits all the rooms. It's gone. Somebody musta taken it when I was in the can."

"All right. You stand back over there out of the way. Number three?" the cop asked, drawing his gun.

Sean nodded, and the cop stepped onto the porch and edged his way to the door and stood on one side of the doorjamb, his back against the motel wall. He knocked hard on the door with one hand and held the gun in the other. No answer. He rapped hard again and again only silence.

"Police, open up," the cop shouted. "Just want to see if everything's okay." When no one answered, the cop moved to the front of the door and kicked it hard directly over the door handle. The flimsy door splintered, and the doorjamb came loose from the wall, sending the door flying inward. The light was still on. Elaina hadn't turned it off when she left. The cop saw the dead body of Harris first and held his gun out in front of him as he entered. He saw the blanket covering Joel and went over to take a look. He lifted the blanket, saw Joel's pale face, and put the blanket back again. He searched the rest of the room, and when he was satisfied that there was no else there, he reholstered his weapon and radioed the station.

"I got two dead bodies here at the Candlelight Motel off of the interstate on Campbell. I need a meat wagon and a team. At least one of 'em is a gunshot," the cop spoke into the radio. He was about to go to the car to get some crime scene tape to secure the scene when he swore the blanket covering the one body moved. He jumped and stepped back just as Sean entered the doorway to see what the cop had found.

"What happened?" Sean asked, stepping into the room.

"Jesus!" the cop breathed as he stared at the blanket. He turned to Sean and shouted, "Get out. This is a crime scene — you can't be in here." He turned back to the body under the blanket and bent down, pulling the blanket all the way back this time. He stared down at the body that didn't seem to be moving, and he noticed a bead of sweat on the young man's forehead. He bent down to check the man's pulse and got another shock when his arm jerked convulsively for a moment and then stopped. Sometimes dead bodies jerked with post-mortem muscle spasms, but he'd never seen one sweat before. He put his hand on the man's throat and felt a weak and irregular heartbeat.

"Hey!" the cop shouted to Sean. "We got a live one." The cop stood and radioed for an ambulance and then knelt next to Joel, who appeared to breathe only now and then, and gave him mouth-to-mouth resuscitation as he waited for the ambulance and the meat wagon to arrive.

CHAPTER 34

Just After Midnight
19 December 2002

ELAINA stared out the broken windshield of the upside down Toyota and saw only dirt and snow. She glanced over at Luke, who seemed unharmed but was crying quietly, hanging upside down, suspended from his seat belt and trying to hold himself up with his arms outstretched toward the ceiling of the truck. Elaina braced her arm against the ceiling and unsnapped the buckle of her seat belt with the other hand. She fell downward toward the ceiling in an uncomfortable position, her legs falling forward toward the windshield, as if she were doing a backwards somersault. She took advantage of the position and kicked out the remainder of the glass, and then on her hands and knees, she crawled over the gear shifter and over to Luke.

"Luke, are you all right?" she asked, checking him out.

"Mom," he said through his tears, "get me out of here."

"Okay. Keep your arms up like that, so you don't hit your head when I unfasten your belt."

He stretched his arms out farther, and she leaned around him feeling for the buckle. When she found it, she pushed the red button and the belt released with a snap, sending Luke down into a handstand before he collapsed onto his knees. Elaina grabbed him up in her arms and hugged him, then pulled back.

"Are you hurt anywhere? Is anything broken?" she asked, and miraculously he shook his head. The Toyota's roll bar just behind the cab had held and kept the roof from caving in during the roll, and amazingly the sides of the truck, although badly dented, did not cave in to the point of injuring them.

"We've got to get out of here," she said. "Go through the window and be careful of the glass." She followed him through into the snowy ravine. Scrambling to her feet, she looked up the hill and saw lights coming closer. "Come on," she said. "Hurry."

They had a bit of a head start on the army Jeep, and their roll down the hill managed to put more distance between them and their pursuers. She pulled Luke by the arm up and out of the ravine, and they ran for the trees.

The Jeep stopped at the top of the hill, its occupants looking down at the wrecked Toyota upside down in the ravine. General Speare jumped out of the vehicle and ordered some men down to check the truck.

"Better call an ambulance," Speare said solemnly.

"But Sir, I thought their presence was to be kept quiet," a private named Medina, driving the vehicle answered.

"I'm not going to let a civilian woman and a boy die, just to cover up whatever Tessier's done," he answered.

Private Medina made the call, and the general made his way back to the warehouse.

"What's Tessier got to say for himself?" Speare demanded, approaching the MP's.

"He's dead, Sir. Shot in the back, inside." The MP pointed toward the warehouse.

"What the hell is going on here?" Speare demanded. "I don't know what his family knew about this project, but I want an armed guard on them, and they are to be taken to a military hospital."

Speare's radio made its ssshhh noise and Medina spoke.

"General Speare, Sir," Medina said hesitantly.

Speare removed his radio from his belt and pushed the button to talk. "Go ahead."

"They're gone, Sir," he began. "They're not in the truck. It looks like they kicked out the windshield and took off. There are footprints in the snow leading into the forest, Sir."

"Go after them! They couldn't have gone far," he shouted. "We can't let them get out of here and talk to the public before we find out what they know."

Speare turned to the MP's and shouted his orders.

"I want a search party out there right now! Get me a helicopter, too." The MP named Zimmer radioed for the helicopter and search team. "Call the local police and request a road block," Speare ordered with stern solemnity.

"Sir, we could get a road block up faster ourselves," said Zimmer.

"That would be kind of hard to explain to the public, don't you think? It's better if they think it's just another escaped convict," Speare reasoned, thinking he was going to end up taking the fall for whatever Sorenson had been up to with Tessier at the Department of Scientific Research. He'd given them too much freedom up there. He knew, of course, about the project and the veterans in the project, but he didn't know the details or how Tessier's wife and child had gotten mixed up with an escaped subject, and how Tessier had kidnapped the kid and put a hit out on his wife. That is until he got the call from the Secretary of Defense, telling him that Sergeant Joel Carpenter was recovering in a local civilian hospital surrounded by police protection, and that he was telling them stories about Tessier's wife going alone to confront Colonel Tessier about getting her kid back. He'd been extremely disturbed to find out that all of this had gone bad five days ago, and no one had bothered to inform him, and now the television stations had gotten a hold of the story, and the FBI was leaving messages on his answering machine. And this day from hell just kept getting worse.

Elaina and Luke ran blindly through the trees, branches and leaves whipping their faces and cutting their skin. Luke stumbled and fell, and Elaina dragged him to his feet, continuing to pull him down the hill through the thicker part of the forest. She was out of breath, and her lungs ached with every intake of air; her legs felt like rubber as she struggled to keep her balance. They came upon a shallow creek, and Elaina pulled Luke, splashing through the freezing water. The snow fell heavier in larger and larger flakes, coming more quickly than before, and Elaina could no longer feel her freezing, wet feet, which made it even more difficult to keep her balance.

On the other side of the bank, the snow was deeper and hard where it had built up over the winter, avoiding the melt from the shade of the surrounding trees. They crunched across the hard snow, and the hill became very steep. They held onto the jagged bark of the pines as they ran down the snowy hill. When they reached the edge of the forest, Elaina saw a precipitous rock formation that led down an almost vertical hill to the bottom of a road. A civilian road. It had to be outside the post. She saw a truck for a major grocery chain speed past as she watched.

All of the sudden the sound of a helicopter surrounded them and seemed to come from every direction at once. Elaina looked up and saw lights from the helicopter above. Momentarily blinded, she shielded her eyes and took Luke by the hand. She stared down at the slippery, partially ice-covered rocks below her and tried to build the courage to begin the descent.

"Come on," she told Luke. "We can make it."

She said a silent prayer, and then over and over in her mind she repeated the words Joel had told her. *I have everything I need to do whatever I need to do, if I just believe it*, she said in her mind. Elaina stepped down, testing her footing on the rock and moved forward, her body going down the hill sideways.

"Like this," she told Luke. "Go sideways, and it isn't as hard."

Luke followed, leaning his weight on her whenever he lost his balance and nearly causing her to lose her own. They started to build up speed as the rocks grew steeper. She couldn't see for sure where she was stepping much of the time because the only illumination in the dark area was the moon, until the swirling searchlight from the helicopter suddenly illuminated their path, touching the ground around them, and then lifting again, leaving them in darkness.

"Hurry, they're coming," she shouted, pulling him down faster to avoid the light. Sirens penetrated the quietness of the night, and Elaina was reminded of the air raid alarms blaring in movies she'd seen while whole towns panicked and scrambled for safety from the impending disaster. The sound seemed to surround them like the whir of the helicopter blades. They ran down the steep rocks faster, spurred on by the sound of the sirens.

She grabbed Luke's arm tightly and ran down the hill at an angle, trying to get more traction. Her foot settled onto a patch of ice, and before she knew it was ice, she put all her weight down on it and began to slide. She let go of Luke and put her arms forward to break an inevitable fall as she slid down, still on her feet. She felt Luke grabbing onto her jacket behind her, and his weight caused her to lose even more of her balance, and she fell on her back. A sharp pain sliced through her kidneys as she slid, pulling Luke with her, still hanging onto her jacket. Elaina slipped to the edge of the rock, and she reached uselessly out to a branch coming out of a nearby rock, but missed it and fell over the edge, hitting another rock and causing her another stabbing pain in her side. Luke had lost his grip on her jacket, and now they were sliding separately. Luke came down fast behind her in the same manner. Going over the edge of the rock, Elaina hit a branch and was propelled through the air, landing on snow-covered dirt and going into a horizontal roll.

Elaina rolled down the steep, snowy hill, perfect for sledding. Picking up speed, she rolled to the bottom of the slope and the start of a road. She hit the ground and came to a stop, head first, her top half on the icy black pavement, and her bottom half rested on the snowy shoulder of the road. She struggled to breathe. The fall had knocked the wind out of her, and as she pushed herself up on her elbows, she was blinded by the headlights of an oncoming semi. She became aware of the horn blaring out in front of her, as Luke slid down behind her and slammed into her back, knocking her farther into the road, directly into the path of the semi.

The semi locked up its brakes and began to fishtail. The truck skidded sideways, the tires squealing loudly. Elaina screamed, and threw Luke off her into the snow and rolled back onto the shoulder, just as the truck skidded to a stop next to her on the road. The driver, a large, bearded, red-haired man of about forty jumped out of the truck and ran to them on the shoulder.

"What the hell—you almost got yourselves killed. Whatta you doing in the middle of the road?" he shouted.

Elaina scrambled to her feet and grabbed him by the arm.

"Help us! We have to go, please!" she pleaded with him, and without further explanation, the driver nodded, opened his passenger door, and helped Elaina and then Luke into the truck.

CHAPTER 35

Afternoon
19 December 2002

ELAINA sat behind the interrogation table while Mike Piganni of the Federal Bureau of Investigation took her statement. She had already given her story reluctantly to the Criminal Investigation Division of the army at Piganni's insistence when she'd agreed to meet him after he'd contacted her at the local Spradley police station where the trucker had taken them. This would make the third time she'd recounted the entire story while a tape recorded her words. Luke was waiting outside, a female police officer entertaining him with a tour of the station.

"How did Speare and his men know where to look for me if Reid was hiding there and didn't tell anyone?" she asked Mike.

"Joel Carpenter told us, and we shared the information

with the CID. Naturally, we needed their cooperation," he explained. "But we didn't know that Speare would find out and—"

"Wh-who told you?" she asked, her heart skipping a beat. A lump rose in her throat, and she had trouble swallowing. "I thought you said Joel—" she began.

"Yes. I thought they told you. Joel survived. He's at Memorial Hospital in Spring Forest," he said smiling.

"But how? I thought he was dead. His heart wasn't beating." She didn't dare believe it was true. The lump in her throat fell to her chest and left a pain there, and her stomach lurched at the hope. "I never would have left him," she said.

"He was in a kind of comatose state when they found him. Barely any vitals. It would have been easy to miss his heartbeat—it was so low and inconsistent according to the paramedics. The police officer who arrived on the scene first saved his life and probably his mind—he kept oxygen going to his brain by performing mouth to mouth resuscitation until the paramedics arrived."

"Is he going to be okay?" Elaina asked, fearing the worst.

"Last time I heard he was getting stronger. They couldn't quite figure out what was wrong with him because he didn't have any apparent injuries."

"I have his medical records," she said, standing up. "I need to get them to the hospital. And the medication. I gave it to the other agent, your partner, as evidence. But he needs it."

"Relax. They thought at first that he had some form of Parkinson's disease because of his neurology. They treated him with the medication they use for that, and he responded well. When he woke, he explained all that had been done to him. They got permission to have a specialist sent in from the Mayo Clinic," Mike said.

"A specialist? How could he be a specialist?" she asked.

"In neurology similar to his, I mean."

"They'll still need his records," she said, moving to the door. And even if they didn't, she needed to be there with him. This was so overwhelming. She'd thought she'd lost him, but he was alive! Her body felt electric, and her knees were weak. She wasn't aware of her legs as she opened the door.

"Mrs. Tessier —"

"Don't call me that, please," Elaina said sharply, and then smiled. "I'm sorry; it's just. . ." she trailed off, and he nodded his understanding.

"I was just going to say that you'll be needed as a material witness, especially to the murder of Tom Pierce."

"I understand. I won't leave Spring Forest," she said. "But I won't be at the house either. Luke and I will be moving out soon. Until then, we'll be staying at a friend's."

She couldn't face sleeping under that roof ever again. Her friend, Val, had already offered to let them stay when she had heard the news.

CHAPTER 36

20 December 2002

L UKE sat in the lounge area of the Intensive Care Unit of Memorial Hospital while Elaina nervously walked down the hall toward Joel's room. The room was brightly lit, and she wondered how he could sleep. He'd always had so much trouble sleeping. She stood next to the bed, the iron rails up, and gazed at his peaceful face. His hair was tousled and waved at the ends, but it was dry. No sweat beading on his brow, no convulsions, no blank stare. She shuddered and put the image of the last time she'd seen him out of her mind. He wasn't dead. He was here sleeping, well taken care of by a team of experts, and they thought he was going to be well again. She reached out and touched his cheek; the stubble had grown into almost a beard now, and it was as dark as his hair.

His eyes opened slowly, and they were as bright as they ever were; they lit up when they saw her. He smiled and lifted his hand. She took it in her own.

"Hey, Sleepy Head," she said.

"I was wondering when you'd get here," he said.

"I thought you were dead." Tears rolled down her face and dropped onto the white sheet of his bed. Again she was reminded of the last time she was with him, and her tears fell from her face to his. Now they were tears of thankfulness.

"Nope. You can't get rid of me that easily," he said.

"I'm so sorry," she began, but he lifted his hand to her lips.

"You don't ever have to be sorry," he said. "I even thought I was dead. I guess it was a miracle."

She stood, unable to say anything and swallowed the lump in her throat.

"How's Luke? I heard what happened," Joel said.

"He's hanging in. He's going to see a counselor," she told him. "It's a lot for an eight year old, a lot for anybody."

"He'll be okay, now. Thanks to you," he said.

"Thanks to you and him. You both saved my life," she said.

"No, you saved your own. I knew you could do it," he said smiling.

"I didn't. Not until I had to," she said, and then she broached the subject that she'd been wanting to talk about. "What's going to happen when you get out of here?" she asked quietly.

"I don't know. They're giving me an honorable discharge and a compensation package. I was thinking of buying some land. What do you think about Washington? Could you live there?" he asked, looking into her eyes.

She held her breath, not sure if she'd heard right and stared at him. "You mean go with you?" she asked.

"Of course, that's what I mean. Do you think I'd ever let you out of my sight again, as much trouble as you get into? They say I'll probably retain some of my precognitive powers, but I don't want to use them tracking you down again," he joked.

She smiled. "I don't know. I kind of liked New Mexico," she said slyly.

"New Mexico was good, but Breckenridge was better," he returned.

"Well, wherever we go, we have to visit my parents first. I owe them a visit, and my mom is anxious to meet you after hearing so much about you."

"How'd it go—with your mom?" he asked, remembering how afraid Elaina had been that her mother would think she was a failure for leaving Reid.

"You were right. She was pretty proud," she said smiling.

The nurse came in with some medication and asked Elaina to step back for a moment. Joel sat up as she gave him some pills to swallow and a glass of water. He saw her worried expression and smiled.

"It's Myotrophin," he laughed. "I haven't taken the Anasymine since we were in the motel room together. I'm finally getting my Gulf War Syndrome treated."

"You don't need it anymore?" she asked, surprised.

"Nope. No more convulsions either. My telekinesis isn't what it used to be. But it's a fair trade off. The pathways in my brain that grew as a result of the drug are still there though. They're permanent. I should be fine as long as I don't over stress those portions of my mind."

The nurse smiled and left the room, and Elaina went over to him and embraced him.

"It was all a lie. They wanted us to think we would die if we didn't take the medication, and it was physically addictive. When anyone tried to go off it, they would have severe withdrawals, which reinforced the notion that they were dying," he said.

He reached over and picked up the newspaper on the table next to his bed. His picture was on the cover. The picture in the file. The picture where she had first seen his face, clean-shaven and in his military uniform. She smiled and reached down and touched the picture. The caption read: DECORATED GULF WAR VETS USED AS GUINEA PIGS. There was a story about Joel. Her name wasn't mentioned. She hadn't given her name, and the authorities said they wouldn't release it or Luke's. She read on.

Speare had been cleared of all charges. Apparently he had not sanctioned the use of the untested drug or the testing of the subjects against their wills. Senator Phillips was indicted for several charges as a result of his deal with Reid to share in the future profits of the sale of Anasymine by pushing the drug through for approval with the plan for faking the test results. They had never gotten that far, thanks to Joel's escape. General Sorenson was dead, and Reid was credited with his death thanks to the security camera the general had installed in his office. No one, unfortunately, had been monitoring it at the time. Reid was also found dead, and according to the papers, his death was still unsolved, but was generally accepted as being caused by a falling out with one of his cohorts from the research facility.

Elaina had told them she did it, and the authorities suspecting the truth, agreed to keep those facts away from the media. After all, no charges were to be filed in his death. Even if Elaina had done it, it was clearly self-defense. She put the paper down and looked at him.

"You're a hero," she said.

"You're the real hero."

"Let's just keep that between you and me," she said and kissed the tip of his nose.

He pulled her down on top of him and kissed her on the lips. She returned the kiss passionately, and suddenly the hospital room faded away, and she was in a sunny bedroom lying next to Joel.

He leans over and puts his head on her stomach, and it is large with their unborn child. "Hey little baby, can you hear me in there? It's Daddy talking to you," Joel is saying to her stomach, and she is laughing.

She broke off the kiss and stood up, looking at him amazed. He laughed.

"Am I?" she asked, and he nodded. She reached down and touched her flat abdomen with wonder. "This is so not fair. I'm supposed to be the one to tell you. You better not tell if it's a girl or boy. I want some surprises," she said very seriously. But she couldn't resist asking, "When?"

"I thought you didn't want me spoiling all your surprises," he said.

"Just shut up and kiss me," she said, and he did.

AUTHOR'S NOTE:

All of the characters and situations in this novel are purely fictional and are a result of the author's imagination. Arrowhead, Milton, Spradley, Spring Forest, and Wilson's Corner are all fictional places. Ft. Powell and Ft. Clairemont are fictional army posts. The Department of Scientific Research and Ft. Clairemont's Medical Research Facility are also fictional.

Although Myotrophin and Pyridostigmene are real medications associated with Gulf War Syndrome and biochemical toxins, respectively, the situations surrounding their use is fictional. No disparagement of their use or benefits is intended. Anasymine is a product of the author's imagination.

Although Gulf War Syndrome's existence is highly controversial, many veterans of the Persian Gulf War are being treated in military facilities for symptoms that are suspected to be caused by biochemical contamination in the Persian Gulf.